THE JOURNAL OF VINCENT DU MAURIER

by K. P. Ambroziak

Edited by Veronica Murphy
Cover design by The Cover Collection

Translator's Note

Up on the Esja, just north of the capital city that used to be known as Reykjavik, a hiker found this journal. He had passed the rock wasteland of Þverfellshorn and the plain of fresh snow, and had reached the grassy peak of Hábunga. As he crouched along the water that cuts through the mountain to wash the sweat from his brow, he saw it. Lodged in a crevice on the stream's bank was a small leather-bound notebook wrapped in plastic. He picked up the treasure, threw it in his backpack, and started his trek down. With the exception of its last few missing pages, the following chronicle is the contents of that book translated in its entirety. The ink and paper have been authenticated, and we believe this journal is an original document from the period of the Red Death.

Dagur Bijarnarson
268 P.C.E. (Post Common Era)

19 September. — Today seems a more fitting day than most to begin this record. With every last drop of blood spoiled by this plague, I am soon to be a relic. I know my invitation to Hades no longer stands, for all those gods are dead and gone, but if I am banished to the halls of oblivion, I want to be remembered. These pages then will bear the account of my survival, my proof of existence.

I have gorged for thousands of years but today starvation nags at the very pit of my core. The temptation sitting mere feet from my chamber piques my voracious appetite. Stephen and Veronica were as surprised as I to discover fresh blood and I knew they found it difficult to resist the smell. Oh, the smell! That enticing blend of sour metal and sweet tonic—intoxicating nectar! We had not smelled blood that fresh since … I cannot remember when … ah, perhaps in the nunnery! I knew if they were clean, I would have to rush them back. All I could think about was bringing fresh blood to Byron, watching him devour it with the elegance I had taught him all those years ago. No longer the gluttonous sort, he would slowly suck the ichor to let his palate delight in all its subtleties. If I could get these donors back to my beloved, I could revive him and stave off his entropy. With three of them, we would all enjoy a much-needed repast even if it were a modest one. This was the reprieve I had hoped for.

"We must make sure they are not infected," I said.

Only my companions could hear me since I kept my voice too low for human ears. I pierced the inside of Stephen's wrist to gain his attention; he was in a daze, mesmerized by the smell. Veronica salivated but had closed her mouth at least; her fangs dropped the moment she smelled fresh blood. The three humans began to fidget. We had been so quiet they must have wondered what happened to us, for they certainly saw the front door open when we rushed in. They probably hoped they had not elicited the attention of the few stragglers wandering outside. One of the men had his hand on the girl's mouth and I assumed she had a hard time keeping calm since she shook beneath his grasp—she smelled extra sweet.

I almost felt compassion for them. They were rather helpless in their predicament with us in their midst and the bloodless stalking the perimeter. They were most likely terrified of being alive, and I thought it strange they had not yet killed themselves. Perhaps human nature made them as resilient as us. We were desperately trying to wait out the plague, hoping for it to vanish as suddenly as it had arrived. Something must have rallied their hope too. It had been so long since I was human, I could not remember how it felt.

There we were in the dark with the bloodless on our heels and humans in our grasp. What was the right move? Speak first or attack unnoticed? I really only had a moment to decide, for they started toward an exit on the other side of the room.

"Wait," I said softly. "Please do not leave." They froze, probably wondering how I could see them in the dark. "I can hear you breathing."

"We're scared," Veronica said, following my lead.

The sound of a female voice eased their fear, for one of the men came forward and shined a flashlight in our direction. He had a pistol in his hand. "We don't want any trouble," he said.

They could see us now and we made on the light blinded us.

"Neither do we," I said, trying to sound nonchalant while faking a squint.

"Are any of you bit?" He asked.

"None of us have been bitten," I said. "Are any of you?" I hoped beyond hope he would answer in the negative.

"No."

Perfect.

Veronica's next move was inspired. "We're lost," she said. "We've been overrun and have nowhere else to go." She topped off her plea with a flush of emotion, as she mustered up a cry. She took to the ruse rather naturally.

Stephen looked over at me. Neither of us knew she was capable of tears. Exasperation, maybe emotional outbursts, but never actual tears. It was remarkable. Veronica's face was awash with crystallized streaks, an effect not lost on the human girl who spoke out from the darkness.

"We don't have much," she said. "We're making do here until they pass." She referred to the swarm we had avoided on the outskirts of town. It had already stormed through, but the three humans did not know that the streets were mostly empty now.

"How did you get past them?" The second man spoke this time.

"We were extremely quiet," Stephen said. "But for the most part, we've been able to avoid the swarms."

"Swarms?"

7

"That is what we call them." I still tried to sound casual—human.

"We don't have any food left if that's what you're after," the man with the pistol said.

Your food? You are food.

"Oh no," I said. "We do not need your food."

The man's flashlight flickered and then went off. I took that opportunity to make my move. I lunged forward with Veronica and Stephen, and together we pounced on the trio. I took down the man with the gun, which was of no consequence since he could not see me coming in the dark, and his pistol dropped to the floor when I pierced his neck. The taste of the nectar almost made me lose my senses. Stephen grabbed the other man while Veronica leapt on the girl. I planned on saving those two for Byron and the others.

"Leave them untapped," I said before burying my fangs in the man's neck a second time.

"Please!" Veronica begged. "Let us taste."

I had taken the first bite to test it, to make sure the man told the truth when he said they had not been infected. My second indulgence was for pleasure. With the man's blood heavy on my lips and in my throat, I passed him off to Veronica. Stephen would want her to feed first. He would always put the needs of his beloved before his own.

The three of us drained the man completely, sucking him dry to reinvigorate ourselves with his blood. The ichor coursed through me, renewing my senses and giving me that full body high that made me feel invincible. The girl had passed out the moment we attacked, and although it was too dark to see me put my fangs into the neck of his companion, the other man, held down by Stephen, resigned himself to his fate. He knew he was done for and blubbered like a child.

"Shush!" Veronica scolded. "You'll raise a swarm with that noise."

"We are not going to hurt you," I said. "Not now."

The plan until then had been to get the blood into our system, but we still had to design a way to get the humans to the cathedral. I assumed it was as simple as putting them on our backs and carrying them through the streets and the field, but when I heard the howls outside the trattoria, I knew our escape would be more difficult. They were drawn to smell as well as sound, and the dead man's viscera at our feet were piquing their curiosity. It would not be long before the few became a swarm.

"They're here," Veronica said.

"Oh God! Oh God!" The man cried again.

"Shush!" Stephen reacted instinctively and covered the man's mouth, but chipped one of his front teeth, cutting his lip and knocking him out. When the blood gushed, the scent of sweet nectar hit the air. "Oops." Stephen looked at me sheepishly. They were like children these two.

"Lick it up," I said. "But keep him alive."

He shared the morsel with his beloved, and while they slurped up the blood on the man's swollen mouth, I drew up a plan. We could not pass through a swarm in the streets, and the scent of the flesh would drive them through the walls, but if we could get out another way, the dead man's body would distract them long enough for us to flee.

"Wait here," I said.

I went down a corridor and followed it to a salon at the back. On the way, I noticed an open

9

storage chamber. Its shelves had been raided, culled by starving humans; broken jars, smashed bottles, human waste, dried bones, and empty cans harassed me with their offensive smells. Humans had a high tolerance for rot, and it seemed as though these three had lived here for more than a few days. The pile of fresh feces in the corner of the chamber was a most cringeworthy sight.

When I reached the salon, the windows greeted me with some fresher air. They had been smashed and resealed multiple times with the floorboards, but despite the coverings, the air was a relief from the stench of human excrement. There was a bar along one wall toppled over on its side with a heap of barstools and ashes piled up against it. The remains of several charred corpses lay on the floor next to the stools. When I saw the sealed door, I threw myself up against it, listening to the narrow laneway at the back. Quiet and empty, we would make it our exit route. I rushed to get the others.

"Grab them both," I said.

Veronica carried the girl in her arms and Stephen threw the man over his shoulders.

"We have to move quickly," I said.

We were still vulnerable to a swarm, despite our having been strengthened by the blood. Even with the two extra bodies, I counted on our being able to spring onto the roof where we could better escape. The darkness would play to our advantage, but I had not decided how to deal with the scent of the humans. That would be our obstacle.

When we stepped into the laneway, I spotted a few bloodless wandering past it on our left. I hoped they were making their way to the front of the trattoria. The howls of a swarm increased, but the mass of them was far enough on the other side of the building, though I did not count on it being for long.

"We need to go up," I said.

I took the man from Stephen's arms and insisted he scale the brick. He hoisted himself up halfway, grabbing hold of the wall, and then propelled his body onto the roof. It was a relief to see him bound so quickly through the air, the human blood having replenished him. He leaned over the side of the building and gave us the all clear.

I had not expected bloodless on the roof. They did not seem evolved enough for tactical matters. Once I had seen several skirt a fence rather than go over it when the latter would have been the optimal choice. It was questionable whether they were fully thinking creatures or mere beasts, but I would never underestimate my adversary, and so I renewed my effort to get us onto the roof and out of there as discreetly as possible.

"We will toss the girl up first," I said.

I put the man on the ground, and grabbed hold of the girl's legs. Veronica took her by the arms and together we threw her up to Stephen. Her limbs flailed like a ragdoll, but he caught her at the top and laid her down on the roof. He gave us the signal to toss up the other. The howls increased and I hurried to ready the man. Veronica took the arms and I the legs, but this time we launched the body a little too softly. Stephen made the catch but not without pulling the man's shoulder from its socket. Unfortunately, this woke him from his unconscious state with a scream.

"Cover his mouth," I said.

Stephen pulled him up onto the roof and did one better. He knocked him out cold again, though it

11

was too late to salvage our discreetness. The scream had alerted the swarm to our position, and several bloodless rounded the corner to get to us. Within moments, new swarms formed at either end of the laneway.

"Go," I said to Veronica. She scaled the wall as easily as Stephen, and when I saw her safely up top, I threw myself onto the bricks. Several bloodless reached me, tearing at my boots with their bony fingers, but they could not gain a grip, as I kicked them off my feet. I was relieved when none of them attempted to scale the wall and climb up after me. When I looked back down at the rotting faces, smacking their jaws to get at me, I shuddered at the thought of being pulled down into them. By the sound of the howls echoing up through the trattoria, some of them had retreated inside and were newly enthralled by the bit of flesh we left behind. It would not be long before the rest of them tore down the walls with their stampede, plowing through one another to get to the human remains lying on the floor.

From the roof, we were able to locate an escape route near a button store farther down the lane, and we made our way from the town and into the forest almost as swiftly as we had arrived. The girl had been unconscious since the trattoria and I held her to my breast to shelter her from the wind. I wanted to prevent her delicious scent from piquing the nose of others, though we did not see too many in the forest now.

Our flight through the cool air revived her and she moved in my arms. I looked down to find her staring up at me. Her neck was exposed and I saw the blood flooding her veins with its sweetness—I could feel her skin throbbing, as the hot serum rushed beneath it. My need to taste her was strong, but I tempered my desire with thoughts of Byron. I could not wait to bring him the prize I held in my arms; I would be satiated just watching him guzzle every drop of her blood. "We must hurry," I said.

When we reached the field, Veronica ran ahead and readied the passage. She held the hatch open for us and I went down first. The girl was quiet, though she was fully awake. Stephen followed me, carrying the man with his arm still dangling from its socket. Veronica was just about to make her way down the steps when she was caught in the grip of a jowl. The bloodless had come out of nowhere, skulking silently in the dark.

"Stephen!" Her call tore through him and though he had already reached the bottom step, he threw the man down and bolted back up to help his beloved. I had placed the girl down as well and was about to run up to give them help when she tugged at the cuff of my pant.

"Don't go," she whispered.

I barely gave her a glance, shaking her hand loose. I rushed up the steps to find six or seven bloodless swarming, their howls escalating so they were soon baying at the moon. Stephen had freed his beloved from the grip of the first and planted his dagger deep in its jowl. Veronica tore the mandible of another with her bare hands. The fresh blood had renewed our fangs and talons and made them worthy opponents for bony fingers and rancid mouths. The bloodless could not break skin, for the texture of ours had become as solid as marble again.

I let my talons loose and sliced the necks of two that came forward while Veronica and Stephen dropped the last three, as a few newcomers darted across the field, catching the human whiff that hung in the air. We flew down the steps and I slammed the hatch, locking us in with the iron bar and metal chains before howls of a second swarm reached our threshold. As we headed down the tunnel to safety, the baying of the bloodless faded.

20 September. — When I realized we could run out of people to feed on, my fangs ached for want of a fresh bite. Three months in and I knew the gravity of the threat—the plague was quickly robbing us of our precious resource. It was then that Byron suggested we stockpile as much blood as we could find, foraging clinics, blood banks, hospitals, med vacs, even military facilities for every last drop. We subsisted on the reserves for a fair amount of time, longer in fact than I expected, but feeding on portioned blood is no way for a vampire to live. Our rations are all depleted now and I am desperate again. Byron has taken a turn for the worse, and I fear this is his end. But Maxine's discovery gave me hope. I did not know if the information she had gathered was worth her life but if it proved true, we would stave off the hunger for a little while longer.

It pains me now to recall Jean's face, as he watched his beloved consort change before his very eyes, her beauty fleeting as instantly as the gasp of a dead man. When she had returned from that fateful jaunt, she had whispered to her maker in their tongue, her French betraying her fear. "Je me suis fait mordre par les monstres." *I was bitten by the monstres.*

"Mais comment?" Jean's disbelief hung in the air long after his voice echoed through the cathedral.

14

I asked her where she had been. I was in a foul mood, starving as I was.

"I went to ze trattoria," she said, "where we found zat boy."

"Foolish," I said under my breath.

The boy had already been infected and was on the verge of his transformation. His insides sat atop his outsides and he smelled rancid. He was unconscious, just barely breathing, and my clan was furious with me for refusing to feed on him. It took some convincing to assure them his blood, should it not poison us, would taste putrid.

"I 'oped zere would be others," Maxine said, "'iding zere." She choked a little.

"Reposes-toi, ma douce." *Rest, my sweet.*

Jean took her by the hand and led her to a pew. He wrapped his arms around her and pulled her into him. She could no longer see the look of horror on his face, the same one the rest of us will never forget. "But I was careful," she whispered to him, as they sat.

"Obviously not careful enough," I said since it was beneath me to cloak my scorn. I expressed my anger at her reckless behavior openly, though I admit scolding her then is something I regret now.

"I made my way to ze alley at ze side," she said. "Zere was nobody zere, but I smelled eet." Her eyes betrayed what *eet* was. "I smelled zat peppery sweetness and I knew it was fresh so I headed for ze trattoria when suddenly I 'eard zem."

"The bloodless?" I asked.

"No, ze 'umans."

"Where?"

"Inside," she said.

"You heard voices?"

15

"Yes," she said. "I'm sure of it. I went to ze door and sniffed ze air. Zat's when I knew I smelled eet and zen I 'eard whispers, a single voice, and zen … zen … I was captured."

Maxine looked at each of us, the sting on our faces making her tremble. She had been caught up in a swarm of infected people we had come to call the bloodless. The plague consumed the humans and robbed them of that delectable ichor we were wont to devour. Losing our precious resource was a reality we still denied.

"Zey surrounded me and I could not escape. Zey pinched me with zeir teeth and dug zeir dirty bones into my skin." She held out her arms to show us the wounds she had suffered. I was horrified by the sight of her torn limbs. Mangled teeth and bony fingers had punctured her marble skin and ripped out chunks of vampiric flesh. Her body would not recover without fresh blood. "I barely got—" She slumped forward and grabbed her stomach, as she let out a shriek.

More compassionate than I, Byron insisted on examining her. He wanted to inspect the wounds that would prove fatal. Jean held Maxine in his arms while Byron studied her limbs. Her flesh blistered, macerated as it was from lack of human blood.

"Comment est-ce possible?" Jean's eyes were wide.

"She went out alone," I said.

I was callous in my treatment of her but I could have never known what was coming. I believed it was as simple as Maxine having flown too close to the sun, her wings now melting. I was angry with her for daring to go out unaccompanied, and though I am not her keeper, I am somewhat responsible for her. I am the one who led them here, I am the one who promised to keep them safe. But if I am being totally honest, it is more than that. Her vulnerability frightened me. It meant this plague could strike me down too.

We stood around waiting to see what would happen next. I had never seen a vampire succumb to human frailty. We had never been infected by disease; no reports of vampires contracting HIV, Hepatitis, influenza, bubonic plagues, black plagues, green plagues, or any plagues for that matter. We had assumed this virus like all the others could only infect a mortal. But we were wrong.

Maxine writhed in the pain of her torn flesh, as she clung to her existence in the arms of her maker. "It burns," she said. "It burns."

It was not until her body heated that we knew she was infected. My sweet Byron tended to her all the while, as weak as he was. He tried to quell her pain with ointments and a sugar serum he had concocted in his chambers but even with all his scientific brilliance, he could not heal Maxine.

"Nom de Dieu," Jean said. "What should we do?"

"We wait," Byron said. He insisted we watch Maxine with diligence in case she changed.

"C'est pas possible?" Jean said, numb with disbelief.

None of us were ready to accept the reality that Maxine could morph into one of them, transform just like the humans do when they are infected.

"But she cannot," Elizabeth said. She was Maxine's dearest friend and her only progeny. Maxine had made Elizabeth so that she would have an eternal playmate—she was only a child when

Jean made her his vampire. For some three hundred years the two girlish vampires had spent a childhood together, both made from the same eccentric venomline. She clung to Maxine, holding her maker's hand in hers, trembling at the thought of losing her. "You can't change," Elizabeth said. "I won't let you." She turned to Jean and pleaded for him to help his beloved. "You must stop this or she'll be lost to us forever."

I do not think Maxine's panic set in completely until then. When she heard her playmate's plea, she cursed and screamed. "I don't want to be one of zem. 'Elp me! Arrêter cette folie! Arrêter ma douleur! Jean, je t'en prie."

I pulled Byron aside and asked him what he thought would happen to her.

"I cannot know for sure," he said. "But her transformation, should it come, will come quickly."

And so it did. One moment she thrashed in Jean's arms, screaming at the top of her lungs, the next she was as rigid as stone.

"Jean," Byron said. "Step away."

Lost in the horror of the moment, Jean had to be pried from his demoiselle, too distraught to let her go. "Quelle horreur!" His cry echoed up through the spire of the cathedral.

"What should we do?" I asked.

Byron shook his head as if to say there was nothing we could do, but when Maxine opened her eyes, it was decided. She was reanimated, but would never live again.

It is difficult to describe what I witnessed in the chancel, for I still deny its truth. Maxine's metamorphosis was quick, though the actual transformation seemed in slow motion. First her

18

visage contorted into an expression of permanent horror, like Frankenstein's might have looked when he first reanimated his patchwork. But Maxine's contortions escalated and soon her nose and mouth began to fuse into what looked like a pointed beak; her skin twisted and became taut around her lips, which swelled like her eyes, bulging more greatly than those of a pop-eye fish. I looked away when her neck stretched wide with the tearing of her tendons and when her talons ripped through the tips of her toes, her newly clawed feet breaking the soles of her boots. She seethed and released a trill before she lunged at me, snapping her fangs. I did not hesitate to defend myself or my clan. I have no remorse for doing what I was forced to do, but the image of what I have done—what I had to do—is seared in my brain, too wretched to recount in full. I wonder if some things are not better left abandoned on the shores of Lethe.

Later. — Soon after we returned with the humans, they became a source of contention. Jean wanted the man, Elizabeth the girl, but Byron decided for all of us. He insisted the man and the girl be locked in a chamber while we made our plans. He was always the coolest head when vital matters were at hand. "They will be rationed," he said.

"I agree," I said. "But how long will two humans last with six hungry vampires?"

"We will take small sips." He smiled, though I did not. He knew a sip would not suffice. The only way for him to recover was to drink three, four, maybe five men at a time. His diet was deficient, he was malnourished and fading rapidly. "Cull their blood," he said.

"What?"

"Draw from the man first." He handed me a syringe from one of his medical bags.

"You want me to extract his blood with this?"

"I am too weak," he said. "Jean and Elizabeth are too hungry, and the other two are … well, you know."

"As you wish."

When I visited our captives, they were both conscious and aware of their new surroundings; they seemed to know we were not exactly the cavalry come to save the day.

"What happened to Salvatore?" The man played it tough, though it was obvious he just wanted to cry.

I ignored him and busied myself with attaching the syringe to the vial. I was in fact just biding my time. I had to work up the courage to draw the man's blood. I do not like needles and the thought of poking him with one made me queasy. I reminded myself it was for Byron and that meant everything—there is nothing I will not do for him.

"Sir?" The girl spoke softly. She seemed braver than the man—if at all possible. "Thank you for saving us," she said.

I looked at her, studying her for the first time in the light. She was ragged looking, dirty and disheveled. Her hair was matted and tangled, her clothes torn and she had no shoes on her feet. Oh my, she was a sight! I was repulsed to the point of not even desiring her blood. That was a first.

"Marco is hurt bad," she said.

I looked at the man, he was in rough shape too. He had scars on his arms and legs from battling to survive, no doubt. His shirt was sleeveless and his pants were torn and shredded. He wore boots and a silly looking bandana around his neck. I decided I would not speak to them since it would only make matters uncomfortable.

I summoned Stephen to the room and had him steady the man, as I drew the blood. The needle missed several times, though it was not the man's fault. Stephen held him down, planting his two hands on his dislocated arm, but I was clumsy with the tool—fangs are much more efficient. When I finally pierced the vein with the point of the needle, I whispered for Stephen to look away. I wished I could have too. I felt desperate to taste the blood, as it gushed up the syringe into the vial. It was thick and dark, that serum of the gods. How I miss those days!

I took four vials, two for Byron and one for each of the others. Veronica and Stephen would have to wait for their next fix, though I let Stephen lick off the blood that had dripped onto my finger in the clean up.

"Enough," I said, as I pushed his head away; he would have devoured my whole hand had I let him. I ordered him to keep guard at the locked door with our captives safely tucked inside. "No one gets in or out," I said. He obeyed, standing at attention as though a centurion saluting his general. The lick of blood had made him playful.

I ignored the girl's pleas for my return, as I floated down the hallway to my beloved. When I entered Byron's chamber, he lay in the sarcophagus we had found him in the tomb below the cathedral. He opened his eyes when he felt me at his side.

"My sweet Vincent," he said. "How was it?"

"I will tell you another time. For now, I need you to drink this."

He sat up and took the vial I offered him. With his beautiful sharp teeth, he tore off its cap and downed the drink. When I handed him a second vial, he finished that off too.

"How do you feel?" I smiled, certain the drink had revived him.

"I fear it is too late for me, sweet love," he said, as he lay back down.

"I will bring you more then," I said. "The entire man if I have to."

As I turned to go, he stopped me, though not with words. His mind called me back; this was our union. As bonded vampires, we no longer need speech to communicate. He can speak into my thoughts, and I his, but since his falling ill, he has not been able to converse with me telepathically. I cannot express how relieved I was the power had returned. I rushed to his side, but he was more depleted than before. That bit of telepathy had zapped him of all the energy he had received from the blood. I searched his eyes, fearing nothing would bring him back.

Not ready to accept his fate yet, I left him to fetch more blood. I recruited Stephen's help again, this time drawing from the girl.

"Please," she said. "We are starved."

As are we, I thought.

I siphoned more blood from the man and when I had taken the most I could from both of them without draining them completely, I ordered Stephen to get them some food. The ecclesiastics had left a pantry full of preserves and canned foodstuffs. Useless to us, they had gone untouched since we moved in. We lost our appetite for food when we lost our only true sustenance.

Stephen returned with a feast, and the two humans, near fainting, gorged on the spread of viands. The food appeased them, making them appreciate their captivity. I tossed Stephen two vials of the man's blood before I rushed back to Byron. "Savor it," I said.

When I brought the new vials to my beloved, he consumed them more reluctantly. "I have barely kept the others down," he said.

It pained me to hear of his suffering; I would give my life to save my beloved.

"What can I do?" I said.

"One must resign oneself to defeat." I could not accept that. This was not his end. There was a way to bring him back—there had to be.

I coaxed him to take a sip of the girl's blood, reminding him the sexes carry different properties. I hoped hers would impact him greatly. He took the vial, forcing a smile. He tore off the cap and raised the container to his lips, tipping the end up gently and letting a few drops hit his tongue. I waited for him to take a proper swig. "Does she taste as sweet as she smells?"

He took another swig and rolled the serum around in his mouth as though sampling a Beaujolais. When he finally swallowed, he grinned. "Saccharine," he said.

I had only tasted blood that sweet once, soon after I had become a vampire. I resided in a tomb, living among the dead by day since it felt like the most apt place to be in the beginning. We lived in a different world then and at night I would wander the gardens and fields, preying on any human that crossed my path—I did not discriminate. One evening, taking in the fresh Mediterranean air, I came upon a woman sitting alone between two olive trees.

"Salutations, my sister."

"And to you, my brother."

Her belly was round and full. "May I give you a hand?"

"No, I am well," she said. "Just waiting for the pass to come."

She was about to deliver, sent out to give birth alone in the night. It was not the custom for mothers to give birth to their sons alone, for they would often die before hearing their child's first cry, but this woman and her child were abandoned.

"Shall I wait with you?" I was just a novice then with remnants of my humanity.

When her labor began, I held her hands, letting her use me as leverage. She squeezed me with all her might, but barely crushed my hardened skin, and I was careful not to squeeze back. She squatted between the trees, pushing down on her pelvis with her body's whole force, and the dewy grass beneath her glistened with drops of blood. The smell overwhelmed me, and though I had wanted to wait for the baby, the sight of her torn flesh, bloody and ripe, drove me into a frenzy. I reached down and touched the wet grass below her. When I brought my fingers up to my lips, I was lost. My fangs tore into her neck, and I sucked the life from her, as she delivered her stillborn child onto the slippery grass between her legs. It was the sweetest blood I had ever tasted—dulcet and candied.

The human girl I had brought into the cathedral, the one whose blood stained the lips of my beloved, was pregnant.

21 September. — Once everyone knew about the girl's condition, excitement filled the hours. Each of us desires to have our way with her. Jean is the most agitated. He wants to see the baby to term, raise it as his own and then bite its neck when it reaches the age of twelve. He has not gotten over his Maxine. Elizabeth wants a child companion too, and Stephen and Veronica desire draining the girl of her sweet ichor while the baby's heart still beats inside her.

"I've never tasted blood that new," Veronica said. "Can we please?" Stephen stroked her arm, as she spoke.

"Byron has called a meeting," I said. "We will hear what he has to say."

"Has it revived him any?" Elizabeth asked. None of them had seen Byron since he drank the vials, but she found her answer in my pained expression. "I'm sorry," she said.

"Il s'en sortira," Jean said. *He'll recover.*

We were gathered in the chancel, waiting for Byron and listening to the howls of a swarm, as it glided past the building. The humans are tucked away, deep inside the belly of the cathedral where nothing can get at them. When Byron finally appeared, looking sallow and weak, my heart sank. Stephen ran to his side and gave him his arm. I had offered to bring him to the meeting, but he refused my help. I suspect his infirmity shames him, for he often tries to hide his suffering from me.

25

My sweet Byron, how it is difficult to see you these days—my whole world is cankered, as thoughts of your demise plague me. The anguish often brings me to my knees when I am alone in my chamber. I do not feel your frequency run through me anymore and it is the most sublime sense of abandonment.

"We must deal with the girl and her child bravely," Byron said to the group.

"Can we keep it?" Elizabeth asked.

"Ça suffit." Jean chided Elizabeth as he had Maxine.

"I have given the situation much thought," Byron said, glancing over at me with his electric eyes, forever burning into me with their scrutiny. "I am not long for this world, and if we do not do something, neither are any of you. That child may be the answer to this plague."

"Quoi?" Jean asked. "What can you mean?"

I knew what he meant. Byron had spoken to me the previous night, invading my thoughts, as I kneeled in my chamber. He believes the child will save us all; he envisions a new human race, a healthy nation that will rise and prosper and outlive the plague. But only with our help, for the fight will be long and difficult. With our protection, the healthy humans can propagate a new generation, and Byron believes that the girl's child is a scientific sign, a guarantee in fact, that rebirth is the solution. The mortals are the answer to our survival, just as we are to theirs. "If enough humans survive, a resilient group can rise up and overcome," I said.

"Exactly." Byron looked at me when he spoke. "We can keep her safe and her child alive and perhaps even find others to protect."

"But how?" Elizabeth asked.

"Willpower," Veronica said. She was the most optimistic of us, the one with the strongest sense of humanity. Both she and Stephen were still young vampires, which meant they were the most capable of mustering up compassion for a human.

"It can be done," Byron said. "It must be done."

"It will be done." I gave him my word then and there. I wanted him to know I would suffer for him, I would starve for him, I would be human for him.

22 September. — When Byron asked for the girl to be brought to him, I questioned his motives since her blood did not appeal to him. "Is that a good idea in your condition?"

"I would like to speak to her," he said. "It is the only way I can know what action to take. Scientifically speaking."

"Scientifically," I said. "Of course." I was not worried he would struggle to resist her, but I was still annoyed.

It is difficult to explain why I feel insecure, why I doubt him. Perhaps it is because he has grown cold and distant, and hard toward me in ways. His affection is mute, if not dead, since nothing is left for him. We do not talk about it, and I do not want to bring it up. I am afraid if I raise the subject he will simply agree with me and that will be all of it. And I am not ready for that. For now, the memory of his becoming mine consoles me hourly. If Byron cannot await me in the realms of Hades, or at the gates of Paradise, this moment shall be our eternity.

The gratitude he showed me at his vampiric birth is still a comfort. After I gifted him with my power, he took my hand in his and kissed it. He thanked me with a sincerity I had never known before. Few show appreciation for their transformation since regret is common. At the beginning, self-pity lingers and the novice may easily forget the miserableness of his mortal life, causing him to mourn a chimera. But not you, Byron—not you, my beloved. You caressed my hand at your revival, and touched me as though I were a god who redeemed you from hell. You understood this privileged life, this gift of immortality, from the start. You knew even before I came for you that the vampire is superior to all other life forms—human, especially. I will never forget that first night when you were still a bloodhungry man and I made you mine without a second thought because I knew you were worthy of me. From that first show of gratitude, my beloved, to this moment now, I have not lived without you. For a century and a half, we have been lovesick and debaucherous in our exceptional union, and you, my darling, forever the scientist, have explored your gifts with fervor. We could never resist the occasional bout of torture, though most were in the name of science, were they not?

When the outbreak began, in fact, Byron was one of the first to experiment on the sick. "There is a cure," he had said. I knew if that were true, he would find it. "I think it is simply a rapid growth of cells that attack the nervous system and eventually contaminate the brain, spreading almost instantly, like some accelerated version of Proteus syndrome."

"My darling, I am not quite as gifted in the disease department," I had said. "Proteus syndrome?"

"It is not a disease so much as an atypical bone growth caused by tumors. But this affliction seems to be developing on and around the spine and causing a type of deformation to the brain that makes it defunct."

"If they are braindead," I had said, "how can they function?"

"They are not braindead so much as automated."

"But what makes them desire to spread their affliction?" By then we had seen the bloodless attack the unafflicted and turn them, as they say.

He smiled at me and winked. "Man at his very root is steered by malice, is he not?"

At the time, Byron believed the plague was not simply a physical contamination but also a moral one. The bloodless were driven by a desire to find company for their misery. Like the fallen angel, they wanted to bring a barrage of cohorts down with them.

"It is as if they suffer a social disorder," he had said. "Some kind of narcissism that impels them to make reproductions of themselves."

We would have never called them bloodless if they had not wreaked havoc on our way of life. The affliction spread at incalculable speeds, taking only several weeks for the plague to be considered a full-fledged pandemic.

Byron performed dissections on the few bloodless we could get our hands on. At the beginning, when we were still feeding easily and Italy had only a few reported cases, he insisted on experimenting. If there were scientific findings to be had, Byron would have them. Test subjects were not difficult to acquire, the stink of the bloodless was easy enough to sniff out. As I have said, when they are not in a swarm, they are harmless. A well nourished vampire is far stronger than an afflicted human, even if it has just turned.

"I have a lead at Santo Padre Gio," he had said one evening.

"In quarantine?"

"Yes, but Ernesto is there to let us in."

One of Byron's human friends was a hospital orderly. He had been giving Byron blood, tissue samples and other sundry medical supplies for years. Byron had known one of his ancestors in medical school and used that as his introduction. He claimed his own great-great grandfather had been a friend of Ernesto's ancestor. Since he knew so many details about the man's family, it was easy for him to ingratiate himself with the human. How Byron resisted digging his fangs into the boy's neck, I will never know. Every time I saw him that was all I wanted to do—he smelled delicious. We had an endless influx of specimen until things got worse and Ernesto disappeared. But the night we went to Santo Padre Gio, he was outside smoking a cigarette from the unending chain of tobacco he pumped into his system. He tossed the butt onto the pavement and pulled out a fresh fag before he let us in the backdoor. Down to the basement, he led us through a hallway and several locked rooms. "I made keys," he said. "You're on your own from here."

He pointed out the direction using the mallet he had on him for protection. The blunt hammer had become an accessory on his newly weaponized belt. With the unlit cigarette dangling from his bottom lip, he gave us his usual speech. "I've shut off the monitor but you only have a minute or two before someone shows up."

"Is she sedated?" Byron asked.

"No, but she's unconscious."

I admired his glibness. Her unconscious state meant that she was about to change and would soon be reanimated. He should have been frightened since his mallet was no match for the bloodless. "You never saw me," he said, as he headed back to his smoking section outside.

"Come Vincent."

I followed Byron through the hall to a door at the end. I was surprised how empty the world looked; there was not another soul to be seen. Byron unlocked the door and we slipped in. We had already made a plan to get her out of the building unnoticed. I would toss her over my shoulder and we would creep through the halls with the speed only we could attain. We would be out the door within seconds.

We found the girl chained to a bed, her arms and legs in irons. Ernesto had given us keys for the shackles and Byron raced to set her free. She remained senseless, as I carried her out. I wondered how such things were possible; I could not imagine this young girl transformed into a beast suddenly upon waking. She seemed weak, and I was strong. I still recall it vividly. I was not convinced these things were a threat to us; their smell of illness and death was too pungent for any vampire to desire, and so feeding off them was out of the question. I had not thought of the other difficulty they posed, the one we face now.

When we got back to our lab, I assisted Byron. I placed straps about her limbs and head, as she stirred. She squirmed a little and tried to resist the force of my hands, but failed. When she was safely locked down, her legs twitched and her torso contorted as though she attempted to ply herself free. When her face began to morph, her lips and nose peeling inward, making her teeth jut out, I could hear her jaw and cheekbones crack. Her teeth looked like any other, but they were backed by an almost superhuman strength.

One of the affliction's side effects, what Byron calls its X factor, is the resilience and strength of the atypical bones. A wolframlike hardening occurs with the heating of their fevered bodies. The power of their jaws is like that of a crocodile's, and they can snap their blunt teeth shut with enormous force. I wondered if her lack of fangs enfeebled her and stuck my hand in her open mouth. She snapped down on one of my fingers but could not gain a grip on my hardened flesh.

"Do not play," Byron said.

"She is too weak to be any kind of threat."

"For now." He looked at me intensely.

"Are they getting stronger then?" I asked.

"No," he said. "But we may weaken."

His words stung, as he predicted something I did not foresee. The plague was insidious, and not just for what it did to humans, but because it robbed us of our natural resource. At the time, I could not understand why he was so interested in finding a cure for the humans. But now—of course now—I do. Now I see everything. He was not working to save them; he was doing it to save us.

As I walked down the cathedral's corridor to fetch the pregnant girl, I thought of the afflicted one. As it went, she was only the tip of the iceberg. After dozens of experiments, Byron had still not made any progress. He was convinced he knew how the disease affected the humans but not what would prevent it. He was frustrated with his lack of advancement in the end. He had dissected spines of active bodies, as they lay on his table; he had cut off the top of that girl's head, peeled back her scalp, and studied her reactions, as he touched different parts of her brain through a deformed cranium. Byron had done his best, and had gotten ill over his obsession. He skipped out on feedings and unless I brought him fresh blood, he would neglect to recharge himself altogether. He was already weak when the rations ran scarce. I blame myself for letting him become so engrossed in the dying that he forgot how to live. Why did I not force him back to health sooner—why did I let him obsess so?

My heart was heavy when I reached the girl's chamber, and I sent Stephen to check on Veronica before I entered her room alone. We had set them up rather civilly, deciding it was useless to treat them as prisoners. We fed them and gave them simple necessities such as access to a lavatory, soap, fresh clothes, and medical attention. We would not resort to savagery just because the world had ended—we found ways to continue simple luxuries like running water. Jean had tended to the man's dislocated shoulder, putting it up in a sling after snapping it back into place. He found it difficult to resist the human, but he was, as we all were, aware of the greater good of our actions. Besides, we are not so incapable of abstaining, even as we starve. We are far more disciplined than humans; our cruelty has some limits.

When I entered the chamber, the man rested on the bed with his eyes closed and the girl sat on the settee with a paperback copy of *Paradise Lost* propped in her lap. She looked completely different. She was revived and pleasant, appearing fresh and clean in one of the long robes we found in the nunnery. She had washed and combed her hair and wore it down and pulled over one of her shoulders. She smiled when she saw me.

"Hello," she said.

I asked her to come with me.

"Is everything okay? Are we still safe?" Her naiveté was refreshing.

"You will not be harmed." I spoke with a soft tone, an attempt to reassure her, but I could not know if she trusted us yet.

"Marco," she said.

He opened his eyes and then snorted, as he bolted up.

"Just you," I said.

I smiled at her with a closed mouth, not wanting to risk exposing my fangs, especially since the aroma in the room teased them. My teeth were itching to drop.

"I can come too if you want," Marco said.

"Just her." I held out my hand for the girl. She got up from the settee and gently placed her book to the side. She came toward me and hesitated before taking my hand. When I touched her skin, mine tingled. I could feel the blood pulse through her veins. Pulse-pulse, it cried. Her smell intoxicated me; that candied serum had come alive with the nourished baby inside her. She put her hand on her belly, as though she knew my thoughts, and looked me straight in the eye when she spoke. "Thank you for saving us."

Her voice was barely above a whisper, and though I knew she meant Marco, her hand on her belly was fitting all the same. She did not show yet, and may not have known she was pregnant. I released her hand once we exited the chamber and headed to see Byron. When we entered, he was poised at his desk, making on he was human I suppose. I had not seen him sit there for weeks. Though we would normally be in the shadows, he wanted to make her feel welcome and had lit candles all around his room.

"Good evening, my dear." He greeted her with warmth, and I thought it was the physician in him that held regard for human life, something he had struggled with when he first became a vampire. All that killing, all those abuses against his Hippocratic oath, made him feel guilty for using man so selfishly. "Please sit," he said.

She could not be more than fifteen; she looked like a child.

"Thank you for saving us," she said.

"It is our pleasure, my dear." He smiled with his mouth closed, wanting to keep his fangs from showing too, no doubt.

We had decided against sharing our true nature with them; we assumed they did not suspect us of being anything other than human since they had not seen us do anything that would give our nature away.

"Are you comfortable," he said. "Do you have all you need?"

"Oh yes, sir, thank you." She shivered, as he sat down beside her.

Byron must have frightened her. He looked like a corpse; pale and skeletal, his eye sockets sunk into his skull. The handsome man I once knew was gone.

She looked up at me several times during their conversation. She smelled so good I had to stay as far away from her as I could. I practically hugged the door by the time she sat down. Byron could see my difficulty. "Vincent," he said. "You may leave us if you have more pressing things to tend to."

He gave me the exit in kindness, but I refused to leave him alone with her. "I am fine."

He dismissed my unease and returned to the girl. "My dear, we drew your blood because we had to run some tests. I am a doctor, you see." She smiled at him and nodded. "I hope we did not cause you any grief," he said.

"Umm," she said. "We were a little scared at first. After what happened at the trattoria and all. We didn't know there were still decent people out there." She looked at me and smiled again. "We've seen some horrible things," she said. "Just horrible things going on out there." I suspected that comment did not refer to the bloodless alone.

"Have you come across other people?" Byron asked.

"Several," she said. "Yes."

Byron waited for her to continue. He hoped she knew where we could find others.

"We were actually hiding from some of them when you found us." She glanced over at me and then back at him. "The three of us—" She stopped herself, uneasy about what happened to her missing party. "I mean, there were three of us and then when we got here there was just Marco and me."

"What happened to your friend?" Byron asked.

"I don't know really," she said. "The last thing I remember is your voice." She looked at me again. "Your soft voice," she said to me. "It sounded like we were going to be safe. Your voice just stuck in my mind and then I, well, I … I guess I fainted."

"I see," Byron said. He was as relieved as I that she had not seen the three of us gorge on her friend. "Who was the other?" He asked.

She took a deep breath and sighed. "I didn't know him really well," she said.

"And Marco?"

"He's my stepdad." She wriggled in her seat, her admission making her uncomfortable. Perhaps she was lying, or perhaps she was ashamed of something else entirely.

Byron put his hand on hers, causing her shoulders to quiver. "My dear," he said. "Do you know you are pregnant?"

She looked stunned for a moment and then closed her eyes. "Uh-huh." She covered her face with her hands and fell into Byron's lap. He looked up at me, as he petted her freshly washed hair.

"Shush," he said, soothing her with his strokes.

The sting of jealousy touched me—just a dart, pricking my side with the force of a pushpin. It was ridiculous really but the sincerity in his voice and his tender touch on the girl's hair made me rage. He was honest in his sympathy for her. His affection for the human had gotten the better of him and I saw him crumble beneath it. I left the room, stifled by the show of emotion and the sickeningly sweet smell of the human.

26 September. — This day. Today … Today … To … Day … T … D … Y … Byron is gone and I cannot weep, I cannot die. My reality hit me when he locked himself in the sarcophagus. All I could do was sit by him, as he writhed inside. Only when the movement stopped, when the thrashing ceased, did I open the lid. Nothing but ash remained. Ashes, I want to consume. I will consume—his ashes—tonight—this night! This night … I will make him mine again.

... — It feels as though the days escape me, as though there is no more reason to keep track of time's passing. All feels lost, though I will go on. I will go on for you, Byron. I will push aside the feelings of pointlessness and come out from your ashes. We lay together in your sarcophagus for long enough. The only thing that can save me from this pain is my responsibility for the others. They need me.

29 September. — The situation is hopeless. We are forced to the lowest means for survival, culling blood piecemeal as though we could stand to live this way. The little taste we consume barely gives us vigor, let alone satisfaction.

My sweet Byron! How my heart aches for your passing. I know you were unable to carry on. I could only hang my head in misery, as I watched your graceful form disintegrate—bloodstarved. You became dust before my eyes and I will mourn you until the end of time. You were my first and only companion, and so you shall remain.

Adieu, sweet Byron. May I see you always in my memory as you were in your moments of splendor—gallant, charming, vampiric, a villain for the ages!

30 September. — Byron had a fondness for the pregnant girl, and tended to her needs until his demise. She was in his care because he was adamant about seeing the baby to term. None of us understood his logic, or why he wanted to torture us so. None of us would be able to resist the candied smell of a bloody newborn. Her baby would be devoured the moment it touched the air, and then she and her stepfather the moments after. "You need to see this through," he had said. "You need to understand what this means."

"It is perverse," I had said. "We are not supposed to save them—just the opposite in fact. I brought them back here to save you."

"She is the answer we have been searching for—"

"How?"

I was frustrated by his inability to see that her pregnancy was the one thing that would save him. "Devour her," I had said. "You can have her all to yourself. It will revive you, reverse your decay—the blood of her child will enrich you. You would be rejuvenated if you would only feed on the girl."

"She is not to be touched," he had said.

We argued like this until our last hours together, but he knew I would obey him. I may have been our clan's leader but I was subservient to Byron. My union with him had dictated it so. I had fastened myself to him, and because I had made him in my image, I could no longer live without him. I was at his mercy, though the others did not see our truth. In front of them, he was the subordinate vampire.

"One day, Vincent, when I am long gone, you will understand this sacrifice."

"Enough!" I promised him I would abide by his wish.

"And the others?" He had asked.

"They will follow my law."

He came to me then and took my hands in his and thanked me with the same gratitude that had melted my heart at his vampiric birth. His kiss was like the drop of heaven I shall never know.

Later. — I am sorry, Byron. I regret my blindness to what you were doing for us. But even more, I regret not telling you I love you for it.

2 October. — Veronica grows weak, as does Elizabeth. The female vampires suffer more without blood. I have ordered Jean to draw from the man again, but to leave the girl untouched. Though we had kept them in the same room, Byron wanted them separated when the girl confided that Marco is the father of her child. She claims it was consensual, but regrets the outcome nevertheless.

When she told us about their escape from their home, she was curled up on the sofa, her legs tucked under her robe. She was still too thin to show but Byron figured she was about five months along. "He saved me but not …" Her words drifted. "He didn't mean to let go of her but we were surrounded and he had no choice," she said.

She told us they made it to a natatorium where they met up with Marco's friend, the third man from her party.

"Salvatore let us in since the neighborhood was already overrun with them. We had stayed in our

40

house long after the neighbors moved out. I think we were the only ones left on the block. Marco insisted we stay until the carabinieri showed up. He said they'd come for us—he said radio reports said they'd come to our neighborhood too." She twisted the fringe of her robe between her fingers, as she spoke. Curling and uncurling, she mangled the wool beneath her sweaty palm and I could smell her perspiring beneath the heavy fabric. "When the creepers—that's what Marco calls them—when they came to the neighborhood in crowds, he decided to leave. We snuck out one night, me and him and Lucia."

"Lucia?" Byron asked.

"Lucia was my sister. She was—" Her voice got caught in her throat, but she cleared it and began again. "I can't even remember her face now, you know?" She looked at Byron with sad eyes and I tempered my sting of compassion. "Marco couldn't save her, but I got away and headed to the pool. Marco said he knew how to get in."

"Were you pursued by the creepers, as you call them?" Byron asked.

"Yes," she said. "Like a pack of wolves or something, they chased after us." Marco led them through a row of bramble bushes, she said, and the thickets scraped them when they passed. But the thorns did more damage to the bloodless, as their skin got caught on the points. She turned back and saw the face of one peel right off, she said, as it ran through the bush after them. "The pool was just on the other side and Marco pulled me by the arm because I couldn't keep up. He finally picked me up and ran with me all the way to the courtyard on the other side of the building. We saw a few creepers

41

reaching through the gate, and that's how we knew there were other people inside."

Marco yelled for help when he saw Salvatore at the gate, and assured her they would be safe inside. "We just made it," she said. "Creepers crowded in on us, and Marco shot at a few of them too."

"Did the bullets stop them?" I asked.

She looked up at me with surprise, having forgotten she was not alone with Byron. "No," she said. "They just kept on."

Byron glanced at me. Nothing short of lighting the bloodless on fire would stop them. My beloved had discovered that only cremation could prevent reanimation.

"I was never so happy to see the inside of that public pool," she said. "It had little windows way up high at the top near the roof so it seemed safe, and the only way in was through the door Salvatore had chained back up after he let us in."

"Were there others with you?" Byron asked.

"Several families," she said. "The pool was drained and cots were set up on the floor."

"How many people in total?"

"Let's see," she said, as she counted her fingers. "Eleven including us."

Byron did not look at me but I knew what he would ask next. "Are they still there?"

"No, no, no," she said. "Oh-no." She seemed fearful of the memory but Byron pushed her, wanting to collect as much information from her as he could before he left us. He made notes, compiling a dossier for me to use after he was—it was that night, after she left him, that he withdrew into—his sarcophagus.

"What happened, my dear?" Byron brushed his hand across hers, and jealousy's sting bit me.

"Well," she said after taking a deep breath, "we lived for several weeks in quiet. I think it was weeks—I spent most of my time with a boy from my school. He was there with his family, and they were holding out too." She and the boy played board games, she said, while the adults played poker around the pool. A third family was there, and the mother nursed their baby at night while the two young boys and their father slept. Evelina and the new mother were the only females in the group, and she seemed timid when Byron pointed that out. I suppose he wondered if she knew to whom the baby belonged, though to me it did not matter.

"Creepers hadn't bothered us since the day we arrived, and so we went back to just waiting for the carabinieri to come. Sometimes we'd hear machine guns outside and every time we thought it was them. But they never came before the day—" She stopped herself.

Byron's hand rested on hers, and he petted her when she fell silent. I subdued my rage—never had I been jealous when we hunted women and men for sport, but this was different, this was unnatural. He did not intend to harm her and his affection seemed too genuine for my taste. I was utterly sick inside.

"Niccolò and I played with the two young boys—Niccolò is—was—the boy from my school," she said, "when all of a sudden we heard a loud crash from the other side of the wall in the courtyard. The whole building shook and then the ceiling started to crumble. We ran toward each other and huddled in a corner. The building tremors slowed but the walls and ceiling kept vibrating.

43

Marco said it was an earthquake, but the others thought it was a bomb. When it was over, the men went to see the damage and came back saying we were all done for. The wall of the courtyard had been knocked down and creepers climbed in and were pressed up to the inner wall, which gave way too." She took another deep breath. "The bomb or earthquake or whatever it was never even stopped them. They came at us. 'Run up the steps!' Salvatore yelled and we made our way up to the back of the building. I didn't realize the others were missing until we got out on the other side. Creepers were everywhere—I don't know how we dodged them all but we got away." Her voice cracked. "The family with the baby—Emilia—taken down." She covered her ears. "I can still hear their screams."

She may have meant the human cries or bloodless howls. Since we had never heard a firsthand account of a human attack, I was riveted.

"Niccolò ... Niccolò ... he ... didn't make it because he tried to save Davide and ... Antonio ... when their dad fell he turned back to get them." She held her hands more tightly against her ears, but Byron seemed transfixed.

"How soon did you get to the trattoria?" He asked.

"We only just got there a few days before you found us." She looked at me, letting her hands fall to her lap. Her face was swollen with sorrow. "The pool attack happened months ago," she said.

I had hoped there were others, as did Byron. "Rest now, my dear," he said. "Vincent will take you back to your room."

She kissed his hand and thanked him with a gratitude like the one that had melted my heart all those years ago; hers, it seemed, had the same effect on him.

"You must keep her safe," he told me when I returned to his chamber. "Her child too."

These were the last words he spoke.

3 October. — I told the others the girl was to be treated with care. "Swear an oath," I said. "Each of you will help me keep her and the baby from harm."

"Tu as ma parole," Jean said.

"Yes, Vincent," Elizabeth said.

Stephen and Veronica also consented.

"Eef I may ask," Jean said. "Why?"

"It is for our own good," I said. No further explanation was needed since the clan would not challenge my command; the problem lay, however, in convincing them it was my desire. "She may be the solution," I said. "Somehow she holds the key to our survival." I wanted to believe what I told them as much as I hoped they would. I put all my faith in my beloved Byron. I could do nothing else. "The man will serve as sustenance for now," I said. "But we will have to go on the hunt again soon, and if lucky, we will find others. We must believe these are not the last two humans on earth."

"Perhaps we should move on," Elizabeth said.

The others looked at me with a similar design in mind. It appeared they had spoken about it in private. "I will take it into consideration," I said. "But it will be difficult to move with two humans and a third on the way." Elizabeth looked down at the floor; she knew I was right. "For now," I said, "let us continue to hunt after dark."

The howling had ceased and the shadows on the walls were minimal, as only a few stray bloodless wandered past. Since we lived in darkness and spoke in hushed tones, we were undetectable to them, and as long as we kept the humans tucked away, our cathedral would be safe.

"How is the man doing?" I asked.

"'E's wavering," Jean said.

"Let us make sure he eats enough."

"Well, that's just it," Stephen said. "They're going through the rations quickly."

Scarcity of human food was not something I had thought about. Foolishly, I had forgotten they also needed to eat. "Our next run into town will have to be for food then."

When our meeting ended, I went to talk with the man. Byron had ignored him, but I wondered if he did not have additional information for us. He had given up reclining on the bed and was on the ground doing sit-ups. He stopped when he saw me and fumbled to get up from the floor. His injured arm was still bound in a sling. "Listen," he said with a slight lisp from his cracked tooth. "I'm going to come right out and say it. We'd like to leave. We thank you for your hospitality but we'd like to take our chances outside."

"Do you think that is really wise considering her condition?"

"Her condition?"

"Your stepdaughter is pregnant."

He was shocked—too shocked. He looked at me in such a way that I wondered if he knew it was even possible. Perhaps the child was not his after all. "Maybe your friend took liberties with the girl," I said.

He scratched his head with his free arm. "That sonofabitch!"

"She seems to think you are the father though," I said.

"She—what—I ..." His flushed expression evinced his guilt. He sat down on the bed and put his head in his free hand. "Oh my God."

"He will not help you," I said. "But I can."

He resigned himself to staying, knowing he could not escape with her in that condition.

"Do you know what happened to your friend Salvatore?" I asked.

"He—he—he," he stammered.

"Yes," I said. "He what?"

"The creepers—they attacked him in—the—the—the trattoria."

"I see," I said. "Do you need anything, Marco?" I wanted him to think our intentions were good and that we were concerned for their well-being—which we were, essentially.

"Uh," he said. "No, thank you." He cleared his throat. "But can I see Evie?"

"Not now," I said. "She rests most of the day." I turned to go but he stopped me.

"What's your name?"

I offered him the most troubling smile, fangs and all, and extended my hand to shake his. "Vincent Du Maurier."

He looked down at the floor, as his hand shot out to meet mine. He trembled when we touched. "Will there be much more blood drawn?"

He knew the answer, but I humored him. "As much as we need," I said.

I flew out of the room before he registered the door open and close again, and passed Jean in the hall with his readied syringe, as I headed back to my chamber.

47

Later. — I pored over Byron's most recent notes. Nothing in them made much sense. I found in the midst of them, however, some kind of chart he had drawn. It had arrows and lines pointing away from one central source—Evelina. She liked to be called Evie, but he was a stickler for formalities. She was at the heart of most of his diagrams. He had outlined the process of delivery very nicely for me, delegating each of us a task when the baby comes. He had given me a list of things she would need between now and then, and even drew up a list of things the baby would have to have as soon as it was born. On almost every page, he had jotted in the margins: *We must keep her alive! She must not be tasted*, and I assumed he had intended the directives for both the bloodless and us.

4 October. — Before we headed out to hunt for human food, we fed on our ration of Marco's blood—a meager portion, I might add, that is now used up. We needed to find sustenance for ourselves, as much as we needed food for the humans. We planned on going to an area of town we had stayed away from for some time, an antiquated section that housed spice markets and butcher shops, apothecaries and fruit stands. I thought if there was food tucked away somewhere, it could be in that area since the market had plenty of underground nooks and storage spaces. It was easy enough to get to, as we flew through the fields practically unnoticed. Only one straggler crossed our path, but we traveled so fast Stephen knocked him over, as we passed him by.

The entrance to the market was once barred but now the gates were toppled over, trampled by a swarm no doubt. I was surprised to see the main street marked with piles of ash, as if a fire had ravaged the place and burned everything in its path.

"Who could've done this?" Veronica asked.

"Must have been humans, right?" Stephen said.

They both hoped we would stumble on some poor fools hiding out, as I had until then, but the smell of burned flesh was thick and my optimism was swept up in it. I motioned for the two to stay close, as we went through the market stand by stand. The spice shelf whose sweet aroma once wafted through the streets was now in embers; its herbs and dried fruits turned to char. The rotting apple stands and lettuce carts were toppled over and burned, while singed rugs and baskets clung to rusted hooks from the awnings, just barely buoyed up in midair. The scene was a postcard from a city struck by the ash of a volcanic eruption, the scorched wares a shadow of a world we had known.

"It smolders still," Stephen said. "They may be here, whoever did this."

It had been set to flame not all that long ago, though I believed no human had done it despite Stephen's hoping so. "Not they," I said. "He."

"Who?" Veronica asked.

"Vlad is here," I said.

The ruler of the House of Dracul had arrived, no doubt to rob and pilfer what blood was left on our coast. I knew he would eventually pay us a visit, I had just thought it would be under better circumstances. Jean is one of Vlad's descendants; made from the venom of the famed impaler, he is his first progeny. He grew dispirited with the Romanian

49

boar and defected soon after we met in France. I taught Jean that the life of the vampire need not be as base and brutal as the one Vlad had offered him and he embraced my customs, striving to be a cultivated creature like me. Though most vampires are bound to the one for whom their transfiguration is owed, they are free beings nevertheless. When Jean decided to leave his boorish maker, Vlad could do nothing but give his progeny his blessing, if only reluctantly. The originator's venomline, however, will always retain some sway, and so since Vlad made Jean and Jean made Maxine and Maxine made Elizabeth, he has influence over all three of my clan members. The head of the House of Dracul has never recovered from the loss of his oldest progeny and since we are all desperate for blood now, he seeks out his descendants both for comfort and as his army to overtake the deserted world.

I had sensed his coming for days, though I tucked my suspicions aside to mourn the loss of my beloved. It was clear at the market that I could avoid him no longer since he would come for Jean, and perhaps the girl. "We have to go," I said.

"Is he dangerous?" Veronica asked.

"He could be if he realizes we have fresh blood," I said.

Neither of them knew how savage Vlad could be or the threat his presence posed to our captives, though I did not doubt Jean and Maxine had told them stories. Reports of Vlad's conduct perpetuated his frightening reputation for centuries; he came from a long line of agitators. During the Black Death, in fact, an ancestor of the Houses of Dracul and Bazaraab decelerated the recovery of the masses. Toktomer was a banished prince of the

Mongol Empire and became a vampire out of sheer
necessity, for he saw it as his only way to rule. I was
not aware of his turning until later, when its myth
spread far and wide among us. A female vampire bit
him, a slave he had captured. He had been at war for
years, leading his army as a Mongolian exile in
Crimea, and as the story goes, he found a girl
wandering along the pass one evening near his
camp. She was only eight or nine, but seduced him
still, and he took her in, calling her his child bride,
teaching her to fight alongside him. She had been
one of mine for a thousand years, and fed on his
troops one by one until he realized something was
amiss.

One night, he left his tent to find his child bride,
who had disappeared in the shadows. He told his
men of his search and went on foot into the
wilderness, lost amidst the darkness of a starless sky.
He still had not returned by the following morning,
but two nights later, in the light of the full moon, he
came back to his troops, changed and more vicious
and as white as a ghost. He resisted the blood of his
men, for he needed them for battle, but his enemies
saw no mercy. And though no one knows what
happened to him in the wilderness, some believe he
saw his child bride feed on another and went mad,
forcing her to turn him out of jealousy. That he
would become unconquerable was an afterthought.
The myth claims that once he was transfigured he
destroyed his child bride since she was never seen
again. But this I know to be a lie for reasons not
worth explaining here.

Some claim that the high numbers of death
during the black plague can be attributed to
Toktomer's family of vampires. He had rallied the

Houses of Dracul and Bazaraab to feast on the blood of the healthy in droves, as they ransacked towns and villages, fields and tracks across Europe, targeting children and men, intending to amass greater power. Many of us steered clear of their destructive path, though our livelihood was never threatened since it was impossible for them to consume our entire source of sustenance. In the end, man rose strong to outlive that plague, and though the record books estimate the Black Death wiped out a third of the population, I presume Toktomer and the Houses of Dracul and Bazaraab killed at least a quarter of those.

We left the smell of the burned flesh and stole through the fields where the scent of the bloodless masked all others. "Wait," Veronica said. "I hear something."

We turned our ears to the wind to better hear the faint hum of frequency that rippled on the air. I recognized the tune of the impaler and assumed he too would be warned of our approach. We doubled our pace and when we reached the cathedral, I sent Stephen and Veronica down through the passageway to safety. "I won't leave you," Stephen said.

"You must lock the hatch," I said. "I will be in soon."

"How?"

"I will find another way." I had no time to dispute and pushed him down into the opening. I sealed the door myself from the outside and waited to hear him lock it. From there, I crept the quarter mile to the rear of the cathedral. The swarms were gone but a shadowy figure was perched on the roof and disappeared when I approached. Vlad's frequency vibrated with a dull hum until it faded and I was alone again.

As I clung to the brick of the rear wall, I made my way to the east side of the cathedral, peeking around the corner to find an empty yard. Not even one lone bloodless wandered past the walls. I clawed my way along the side, beneath the stained glass windows, to the front courtyard, where again I spied nothing. But the air was no longer silent, for the low rumble of feeding bloodless echoed in the darkness. As I rounded the corner, I anticipated the swarm, one much greater than I had ever seen, feasting on a carcass. The flesh hypnotized them, as they tore it apart and pulverized everything including the bones. I did not need to see what caused their frenzy, for I knew it was the newly drained body of Marco.

Later. — Jean was forced to give up Marco when Vlad found his way into the cathedral. "Je n'ai rien pu faire," he said.

"And the girl?"

"À l'abri."

She was safe. He sent Vlad on his way, satisfied with the man. Jean heard the frequency too, knowing his maker was here. For several nights, he had anticipated his arrival, sensing its coming as I had. "I would not have left if you had confirmed my suspicions," I said.

"Forgive me," he said. "I zought zat I could 'andle 'im on my own. It was more important for you to go."

"Are you sure he is gone?"

"'E took all zat 'e zought we 'ad."

"Our only donor," I said.

53

Vlad had come in through a hatch in one of the spires on the roof. We had left them unlocked, thinking the bloodless could never climb up. He came alone, telling Jean he had witnessed most of his clan succumb to blood starvation. Toktomer was gone, he said. Like Byron, he had given in to malnutrition, and given up. Often the case with vampires who consumed gluttonously, they suffered greatest with a scarcity of blood. Jean pitied Vlad, waning as he was under the fast. He told his progeny he had scoured high and low for food but had little success securing human blood. Jean appeased his maker, inviting him to stay for a little nourishment. I had taught him the importance of hospitality, but regret it now. He tried to satisfy his maker with a small vial of Marco's blood, but when the impaler tasted it, he went mad.

"I didn't know," Jean said. "I couldn't let 'im suffer."

"No," I said. "Instead we shall all suffer."

Vlad's appeal was a ruse. He hid his true strength from Jean, for he had more than enough force to throw his progeny out of the way and seize Marco. Elizabeth could not help since she had rushed to the girl's side to keep her hidden while the villain robbed our store. Vlad tore the chamber door off its hinges and threw himself on our donor, sucking him dry in record time. Jean watched in horror, as his maker drained the source we had held so dear.

"Why did he leave?" I asked.

"Il n'a rien dit." *He did not say.*

He took Marco's body with him when he made his escape through the hatch in the spire, flashing his bloody fangs at Jean before greeting the darkness awaiting him.

"He used the body as a diversion," I said.

I knew why Vlad left; he was no match for me and a confrontation would surely finish him. My strength will outmatch his any day, starving or not. I am older than he, older than Toktomer and the Houses of Dracul and Bazaraab, and such primacy counts for something in our world. We hold to no hierarchy or seniority, but the sanctity of one as old as I is undeniable. It may sound foolish that we keep tradition, even as we face the possibility of extinction, but we cannot be faulted for our sentimentality. We are fiercely nostalgic creatures, though never to be taken for mawkish ones.

Vlad is no threat now, but difficulty will arise when several vampires know about the girl. If she is the last blood source for us all, she may surely be torn to pieces.

8 October. — We are desperate. The girl grows weaker by the day. We are out of options and have to push on. I regret to abandon the last place I held Byron. He had made the cathedral his home, a final laboratory among hallowed walls. He would grieve our parting too, but it is dangerous to stay. We can no longer make runs into town without endangering both those who remain and those who go. Vlad's diversion beckoned the bloodless to the cathedral, as a church bell calls its faithful to the altar. Our walls will not keep them out forever. Minor tremors rattle the stained glass windows each day, and soon an earthquake will shake the foundation, cracking open our fortification.

I have spent the last two nights planning our escape, and have almost worked it out but struggle with how to mask the girl's scent. Nothing seems to do. Even cloaking her in our clothes, our scent, is weak at best. I have to find a way to get her through the field and dell, all the way to the shore of the river without detection. Once we reach the water, the stream will carry us out to sea, where I am certain we can keep her safe. I have given the others instructions, and assured them we will leave tomorrow at dusk.

Later. — When I went to see the girl about our plans to leave, I told her of her stepfather's death. She had not seen him since we separated them, but seemed to appreciate the privacy. "Marco saved me," she had said to Byron. "I'm grateful for that, but he isn't the most honest man, if you know what I mean." Byron confessed that he did. "And he wasn't much of a father." My beloved reassured her she was safe, and expected me to carry out the task of keeping the man from the girl.

She was asleep when I entered her chamber, a tantalizing vision lying on the bed. I fantasized about seizing her and penetrating her neck; her tan skin, exposed at the round of her shoulder, begged to be touched. The blood pulsed beneath, urging me to taste it. I gazed on her, sucking in her saccharine aroma with each inhale and exhale she took. She is more trouble than I care to admit—but I have shaken off the temptation. It may seem out of character for an old vampire like me to resist such a savory morsel, but actually it is beneath me not to. My long years have granted me a willpower well beyond any other, and I am resilient to desire.

56

I floated to her side and sat on her bed, whispering her name. She was deep asleep and so I allowed my fingertips to touch the crown of her head, brushing her skin ever so lightly before drawing a line across her forehead with my thumb. Delectable creature that she is, my fangs still dropped—they have a mind of their own—and my points pierced my bottom lip, arousing me. I closed my eyes and thought of Byron. Was I really taken with this girl or did I simply desire her because my beloved had admired her so? Perhaps I wanted her because she was one of the last human beings on earth. I really could not tell. When she stirred a little and let out a long exaggerated sigh, I pulled my hand away.

"Why did you stop?" Her voice was faint.

"I am sorry," I said. "I was merely trying to wake you."

She left her head on the pillow and looked up at me with sleepy eyes. "I'm awake now."

"I can see that." She smiled at me but my moment of weakness had passed. "I have news that I fear might upset you," I said.

She sat up and looked at me with wide eyes. "You're not leaving me are you?"

She was so vulnerable, like a wounded animal, and I wondered if she would not be better off as a vampire. "No," I said. "We are not leaving you." She exhaled. "But your stepfather is gone."

She pursed her lips and turned away. "Did he upset you?"

Her question surprised me; it meant she assumed we had harmed him. "No," I said. "He was rather useful to us."

"Did the creepers get in?" Her voice cracked.

57

"We have not been breached." I tried to deal with her as Byron would, but I was not as compassionate as he was. "We have to take you somewhere more safe," I said. "We have to find food too." I told her of our plans and assured her I would let her know when I had worked out the details for her. I told her it was imperative she stay in her room for the time being, as I did not want anyone—or anything—to catch a whiff of her scent.

"I'll stay here," she said. "But please don't forget me."

She was terrified—I could practically smell her fear. For a brief moment—very brief—I wanted to send one of the others in to sit with her, but my sympathy passed and I got up to go. As I reached for the door, she made the offer I loathed to refuse.

"You can have my blood if you need it," she said.

She knows our secret—I am certain of it now.

9 October. — The girl proved easy enough to transport, and we have my beloved to thank for that. An entry in his notes gave me the solution I needed. Sometime in the early stages of his experimentation, he had discovered that the bloodless were unable to detect particular scents. They were acutely aware of the smell of living flesh, but they seemed indifferent to the smell of the vampire. The attacks they made on us were random. They could not have cared for Maxine the night they surrounded her, but probably sensed the humans inside the trattoria. Byron's note read:

Test Subject 56 – incapable of detecting the burning from the candle wax – I held a piece of flesh just out of reach – she clambered to get to it – she fell off the table – her reaction was as expected – the lit camphor oil was different – she did not smell the flesh doused in oil – same reaction with incense, spice, lavender, etc. etc. – no reaction to aromatic perfumes. Conclusion: olfactory organs are limited – human flesh reaction – human flesh covered in perfume no reaction. Must try opiates next!

With this, my sweet Byron, you have given me the answer to getting the girl out of the cathedral undetected.

When I explained it to her, she was surprisingly cooperative. The baptismal ritual was unpleasant, to be sure. Veronica and Elizabeth brought me all the incense oils they could find and we filled a wash basin. The girl covered her hair, her face, her arms, her legs, every bit of skin with the perfume, and then we dressed her in an oil-drenched garment. The smell was repellent to us since we could barely detect the human scent beneath all the perfume.

I paid my respects to Byron's ashes, sealing the sarcophagus forever. I packed his notebooks and put on the overcoat he wore the last time I saw him. My heart was heavy, but I turned my focus to the journey ahead—and the clan, my clan, I was desperate to keep safe.

With all the supplies we could gather, we left the cathedral in a weaker state than when we had arrived. The girl was nestled between me and Jean, as Stephen led us through the passage to the exit. Before he untied the chain from the portal, he listened at the opening for howls, and when he heard none, we proceeded out the hatch.

The earth's full satellite greeted us, as we rose up from the ground. Despite the light of the moon, the field was as dark as ink, but we moved easily through the wilderness. I glanced back at the cathedral only once, and then let it disappear from view forever. Byron's last kiss remained with me, though, as I welcomed the cool air on my skin.

Our first test came at the edge of the dale. The field had been empty, but when we reached the valley, we ran into a swarm too big to skirt.

"Qu'est-ce qu'on fait?" Elizabeth clung to Jean and Veronica linked her arm through Stephen's.

"We move quickly," I said. "Together." I picked up the girl and carried her in my arms. She remained as still as a stone, as the clan folded in around us, and we wove through the valley as a tight-knit cluster. Stephen and Jean held out their blades, slashing at the ones that came within reach. The bloodless swarmed loosely but our smell evaded them and I silently thanked my beloved for providing the solution that made the girl invisible.

The water's edge was a short jaunt from the dale, and I anticipated the boat, if not hoped one would be waiting. That was the only detail I was unable to plan. We had seen boats tied to a dock several months ago but I could not know if they would still be there. I had a back-up plan, but nothing as solid as floating down the river in a vessel. I thanked my beloved Byron again when I saw the small, double-masted sailboat greet us at the shore. Stephen and Veronica went on first, and when they confirmed the boat was empty, the rest of us boarded. Jean set us on the course I had mapped out for him. Never one to refuse commandeering his own ship, he is our captain. Many years ago, he sailed with the Spanish Armada, working his way up from master's mate to midshipman on one of their warships. He probably fed his way up the ranks to

60

commander of the São Cristóbel, but I cannot say for sure. That particular vessel had seen the most casualties during the attack on the British.

I set the girl up in one of the two cabins below. She was tired from the travel and I insisted she rest while we set out to sea. "Thank you for bringing me," she said, rubbing her belly, as she sat on the edge of the berth.

"How are you feeling?" I had to think about her welfare and could no longer dismiss her human needs.

"I'm a little hungry," she said. I avoided looking at her directly. Despite the perfume, she still proved alluring. "You must be too," she said.

"We all have sacrifices to make." I searched the bag of supplies and found the last of the dried apricots, handing them to her without ceremony. "This should help a little," I said.

She took the tin of fruit and turned it over in her hands. She sighed softly and placed it at her side, and then with a coolness that mimicked my own, she pulled up her sleeve and bared the inside of her arm, holding it out for me. "I don't mind," she said. "You have to feed too."

I will admit the offer tempted me, and it took every ounce of willpower to keep my fangs from dropping. I reached for her arm and pulled her sleeve back down. "It is safer if none of us taste you," I said. There was no point in masking our conversation anymore. She knew what I was, what we all were, and she was fearless. "If we do," I said. "None of us will survive."

She sighed again, but this time more passionately. "Will you make me like you?"

I did not need to voice my refusal; she knew she was only useful as long as she remained human.

"I'm … afraid of becoming … one of them," she said.

It was as if those were her only two choices. "Why can you not simply remain human?" I asked.

"There's no more place in this world for humans," she said.

"Then we shall all be lost, my dear." The term of endearment rolled off my tongue as if it had always been mine. But I merely impersonated Byron, stealing what little compassion I could from him.

When I left the girl, she was asleep. Her moment of weakness worries me. If any of the others witness her vulnerability, her generosity, they will not be able to resist as I have.

10 October. — In 1588 on the waters of the North Sea, Jean saw a Siren.

When he was still a midshipman on the São Cristóbel, he kept watch at night. He had passed his seventy-fifth year as a nocturnal, which meant he could tolerate the daylight, but he preferred the solace of the ship in the dark and often volunteered for the post.

As we sat on the deck of the small sloop tonight, he recalled the mythical creature. "She 'ad gold 'air like ze old French coin wiz skin as white as snow and leeps as red as ze blood I seeped." He swore he could hear her singing, calling for him to join her. She danced up and down on the foam of the dark sea, her hair thrashing about in the wind. Her breasts were lush, exposed above the water. "'Er neck," he said. "She showed 'er neck to me wiz ze promise of succulence." He said that he pulled out his telescope to get a better view and when he put the magnifier to his eye, she was but an arm's length away. He reached for her and felt his cold hand burn at the imaginary touch. Her eyes were like fire. "Le Diable," he said. "Le Diable." He was convinced she was the devil. "I pulled ze telescope away," he said. "And she was gone. No'zing but ze angry waves left." He said her song stayed in his head for days, as he longed for her return. "She never came back," he said.

"You hallucinated," I said. "Probably from the opiates in a wounded man's blood."

"Ah, merde." He shooed at the stream we floated down, offering it his tsk-tsk.

I believe Jean saw what he did. I am no skeptic, I am a vampire, and I come from irregular stock too. My mother was a naiad, an early shapeshifter. But that is a story for another time …

12 October. — We have been on the water for two nights now. We are starved and weak, though the girl is safe and we have had luck catching fish for her to eat. Stephen and Veronica found rods and lures below the boat's deck our first night aboard. The perch is a mild fish, despite its pungent aroma, and she eats it courageously, for it is served to her raw. We cannot have the smell of fried fish wafting through the air; cooked flesh may welcome others.

The water is calm, empty, abandoned. My clan keeps watch, as I guard the girl below, afraid they may be tempted. It gives me time to pore over Byron's notes, and I am well aware—

13 October. — My previous entry was cut short when Jean called me up on deck. His excitement was unmistakable, and I hoped his Siren had returned. I had been below since the sun set and when I surfaced I saw the tiny crescent of a moon way up in the sky. The clan was gathered at the helm and I rushed to meet them. "Là bas!" Jean pointed toward the dark shoreline.

"What is it?" Elizabeth said.

Stephen and Veronica were huddled together, she having grown weak and finding it difficult to focus. I wondered when her beloved would beg me to let her feed on the girl. I avoided that confrontation daily. I am by far the strongest vampire on the ship, and I know they cannot defeat me with a mutiny, for I could destroy each and every one of them. Doing so, however, would break me in ways I cannot explain.

"It's moving," Stephen said, as he pointed to the shadow along the shore.

The thing was difficult to see because it was not giving off any heat. At first I could only make out a shadowed outline rustling in the brush, but as we floated along the river's edge, I recognized the danger. The shadows multiplied and seemed to grow larger, as they came closer. Multiple swarms, countless swarms spun toward the river's edge, as we watched the shoreline in disbelief. The howls of bloodless reached us, as they bayed at the passing ship.

"We're safe on the water, right?" Veronica said.

I assured her we were, though I began to doubt it, and within seconds my fears were realized. To my horror, the bloodless dropped one by one into the water. Like rats driven out of a forest by fire, they plunged off the bank and into the river. We watched as hundreds of bodies dove in head first and came back up chomping their wolframlike jaws. Our sails were down since the wind had died and without a drop of gasoline in our tank, we only coasted. As the bloodless moved through the water toward us, all we could do was watch.

"Qu'est-ce qu'on fait?" Jean's look of panic gave me resolve.

"Shall I get the girl?" Elizabeth asked.

"No." I was certain the bloodless could not climb up the side of the sloop, but they were resilient to water and I had no idea what drove them so fiendishly toward us. Swarms made their way through the current, coming at speeds I had not seen them reach before.

"They'll get to the boat," Stephen said.

"But they will not get on board," I said.

I ordered the others to pull up the ropes and ladders hanging over the sides and to release the lifeboat at the stern of the ship.

"What if we need zis to escape?"

"They will not breach the ship." I was adamant on that point.

We stood on the deck, watching the heads in the water get closer. At least a hundred closed in on the sloop, clambering over one another, snapping their jaws like a gaggle of gulls fighting for measly scraps. "Lower ze mainsail!" Jean yelled.

He and Elizabeth let fly the sheets on the mast, trying to catch what bit of wind they could, but it was pointless. The air stood still.

"Should I shoot at them?" Stephen said.

We had found spear guns with the fishing supplies.

65

"It will not stop them," I said.

"They are coming around to the bow!" Elizabeth said.

"The stern too," Veronica said.

In a frenzy, the bloodless surrounded the sloop, getting as close to its hull as possible. From above we must have looked like a cube of sugar attacked by a farm of ants. They toppled over one another, sending each other under the water. I panicked when I realized the weight of them could sink the boat. The sloop would not stay afloat if they pulled it down.

Elizabeth peered over the side and almost fell over when one of them climbed up on top of another and grabbed her hand. Her scream drowned out their howls and I jammed my boot into his jaw. The whole bottom part of his mouth fell away, though it did not stop him. With one more fierce kick, I tossed his head back, severing it from his spine. It seemed the wolframlike bones were no challenge for my adrenaline. Jean gave up the sails and went to the prow, trying to prevent them from getting onto the safety net dangling below. Stephen and Veronica were on the other side of the deck whacking at them with their fishing poles. I had not thought of the girl, even as the bloodless reached the railings and got onto the deck, but her voice snapped me from my fury. "Vincent?"

"Get back down," I said. I growled at her and regretted the look of terror I put on her face. She turned on her heel and practically stumbled back down the hatch. I yelled for Elizabeth on the other side of me—she was the best choice, my only choice. She had shown the least amount of desire to feed off the girl. "Stay with the girl," I said. "And cover her with the oil." Elizabeth was in a daze, still shaken from the grab of one of them. I touched her shoulders and made her face me. I looked into her eyes, pulling her back to me, stopping everything around us, forcing her to see only me. "Elizabeth," I said. "Have you heard my command?" She nodded and gave me a slight smile. "Repeat it back to me," I said.

"Stay with the girl and cover her in oil," she said.

Just then a bloodless flopped over the rail and onto the deck, lunging at her and clasping her wrist. Before she could scream, I pummeled his arm with my bare hands, my adrenaline rush accelerated by the danger. I did not hesitate to crush another as it came over the rail too. I swirled around and grabbed it by the neck, squeezing its throat between my fingers, ripping its head from its body and tossing it over the side of the rail. The one-armed bloodless that had grabbed Elizabeth rebounded and reached for her again. This time she fought him off, piercing his eye with her finger, forcing her entire hand into his socket and then using his head to batter the next that tried to attack her. I threw a few more bodies from my feet and pulled Elizabeth from the fray. As we made our way to the hatch, I body-checked several more, sending them over the rail and back into the black water. I lifted the hatch and helped Elizabeth down to safety. "Protect the girl," I said.

When Elizabeth disappeared below, I sealed the hatch and headed for Jean. I ran to him, and with my rush of adrenaline ripped the bloodless from my longtime friend.

"Le pistolet!" Jean had a small gun strapped to the inside of his leg and tried to get it when several more grabbed hold of him. I reached for his gun and fired off shots—two then three, the bullets did not stop them and my effort was in vain. I hate myself for not stopping the bloodless little girl from coming up through the swarm and digging her teeth into Jean's thigh. The infected child grabbed hold of my friend with her crocodile bite and did not let him go. "Maxine!" His cry of terror reached the stars and if his beloved were there, she would have heard his call.

When I finally severed the child's head and tore her from his flesh, it was too late. She had left her mark on my friend, tearing out his weak skin, as Maxine's had been ripped open. Jean was finished and I knew it. He would turn into a horror just like his beloved, forcing me to end his life. But I did not give up in that moment and freed my friend from the swarm that had breached the prow. When Stephen came to our aid, it was as if the attack had only begun. They persisted, climbing up on top of each other to get between the rails of the boat. Stephen grabbed Jean and threw him over his shoulder. "Get below," he yelled.

We made our way to the hatch, where two bloodless scratched at the portal. I grabbed the first by its soaking strands of hair and yanked its head back, snapping it clean off. The jaw gnashed at me and I launched the head to the stern of the ship. The body dropped to the deck and reached for us, but I stomped on its limbs with vigor. Stephen twisted up the other bloodless with his blade and pulled its insides out. It was not long before more came and I threw open the hatch, sending Stephen down with Jean. The bony fingers of another caught me as I went down, but I was able to shake him loose before sinking below and sealing the portal.

I had no time to survey the deck, but knew they invaded us from all sides. Wet, bloodless bodies tossed themselves onto the sloop, clawing toward us, and the smell of the human. We gathered in the girl's cabin, where she cried and lamented my outburst. Elizabeth consoled her until she saw Jean's wound. I made certain none of the others were injured before turning my attention to him. "Let me see it," I said.

"Je suis finis." The most definitive sentence in French—he was done for. He knew his fate was just like Maxine's and it was only a matter of time before he became one of them.

"Is there nothing we can do?" Elizabeth said. She held her emotion in check, though I could see she writhed inside.

"Let me help," Veronica said. She rubbed a balm on Jean's inner thigh where his flesh was torn out, just as Byron had done for Maxine.

"You 'ave to escape," he said. "Zis is not ze end."

I had run out of ideas. We were never going to get through those monsters with the girl even if we drowned her in incense. They had detected her smell from a distance, and their energy peaked with their baptism in the river. The water made them supercharged, frenzied like vampires to blood. "We are trapped," I said.

"Non," Jean said. He spoke through clenched teeth. The pain was clearly unbearable. "I weel get you out." Despite the anguish, the fever, the unsettling reality of his situation, he proposed a plan for our escape. It was a tactical nightmare, but Jean

69

insisted he had seen it work when a British ship breached the São Cristóbel.

"We have to give it a try," Stephen said.

"And the girl?" I did not believe she was up for the physical will his plan entailed.

"I can do it," she said. Her feminine voice was a stranger among the tenor of the vampires. She was brave, knowing there was a strong chance she would not survive the escape. Byron would have never approved of my putting her life in jeopardy this way, but I had no other option. If she did not survive, at the very least we would.

"This is the only way," Veronica said.

I could barely look at the wasted vampire when she spoke. Her emaciated frame was frail and weak, a constant reminder of my failure to keep them safe. For a moment, I considered feeding off the girl. If each of us nourished ourselves on her blood, we could escape unscathed, we could free ourselves from the deathtrap if only … if only …

And then what Vincent? I heard Byron's voice as clear as when he spoke into my thoughts. *And then what?* "We will try Jean's plan," I said.

I delegated their assignments and encouraged them with my resolve. The bloodless were noisy up on the deck and we could hear them bearing down on the hatch. By now a super swarm had most likely toppled the rails of the sloop, and it would not be long before the deck would collapse, if the boat did not sink altogether.

Jean's plan was to puncture a whole in the ship's stern and escape through the opening into the rush of water. The sloop would certainly sink, but we planned on getting far enough away before it did. The weight of our bodies would sink us, and we

70

could walk along the bottom of the river to the bank on the other side. We do not need to worry about holding our breath underwater—air is inconsequential. But for the girl, time would be of the essence. I planned to cradle her in my arms, hoping she could hold her breath long enough.

When Stephen and Veronica took axes to the inside of the hull, the rest of us waited in the cabin at the bow of the ship. I held the girl in my arms, ready for when the water rushed in. "I will tell you when to take your last breath," I said. She did not move, but I could feel her cling to me more tightly.

When Stephen signaled for us to come, we waded through the cabin to the opening in the hull. We had to go under before we could get out, and I encouraged her to breath in deeply. "One last one," I said. "Hold it." She filled her lungs and closed her mouth. I dunked us beneath the water and headed directly to the opening. Veronica and Stephen had already escaped and were on the look out for bloodless. Elizabeth and Jean followed in the rear. I suppose I should have known. I should have realized that he would save us all.

The girl was tucked into my chest, as Veronica and Elizabeth flanked me and Stephen rushed ahead to the bank. We assumed the other side of the river was empty. Making our way across the silt at the bottom of the stream, we only saw a few frantic stragglers at the water's surface. The bloodless seemed more prone to float than sink, and their legs dangled overtop us, as we made our way across the bottom. When we finally surfaced, I laid the girl on the dirt. Elizabeth examined her while Stephen and Veronica checked the perimeter.

"She's not moving," Elizabeth said.

71

"Is she breathing?" I asked.

The girl's eyes were closed but from where I stood it looked as though her chest was moving. Elizabeth leaned in and listened for her heartbeat. "I don't hear anything," she said.

I bent down and put my hand on the girl's chest. She did feel dead. I touched her cheek with my palm, tapping it softly to revive her. I placed two fingers near her clavicle and waited to feel her pulse—she was not breathing. I coaxed the blood to flow, teasing it out with my dreadful desire to taste it.

"You must bring her back," Elizabeth said. She could not hide her sorrow this time and gently caressed the girl's face with the back of her hand. "She cannot be dead," she said.

I shooed her away and tilted the girl's head back, opening her mouth wide and clearing her airway. I placed my mouth on hers and blew an artificial gust of air from my lungs without thinking about my lips on hers, how close my fangs were to her skin, the deliciousness of her blood and the sweetness of the child growing inside of her. All I thought about was bringing her back to life. I pressed on her chest, counting the pumps in my head—one, two, three, one, two, three, one, two three. I placed my lips on hers again when I felt her stir and gave her another gust of air. When I sensed the jolt of heat through her veins, I pulled my mouth away and turned her on her side before the surge of water erupted from her lungs. She coughed and then inhaled deeply, trying desperately to catch her breath.

Elizabeth's squeal of joy pulled me from my haze, and I let her take my place beside the girl. I did not see her open her eyes, but I knew I had revived her. I tasted her on the tip of my tongue, not realizing I had pierced the inside of her lip with my subtle fangs when I resuscitated her, drawing the smallest amount of blood which lingered for hours.

"Where are the others?" I asked.

Only then did I notice we were alone. I looked to the water and saw a magnificent glow on the river. Stephen and Veronica stood on the bank watching it too. The sloop had erupted in fire, gone up in flames to burn the bloodless trapped on it. The bonfire of monsters roared, as distorted flesh roasted on the boat-sized spit.

"How?" Stephen asked.

"Jean," Elizabeth said, as she came up behind me. "Jean stayed behind."

Veronica turned to us with those awful human tears in her eyes. "He's gone."

I knew it then if I had not known it before. He never planned to leave the sloop. He took the canisters of propane from the galley and the flares from the tackle box, going back up on deck to light his pyre. He would have had to wait for the last possible moment to light the fire, making sure we had reached safety. The torture would have been horrific. He sacrificed himself for us—and I will remember you, my friend, for it is because of you that I am still here.

As the fire burned, I thought of the hell we were forced to face, nowhere now and lost along the riverbank. The girl called me to her and the softness in her voice made me recall the taste. Hours later and it lives in me still. She sat up, her bright eyes welcoming me beside her. She did not look like someone who had barely escaped death. She held a

73

small plastic bag in her hand, and it was not until I sat beside her that I realized what it was. "I saved this for you," she said.

When she handed me my journal, I was touched. She had saved my history in the small pocket of her robe, safely tucking between its pages my beloved Byron's notes. Now it was I who gushed with gratitude. "Thank you, Evelina."

14 October. — We spent the night in the woods without shelter, but dawn has finally arrived to break up the darkness. Mere hours since fleeing the boat, I still mourn my loss. Elizabeth is heartbroken too, though she seems to have converted her sorrow into care for the girl. She has been by her side since our escape and I hope the temptation is not as torturous for her as it is for the other two. Veronica is worse off than ever, and Stephen is despondent. I will take him with me to hunt, leaving the girl with the other two. I see no use in dragging her through the woods. Though I put my faith in Veronica and Elizabeth, I have no other choice. It will be difficult for Stephen to leave his beloved, and I can already see the anguish on his face. Their commitment is inviolable since it is virtually physical. They knew each other as humans, which always makes for a severe attachment. More than a hundred years ago in Budapest, after she was transfigured, she saved him; it is a story worth a few lines in my diary.

Late one evening, as the two crossed Heroes' Square together, they were assaulted. Stephen said the man's eyes raged like a rabid animal, and he was waving a pistol at them. Stephen calmly stepped in front of Veronica and asked the man to back away. He twitched and scratched and then started to retreat

74

but tripped on something and fell backwards. He fired off two shots, one bullet grazing Stephen's shoulder and getting lodged in his neck, the other hitting Veronica in the temple. Stephen recalls lying on the ground, trying to get to Veronica but no longer able to move. "Only my eyes," he said. "I could only move my eyes."

He saw the shadow from the corner of his eye, the presence bending over him and caressing his face. He could feel the coldness, despite his paralysis, and still remembers the smell of lavender. *Veronica-a-a-a.*

"Taci," the shadow said. "Noapte bună."

He saw the shadow take Veronica's body and carry it away. He recalls how they seemed to disappear into the darkness as though the shadow had never even touched the ground. Paramedics soon arrived and ushered Stephen away. He only heard voices in the hospital, apathetic and cold sounds. Nothing seemed real, as he lay in a bed paralyzed from his chin down. In and out of consciousness, he asked for Veronica each time he woke. Eventually, he realized his calls went unheard—the wound had silenced him, the bullet having severed his vocal chords. He lay incapacitated for months, aching for a life that was lost to him forever. Hopeless in his isolation, powerless in his body, he suffered until she came for him. He says he will never forget the moment everything changed, how in the blink of an eye, his life was restored. "I saw the shadow flit across the ceiling," he said. "And then I smelled the lavender."

He did not feel the bite, the venom's rime course through him, the pain of his transformation. His perception was engrossed in the tingling of his newly revived body and the thirst—the burning need for blood. "I thought I was dreaming when I saw her," he said.

Veronica greeted him with his first drink, nursing him to stability. From the moment of their embrace, he knew what he had become. "Wallach is my maker," she said. "And I am yours."

"Wallach?"

"It's complicated," she said.

Wallach is a Romanian nomad, a vampire who mostly travels alone. Nomads are reputed to be cruel, incapable of compassion, but Wallach had been good to Veronica. He had sincerely wanted to be with her, though he cannot change his nature. Abandoned at inception, he is unable to nurture a progeny.

"Why didn't he save me that night too?" Stephen asked.

"He couldn't," she said. "We can only choose one every hundred years."

Stephen said he did not understand what that meant at first, but soon realized the greatness of Veronica's gesture—she had chosen him.

"I didn't know if you'd regret my choice," she said. "It's permanent in the most permanent way." He said she smiled when she said that and he could not resist showing her how grateful he was.

I've always admired their physical bond—their humanlike attachment. They knew how to enjoy their vampiric nature together from the beginning. After they joined our clan, we met Veronica's maker. Wallach had taken up with an ancient vampire named Rangu. Rangu—not quite as ancient as I, but he wishes—claims to be a reincarnation of Vishnu, though not the tenth avatar. These days, however, I wonder if he is not the Hindu god come to herald the end of the world.

Later. — When Stephen and I made our way through the woods, we avoided the bloodless with ease since only a few wandered on this side of the riverbank.

"Wait," Stephen said.

"I smell it too," I said.

Smoke wafted through the trees, evincing the recent dampening of a fire. The bloodless are incapable of mental tasks such as building campfires—I will be devastated if I learn they have developed cognitive ability. The horror on the water had been threatening enough. "This way," I said.

The scent led us through the trees to a clearing with a circle of spears stuck in the ground. The small enclosure looked like a savage's prison, only not to keep the enemy in but out. In the center, stones surrounded a pit of sand. Stephen slipped in between the spears. "The coals are wet," he said.

Neither of us picked up the human scent, not even one that had long since expired. "What are you thinking?" He asked.

I pointed to the small game drying on the line strung between two trees. Stephen smiled. "Humans," he said.

"Grab the meat," I said.

As he gathered the game from the line, bending down to place it in his satchel, a bullet sailed through the trees and grazed the top of his ear. Without hesitating, he turned in the direction of the shot and blasted off through the brush. When I caught up to him, he hung from a tree. He was tied up in a net, dangling from a branch, and I rushed up the trunk to free him with my talons.

"Why can't I smell him?" Stephen asked when he hit the ground.

I held a finger up, directing him to keep quiet. I could hear the man breathing. When another shot fired in our direction, this time nicking the corner of my ear, I knew exactly where he was. I flew through the brush and caught the man before he got away, crushing his windpipe beneath my grip. A gun dangled at his side, as I held him several feet off the ground. The mystery of his elusive scent was solved when we smelled the month's worth of silt and rot from the riverbed. He was covered in a stink that rivaled a sewer.

"Can we clean him before we feed?" Stephen asked.

I assured him we would have to make do, and we each took a nip from the stinking man's neck before tearing through the forest back the way we came with his unconscious body. When we arrived, Veronica was gone.

"She was going mad," Elizabeth said. "I'm sorry Stephen." Elizabeth told us that Veronica ranted about turning to ashes. "I asked her to stay calm for Evie's sake," she said. "She leered at her—and I know that look. When her fangs dropped, I had to send her away."

I chided myself for taking Stephen and leaving Veronica with such temptation. Elizabeth showed me the bruise the vampire gave Evelina when she attempted to put her arm in her mouth. "I was strong enough to get her off," Elizabeth said.

"It wasn't her fault," Evelina said with her small voice. "I know she suffers."

78

I still cannot get Stephen's look of violence and disgust out of my mind. His wound was palpable, as he released his irons. "Do not," I warned him. "You will regret it."

"One sip for Chrissake," he said. "You could have given her one sip." He looked away, ashamed at his outburst, and I knew he would not cross the line. Instead, he ran off in the direction Elizabeth told him his beloved had gone and did not look back, as he disappeared into the woods.

I am torn—heartbroken really. I do not know how to keep us all together. The blood from the man has given my starvation a reprieve, but without Stephen and Veronica, without my whole clan, I am more vulnerable than ever—and so is Evelina. I have decided to wait for them until dusk. I hope for their return before the sun sets.

15 October. — When Stephen and Veronica did not return, Elizabeth and I carried Evelina through the woods to a deserted hamlet on its border. We encountered a few stray bloodless here and there, but the man's blood gave me enough strength to smite them with my talons. We are in a cottage; it is rather small, with a single room, but is isolated enough and seems the safest place for us while I decide what to do about my shrunken clan. Elizabeth watches over the girl, and I have commended her on her discipline.

"You have shown great bravery and sacrifice," I said to her, as Evelina slept at her side. She was touched by my gratitude and I suspect she did not think I would notice.

"I want to please her," she said.

"You do."

Elizabeth resented her transfiguration, though she loved Maxine, and spent years in search of her beloved, one she has yet to find. I worry she may think Evelina is a possible candidate, though she would never change the girl. That, I do not doubt. She must hope, though, that somehow, in some way, she is forging a bond with the human. I will not tell her it is hopeless, that their differences are too great and will eventually get the better of their friendship. For now, Elizabeth has nothing else, and I need her just as much as Evelina does.

17 October. — Byron had mapped out a course of action in his notes. He had designed a plan to repopulate the earth with healthy humans. He believed the bloodless would eventually die off, and the healthy would outlive the plague. *In two generations*, he wrote, *there will be no bloodless left—the infection will die with the last of them.*

I feel an immense weight at this prospect since his conjecture may only be validated if I can keep the healthy safe. How I am to keep bloodless from this new population is a mystery I am determined to solve. Humans can only repopulate if bloodless do not prey on the populace—not to mention the starved vampires, lurking amidst colonies of healthy donors, bleeding them dry.

Later. — I had a dream, or a waking reverie, I conversed with Byron about cloning. *Cloning can either save or destroy the world!* Ah, it is a useless prophecy without scientists and labs. Save the girl! That is all you can do.

18 October. — We have been here for three days and several swarms have passed us, though none have picked up Evelina's scent. She is covered in incense oil.

I have been successful finding canned preserves for her from nearby pantries. The hamlet is surprisingly untouched, as if all its inhabitants got up and left before the pandemic began. The cottages are vacant, none of them harboring the enemy. Elizabeth and I suffer—we are hungry. We hide our anguish from Evelina but if we do not get blood soon, we will be of little use to her.

19 October. — Byron, my dear sweet Byron, thank you for showing me your brilliant mind this morning when I found your entry on blood substitutes. You had hoped it would not come to this since consuming a substitute is a wretched thought and something none of us would desire, but you had been experimenting on synthetics nevertheless. I assume you wanted to spare me the horror of your delving into such grimy waters. I found the formula marked in the margin of your notes, and I can only assume it is a recipe for a substitute.

Since the turn of the millennium, the medical community had made significant advancements in hemoglobin-based oxygen therapeutics. By 2036, scientists had engineered a sufficient and acceptable substitute for human blood. We had never tried it since we never had a need for it, but now it seemed a viable option. I cannot imagine why Byron kept this from me, though I recall an allusion to it in a conversation months before the epidemic. He had been working tirelessly in his lab and when I expressed interest, he dodged my question.

"It is nothing," he had said. "A mere trifle."

Day and night he locked himself in his lab, vexed by the slightest disruption. Long gone were our wicked nights on the prowl for cold women and warm blood. It got to the point of my having to insist he come out to dine on the leftovers I brought him from my hunt. On one such occasion, as I watched him devour the lithe waif I served him, I noticed his malaise. It was as if the human blood did not excite his senses, and his apathy bothered me. "Is something wrong?" I asked.

He insisted he was not hungry and when I asked if he had fed, he changed the subject.

"Do you prefer men or women?" He teased me, knowing I favored the blood of young women. "What about animals?" He asked.

The proposition disgusted me and I showed him so, sticking out my tongue and making a retching sound. "Beneath me," I said.

"I realize, my love, that you have ancient taste buds," he said with a grin. "But we may not always be fortunate enough to choose from where our blood comes." With that, he slipped back into his lab, leaving me to finish the waif he had only just begun.

I assumed his behavior was a result of his exhaustion, overworked as he was. Though we do not need sleep, we are required to rest our minds every now and then. I did not press him, and when the affliction proved resilient and he started his work on the bloodless, his troubling conduct was forgotten.

How could I not know, Byron? You were in the midst of developing a blood substitute that could save us all from anguish. It seems obvious now, but why did you not suggest it when our need for it grew

82

desperate? Why not use the supplement to save us? To save you? My questions are without answers, though his final gift to me stares up at me from the margin of his notes. In addition to the formula, he made a list of the gallons of blood substitute in a cryostat cooler in his lab at our home in the catacombs.

Later. — As I anticipate our arrival tomorrow, I dread my nostos. I have not seen LaDenza since the plague began. When I told Elizabeth my plan early this morning, she voiced her reservations.

"Will we bring Evie?" Elizabeth's sole concern was for Evelina and her child.

"Of course," I said.

"But how'll we get past the creepers?" She asked. "Just the two of us?"

I found it telling she had picked up the girl's term for the bloodless. "We have no choice," I said. "We have to get back to the catacombs."

"What if they're still—" I raised my hand to prevent her question. She knew it meant I had nothing further to discuss and my decision was final.

"We set out when she wakes," I said.

We left the cottage an hour later. I carried Evelina on my back while Elizabeth towed the meager provisions we had acquired. We moved swiftly through the abandoned hamlet, a ghost town without a soul, living or dead. I had found a map and planned our trip along the quickest route back to my home. The catacombs are on the outskirts of a town ten miles north of our current location, but there is an obstacle and it will take us twenty-five to get there. The river through the path keeps us from

83

traveling straight since we must avoid the water at all costs.

My energy waned, hungry as I was, but I conserved what I had in case of an attack. The rise of a swarm is difficult to predict, so I renewed my efforts to listen for howls in the distance. Elizabeth clung to my left side and we cradled Evelina between us. I could not carry her any longer and we were forced to walk at a human pace. I tried to resist frustration when she asked to stop. "Please," she said. "I need to catch my breath."

The last thing I wanted to do was stop, even for a brief moment, but pushing her was pointless. I needed her healthy and alive but had to remind myself of her condition constantly. "We will rest here for a while," I said.

We were in a vineyard and I noticed a small cabin a few yards away. I insisted we go inside for shelter. "I'll go ahead," Elizabeth said.

As she stole through the withered vines up to the cabin, I scanned the horizon for movement. The place was abandoned, and the silence confirmed there were no bloodless for at least a furlong. When Elizabeth waved to me from the cabin, I picked Evelina up in my arms and carried her to safety. The stop was a fortuitous one since we found a fully stocked cupboard and what looked like a fresh pot of coffee inside. Though the pot was cold, the grinds were fresh. Elizabeth opened a can of oysters and a tin of crackers and set a plate for Evelina. "Doesn't it seem like someone is living here?"

"Yes," I said. *Yes, yes, it does!* The thought of also sharing a meal woke my senses.

When Evelina finished eating, she was ready for sleep. I carried her to a small cot in a nook at the back of the cabin and as she rested, Elizabeth and I sat in the main room, where soon the most incredible smell wafted in through the windows. When starved, fresh blood smells delicious no matter the human.

"Shush!" The sound of a male voice broke the silence.

What luck, I thought, there is more than one.

"Someone's inside," the man whispered.

"The dead?"

"How should I know?"

We stood at the door, waiting with readied fangs. I let my irons drop for the simple pleasure of the kill I had long been needing. Elizabeth gave me a look that said she wanted to give chase but I held her back. We hung on the edge of anticipation for what seemed like eternity. "They've gone?" Elizabeth gestured.

I sniffed the air, shaking my head at the fresh blood smell still thick and close. They had not gone, but waited to see if we would come out. I feigned a cough and then baited them with a loud whisper. "Someone is coming," I said.

Elizabeth mimicked Evelina's small voice. "Oh no," she said. "Do you think they'll let us stay?"

We heard shuffling on the other side of the door, and I put my hand on the knob, turning it slowly. Before I could pull the door to me, it swung open and a young woman stood on the step with a rifle pointed at my face. She was dead at the sight of me, for I grabbed her hair and ripped open her neck with my mouth, as the rifle dropped to the ground. I bit into her with my subtle fangs, keeping her alive for Elizabeth. When I had my fill, I handed her off. "I will be back with the other," I said, wiping the blood from my chin. I do not think she heard me, as she was in the throes of ecstasy when I took off.

I raced along the side of the cabin, following the trail of the man's scent. When I got to the rear, he had disappeared into an opening in the wall. With the taste of the woman's blood still fresh on my tongue, I slipped in through the hole after him. I not only smelled him, but could see the large trace of heat his body gave off in the dark. The opening had led us in to the small nook where Evelina slept. Foolishly, the man grabbed the girl from the cot and pulled her to him. She shrieked, woken with fright. He put a small pistol to her head and held her in his arms as though she were his hostage. He could not see me in the dark—and she barely saw him. When Evelina called my name, Elizabeth's anguish met her cry. "Nooo!" She screamed.

Elizabeth's entrance startled the man and he turned to face her, loosening his grip on Evelina. The girl dropped to the floor and I lunged to catch her. Elizabeth dug her talons into the man's neck, causing him to fire off a shot. Luckily, I had the girl tucked in my arms and the bullet bounced off my shoulder and hit a wooden dresser full of clothes. When Elizabeth finished her drink, we exchanged bounties and she took Evelina in her arms. I gorged on the man's blood, tearing him open with my irons and sucking every last pittance of serum from his veins. The satisfaction is indescribable, greater than a scratch relieving an itch.

Our stay in the cabin was short-lived. The bullet exploded in the drawer and set fire to the linens inside. As the curtains rose up in flames, we stole into the night with the girl, feeling high and satiated for the rest of the road.

20 October. — Byron and I moved into the catacombs at LaDenza in the spring of 1901. He had only been mine a short while, though he took to the vampiric lifestyle straightaway.

When I first found him in the foggy hillside of Scotland, an assistant professor of biology at a small university north of Glasgow, I was crossing his family's estate. He was at home for a visit, and I was only there by chance, having made an unexpected stop in the highlands. The serendipity of our meeting is too perfect for the banality of words—and so I will refrain, leaving the mysterious circumstances unexplained. Byron never thought he would leave Scotland but changed his mind when he became immortal—ah! trite and goading word. "I do not want to hunt my own people," he had said. "I cannot be satiated by the same blood that once coursed through my veins." His ancestors had lived in the highlands for centuries.

Byron fell in love with Italy, and so it was here that we spent most of our time. We had been cruising through the countryside, visiting each village as it came up on the road, when on a whim we found the catacombs at LaDenza. They sat below an abandoned cemetery in a pasture somewhere between one town and the next. Overgrown with ivy and moss, the entrance carries the inscription "Memento Mori." *Remember your mortality.*

He laughed at the epigraph when he saw it, insisting we had arrived.

"Arrived?" I asked.

"This is where we shall spend our days." He meant it literally since he could only venture out at night then. "Let us explore," he said. "Shall we?"

87

We went down into the depths of the wasted chambers. The tombs were filled with the brave Latini soldiers who fought in the early fourth century. The surroundings were all but dust and stone, though inside some of the sarcophagi were hidden gems. We spent hours lurking in the darkness, surrounded by the rich history of Roman death, not realizing until the plague the tombs also housed more recent burials.

It did not take much to set up a place for him to work. We cleaned out several of the large tombs making enough space for his laboratory. We turned most of the catacombs into habitable living space but still maintained a residence in the nearest village. We made sure to keep up appearances with the locals. By day Byron did his research down in the tombs, by night we explored the outside world— together.

"It is home," Byron had said. And for over a century, it was.

But one hundred and fifty years after we moved into LaDenza, we were forced out. When the outbreak reached its peak, those recently buried in the cemetery rose and wrangled the bloodless to our nest. One afternoon, as Byron worked on a body, another attacked him. I heard his yell echo through the chambers. I ran to his laboratory to find him cornered behind his autopsy table. The bloodless that lay on the slab was strapped down, but five or six frighteningly decayed corpses were upright and closing in on him where he stood. They were mostly skeletal, deformed and awkward, but strong, as they clawed at him. He had been pinned up against the entryway by their efforts to escape. I grabbed the cattle prod that lay on the counter and smashed the bones to pieces. The shards flew in all directions, the broken bits still moving across the stone floor. I took hold of Byron and rose with him to safety.

"My notes," he cried. "My work."

I promised him we would return, though we never did. Things escalated overnight and the village that housed our apartment was overrun with bloodless. When we fled LaDenza, I never thought I would return again—at least not without him. As I stared at the moss covered engraving this afternoon, I did not recall mortality, just Byron.

I had Elizabeth wait with the girl, so I could go down into the depths alone to make sure the bloodless were gone. The field was empty, though the route between the tombs and the vineyard had not been. We passed several swarms, as we stole our way around them with the stealth we had newly acquired from our feast. The blood of the two humans had been an excellent source of vitality for Elizabeth and me, and for the moment, we have enough strength to outrun, outwit and outlast anything.

The tombs were dark and empty and wet. A flood had washed through and our history was drowned beneath several feet of rainwater. I had hoped we could stay here, but the pools on the ground dampened that idea. I hurried to get what I came for, not wanting to leave the other two alone for longer than I had to.

In the depths of the catacombs, I found the tomb where Byron had spent most of his life. I felt him there among his work, his diagrams and notes pasted up on the walls, his elements and samples lining the counters as though trapped in a still life. Our existence was captured before me like a study on canvas. The bloodless he had strapped to his slab had somehow freed itself from the manacles, and I wondered if its limbs had not simply rotted away. I took a large duffel bag from the cabinet and headed to the compartment in the back. The cryostat blood samples were housed there in a small trough-shape container, its temperature gauge assuring me its battery had been preserved. I placed the container in the bag and headed back through the laboratory.

As I made my way to the entrance, I noticed Byron's lab coat hanging on the rack by the door. I went to it and ran my fingers down the length of its arm. I recalled how comforting it was to do the same when he was in it. A slight touch down his arm would always send him into spells; he had been receptive to all of my affections once upon a time. When I reached the pocket on the side of the lab coat, I touched the small journal tucked inside. I stole the book from the pocket and slipped it into my own, knowing it contained more of the mysteries my Byron had solved. I was so caught up in my memories I did not hear the howl until it was too late and I felt the pressure of a wolframlike clamp on my shoulder, though the teeth could not gain a grip, slipping off my stone flesh.

The fiend came at me again and I whacked it in the face with the duffel bag. It fell back into the water and then leapt up as though the baptism reinvigorated it. I tried to grab it by the throat but only got my hand caught in its open mouth. It snapped its teeth at me, and was met with a jaw full of hard flesh. I used my foot to dislodge my hand from the maw and sliced its throat with my talons. I turned around and made my escape. But I flew through the water only to find myself confronted by several more bloodless, waiting for me near the entrance. The water on the floor of the catacombs had awakened them and they formed a swarm, frenzied by the blood substitute in the duffel bag on my shoulder. They clawed their bony fingers and snapped their jaws but I was unwilling to surrender the one thing for which I had come. I renewed my efforts, slashing my talons and plowing my body into their deformed figures, as I made my way to the stairs that would bring me to the surface. I could not let them escape with me and so I called out for Elizabeth, as I charged through the fray. "Ready the gate," I said.

I hoped she was not under attack too, as I flew up the steps of the catacombs. When I slipped through the portal, she was ready at the gate and slammed it shut as soon as I escaped. I could hear the bones of the bloodless get wracked, as they crashed against the large stone slab rolled into place at the gate's front.

"Well done." The vampire's voice took me by surprise. It was not Elizabeth's, but the low register of Rangu. The godlike Hindu had caught the scent of the girl, coming upon the two of them, as I went down into the catacombs. Luckily for me, Elizabeth was able to distract him until I returned.

He is not a villainous vampire—as I said, he believes he is a god incarnate. He was willing to hear my reasons for not feeding on the girl. "Byron believes she's the key to saving humanity," he said, sounding unconvinced.

"We both do," I said. "She is our hope there will be others."

"And how do you plan on keeping her safe?" He has lived through as many plagues as I and realizes how dire this one is in comparison.

"I will stay by her side until I cannot any longer," I said.

He laughed with a deep, guttural chortle that was both jovial and frightening. "This problem holds no solution," he said. "You are better off accepting our fate."

"Which is what?" I asked.

"Our time has come to its end."

I did not believe that, though I would not argue with one who thought he was the harbinger of the final days. "Where is Wallach?" I asked.

"Searching for his scion," he said.

"Veronica?"

He nodded reluctantly. Rangu did not like competition.

"Does he know where she is?" I asked.

"I think he's looking somewhere about these parts," he said. "He doesn't know she's not long for this world."

"How do you know?"

"None of us are."

Rangu was like that, a prophet without prophecy, just presumptions. He assumed Wallach's punishment for leaving him was never to see Veronica again.

"And Stephen?" I asked.

Because Wallach was Veronica's maker, he would sense her whereabouts, and if he was in the vicinity, it meant she and Stephen were too. My hope that our paths would cross again was renewed.

"When did you last feed?" Rangu asked.

"We have had some good fortune in the vineyards."

"Hmm," he muttered. "You look satisfied." He glanced over at Evelina and I readied myself. I could tell he itched for her, but not if he felt brave enough to face the consequences. "Every now and then I catch one up in my fangs too," he said, concentrating on the girl. "I thought I had stumbled upon a pretty prize when I found Byron's little miracle here." He smiled at her with a closed mouth, trying to hide the fangs that had most certainly dropped by now. "When Elizabeth told me she was waiting for you, I was more than willing to wait for you too. I thought we might feast together."

Despite his agitated state, Rangu looked sullen. It had been a while since he fed.

"I have something that will help," I said. "Byron made a blood substi—"

He cut me off, insisting he would rather starve than drink synthetic blood. He assured me he was in no position to stoop to such extremes. "If it's time for me to part with this body, I shall abide Vishnu's will." His resignation made me think of Byron. "I'm sorry for your companion," he said, as if reading my mind.

"How did you know?"

"I always do."

Rangu took my hand in his and I shuddered at his fragile skin. Our hands remained clasped for a moment, and then he turned to Elizabeth. "Be well bhagini," he said. "May Vishnu watch over you." He leaned in and kissed her on the forehead, and then he faced Evelina, gazing at her for a moment before speaking. "May I?" His voice had fallen into its deepest and darkest register.

She glanced over at me but lifted her hand to Rangu. He took it in his and turned it over. He brought the inside of her wrist up to his nose, sniffing in deeply. He let the smell of her blood wash over him, holding it in his nostrils as though savoring it for later. That is when I realized my mistake. His composure shifted and I saw his mind turn. Who can resist the smell of a fetus? His fangs erupted and he snapped open his jaw, but before he could take his bite, I threw myself between teeth and skin. The look I gave him was enough to set him straight, for he quickly retracted his fangs and feigned a smile before backing away. "I see," he said. "Now I see."

With that, he vanished into the field as furtively as he had come.

25 October. — We are in a villa on the outskirts of Portero, a town abandoned but not empty. Swarms rove the streets, though we reached the hideout easily enough by scaling the rocks around the village. Elizabeth and I took turns smiting bloodless, as we bore Evelina to safety. After our encounter with Rangu, I thought it best to hole up for a while. I have made the villa resilient to invasion and we were fortunate to find canned goods in its cupboards. Evelina will have food for several weeks, though I worry about Elizabeth. We have grown hungry again already, which is why I decided we would sample the blood substitute.

As Evelina slept, Elizabeth and I dined by candlelight in the small kitchen. The cases of blood substitute were sealed, each one labeled and dated in my beloved's handwriting—I felt him with me, guiding me as I made my selection. I chose the most recent specimen out of the dozens of vials, confident we could ration the portions and make them last for weeks. "We will share one every couple of days," I said, holding the vial up to the candle, studying the thick crimson serum.

"It looks like the real thing," Elizabeth said, wrinkling her nose. "Do you think it tastes like it?"

"We can hope."

When I tore off the cap, the pungency of the fake blood struck me. It was similar to the scent I adored, but less fleshly. My fangs dropped and my mouth moistened, as I held the vial up to my nose. The feral scent aroused me, reminding me of every battlefield I had crossed. The stench of wounded blood penetrated the senses more deeply, even if less savory. I have always been a discerning biter, though I have been known to experiment. Every savor of blood is distinct, for every human being is a unique and complicated nexus of nourishment. No two donors taste alike, which makes the pursuit doubly pleasing. I assumed the same would be true for the synthetic blood. I put the vial to my lips and tossed my head back, downing half of the blood in one swill.

"What does it taste like?" Elizabeth was keen to try it, so I handed off the vial without explaining that the texture was wanting, less coagulated than authentic blood, and the flavor was acrid. She emptied the vial into her wide open mouth, and then licked her fangs and front teeth. She shivered and gave me a sour look. "It's horrible!"

She too had a sensitive palate. "Shush," I said. "You will wake the girl."

She shook her shoulders as though freeing herself from the experience. "Will we ever gorge on proper blood again?"

I was glad Evelina did not tempt her. Never had she asked to feed on the girl, and though I cannot tell if she wants to, I doubt she could resist if the opportunity arose. The newborn will be a whole other challenge—for both of us.

"That is the hope," I said. "By saving Evelina and her child, we will not want for blood again." I had my doubts, though I would never voice them. I reassured her our efforts were valiant and we had no reason to fail.

My vampire companion retired to a bedroom where she could daydream of better days, as she suffered the substitute's second-rate blood high. I stayed in the front room, waiting for the sun to rise over the mountain's ridge. The villa is at the top of a hill and looks out over the others. I reclined on the settee while the blood substitute coursed through me. Like lightning running across my insides, it gave me the rush to which I had grown addicted.

When the morning light began to wash the room, I took out the small journal I had found in Byron's coat. I flipped through its pages, remarking his elegant hand. His script was always embellished with swirls and flourishes. He made every word an event, which is why this one entry caught my eye. In big bold capital letters, he had marked *impure* across the page. The word stood alone—the entry before and after it unrelated; one described the earth's rise in temperature and the other was an observation about specimen number ten. I assumed his reference was to the brain he had been examining at the time but I could not make the connection. The bold print was surreal, invasive, innocuous and terrifying all at once. I flipped through the pages to find anything that could be related, and when I came to the last entry, the one dated the day before I yanked him from his laboratory in the catacombs, I found what I was looking for.

The blood substitute is impure. One drop has made my insides feel as though they are turning to stone. The pain is unbearable—cannot let Vincent know.

Byron had not always been secretive, but we never discussed the blood sub—

26 October. — The scream that rushed up the hallway to meet me suspended my horror and reason. I jumped up from the escritoire and ran to the room where Evelina slept, but she too had heard Elizabeth's cry and headed in to see the vampire. We found her toppled over on the floor, her legs still on the bed and her torso contorted and twisted on the rug beneath her. Her face was buried under her hair. She flailed her arms and reached out to me. "Vincent … the pain."

I crouched down beside her and took her up in my arms. Her arched torso vexed and convulsed. I brushed the hair away from her face and was struck with terror. Impossible nature! The expression on her visage was a manifestation of her anguish. Like a statue, rigidity had seized her and hardened her to rock. Her lips were mere lines, as the corners of her mouth had become taut and stony. Her eyes were wide and her brows raised in a perfect arch of petrification. I took her face in my hands but it chipped beneath my grasp. Soon her torso stopped convulsing and became stone too. Lastly, her legs and feet went rigid. I pulled them down onto the floor with the rest of her, but their weight made them crash and smash into pieces. She was a broken cast of slate—an uncanny reproduction—a marble effigy.

"Oh no! no! no!" I could barely hear Evelina's screams, as they filled the room.

She dropped to her knees, beholding her guardian in smithereens. I did not know if Elizabeth's condition was infectious, if she had been attacked and was contaminated, so I tried to hold the girl back with my free arm, but confusion got the better of me, and as I reached for Evelina, she slipped farther away.

"She is stone!" Evelina's voice was so small it was barely audible.

My own suffering sprang up, as the searing pain of a seizure took hold of my head. *The blood*—I could not speak. My brain seemed to rattle in my skull and everything shook around me. The anguish made my body heave, and I felt my gut ripped from my body, as my ribcage was torn apart and my lungs were pulled out of my corse. My limbs cramped as though the very flesh within them was ground up in a grinder. I went blind, as I tried to raise my arms to steady my dizzying head. Elizabeth disappeared, the room vanished, the world went mute, and I succumbed to oblivion until my angel of salvation arrived.

When I finally woke, I was prostrate on the bedroom floor, and the memory of my suffering was fuzzy. She saved me, Byron. Your girl saved me from the painful demise a vampire should never know.

I retched when I saw Elizabeth's fractured body beside me, overwhelmed by my reality. "Vincent!"

98

Evelina threw her arms around my slumped frame. "Thank goodness." Her tender voice calmed my nerves, as she stroked my forehead with warm fingers. "I didn't have the strength to move you," she whispered. "I'm sorry you're still on the floor."

I smelled the blood and my voice was barely a whisper when I asked her what happened.

"I didn't know what else to do," she said. "We couldn't go on without you." She wiped the tears from her cheeks with the back of her hand, revealing the blood. I reached for her arm but she pulled it away.

"You are hurt," I said.

"I'm fine. You're alive." She tried to hide her shame.

"What have you done?"

"I brought you back."

I did not need to ask; I tasted her still. Her blood lived in me, pulsing through me with its candied persistence, daring me to refuse more. I reached for her bloody arm again, this time catching it before she could get away. The wounds were fresh, the blood coagulated on the opening. I pulled her arm to me, holding it up to my nose. I drew in her scent, letting my fangs anticipate the pleasure of piercing her flesh, and then I gave in, tearing into her wounds with my teeth. I sucked the blood from her as if she held a bottomless reserve, the pleasure as intense as my earlier pain. Aroused and wild, I could not stop.

By the time I heard her scream, her anguish had already shamed me. I pulled my fangs out and dropped her arm from my mouth. Evelina had passed out, limp on the floor beside me. I did not let my weakness get the better of me, and rushed to repair the damage. I ran to the kitchen, her generosity coursing through me, and reached for the bottle of grappa on the counter, tearing it open as I returned to her slumped on the floor. I pulled her into my arms and gently tapped her cheeks. When she did not stir, I touched her mouth with the rim of the open bottle, rubbing some of the liquor on her lips. I held her for several minutes before she finally opened her eyes and drank some of the draft. The wounds on her arms had clotted, but would need to be cleaned and bandaged.

"Vincent," she said with her eyes closed again, "do you feel better?"

I had attacked her, gorged on her blood after she had selflessly saved me, and yet she did not fear me. My safety seemed her only concern. When she had heard Elizabeth's scream, she grabbed her small switchblade. The sight of the stony vampire had frightened her, but when I started to convulse she reacted without thinking. She swiped the blade across the inside of her arm multiple times, drawing as much blood as she could. She held her open wounds to my mouth, forcing the blood into me. Once I started to swallow, she cut deeper and drew more blood, feeding me in excess of what she should have spared. Minutes passed, as she let the blood pool in my mouth. She saw my subtle fangs drop and used them to puncture the vein more deeply, stopping only when the symptoms seemed to pass and I regained consciousness.

"I prayed for you, Vincent," she whispered. "I asked God to spare you for my sake."

Her compassion should have overwhelmed me, but I could not forget that her sacrifice would cost me. I desire her blood more than ever now.

"I won't survive without you," she said. "That's why I'm willing to risk my life to save yours. If you die…" She looked away and I did not bother to remind her that her death may very well be my demise too.

Later. — I have left Elizabeth's remains where they are. Ah, sweet Elizabeth! Her petrified pieces lie scattered on the floor of the bedroom. When the substitute seized me, I dropped her and she crashed to the floor, her stony frame smashing into bits. She is now a heap of dust just as Byron had become. Ashes to ashes, dust to dust—her end terrifies me for many reasons.

Evelina's blood acted as a transfusion, purging me of the tainted substitute and rendering it harmless. I do not know if I would have succumbed to the same fate as Elizabeth, but I would have eventually walked the path that Byron had. The substitute had contaminated my beloved and slowly eaten away his insides.

The blood that courses through me now is the same that saved me from that dreadful fate. I will never forget what the girl has done, but I must abate my hunger without tasting her again.

1 November. — We have been here for six days. I recovered within hours of drinking her blood, and the girl is healing too. Her wounds are hidden beneath bandages, though I force her to check them every few hours. The smell of her blood lives inside me and I cannot shake my hunger for it. It is the child that makes her cocktail so enticing. The sugary bite of her ichor, the baby's blood, is dangerously addictive. Byron warned me of this. I will not taste her again.

The scape outside is relatively quiet now, and the few bloodless that have passed by have not detected the girl. But I am more concerned with the arrival of other vampires at the moment. I am on constant watch.

The girl eats well and rests often. We have lived in the same room since the incident. She will not leave me, sleeping at my side mostly. She is attached and I do not know what else to do but let her indulge in this bond. I confess her presence comforts me in ways. I do not desire isolation, nor do I want to remember all that I have lost, but today she asked me one of those questions that forced me to recall my situation.

"Where did Veronica go?"

We had not spoken of Veronica since the night she disappeared, and I knew the girl felt responsible for the vampire's suffering. "We cannot know," I said.

"You don't sense each other?"

"Most of us do," I said. "But Veronica is too weak to emit a frequency."

"A frequency?"

Though Evelina would not understand and I was in no mood to explain, I gave it my best effort. "We give off an auditory emission when others are close," I said.

"Like bats?"

I hated to admit it, but it was similar to the biological sonar used by certain animals.

"Bats send out a signal and listen for its echo to locate objects and guide them in flight," I said. "The signals we send out are not in our control. We are stimulated by others and automatically emit a call—a unique frequency undetectable to any but us."

Mortals will never comprehend our nature, despite an attempt to understand it. We are collective creatures, not solitary, and though we do not seek one another out, we know when we are near.

"So you can tell when another vampire is around?"

"More often than not," I said.

"Not always?"

"As I said, some of us may be too weak to emit."

Though I am extremely skilled at controlling my own frequency, something I did not bother to explain to the girl, on a few occasions a vampire has caught me off guard. Some wield their nature with greater precision than others.

"Is Veronica dead?"

"We cannot die," I said. "We can only move into a state of nonexistence." It seems like semantics, but to me there is a grave distinction. "Veronica may be gone, but she is not dead."

She thought about the difference for a moment. I could see her mind working it out. "Do you believe in heaven?" She asked.

"Is one life on earth not enough for you?" My question cut and her look of embarrassment shamed me. "Veronica cannot continue to exist without proper nourishment."

"She can't survive without human blood, right?"

I smiled, though I have no idea why. "Yes," I said. "None of us can."

"Will you consume mine after the baby is born?" She was stoic, disturbingly deadpan, and I

103

hesitated before reassuring her I would not. "And my baby's blood?" She asked. "Will you consume it?"

The girl believes she is kept alive to restore the vampiric race. It is as if she does not realize the human one hangs in the balance too.

"Are you frightened of me?" I asked. She did not flinch. "You should be," I said. "I am not your friend."

Her cheeks flushed, as if her blood wanted to tempt me. "But you were human once too, weren't you?"

"Many lifetimes ago—too many to recall," I said.

My lie was somewhat the truth—I no longer entertain human sentiment, but I will never forget the mortal I was.

Later. — My genesis is primal. I am the first of our kind, though my mortal origin may be more compelling since I am a legend. A great-grandson of Zeus, I was born to a warrior father and nereid mother. My Thessalian name is Achilles and though my history has been spun in epic tales, the truth is my mother is in fact only part human, a sea goddess with a gift for shifting her shape. My father worshipped Thetis from the moment he trapped her in his nets and her father Nereus offered her up to him as a gift. When King Peleus married his water-born bride, she promised to forego shifting while she remained his wife, but only if he gave her a son. She was a mere woman for years, until his death, but I was born into my full inheritance—I was a demigod.

My mother, known for her volatile moods, probably an offshoot of her denying her true nature, began plotting shortly after I was born. She was determined to make me immortal like her, though my father could not understand—he was a brutish man. I was just a baby at the time, but I recall my mother's attempts as if I had witnessed them as an observer, not the sufferer. Each time she botched my deification, she made me more sacred.

Her last attempt had me submerged in the Aegean Sea. Nereus was present, and my mother's nereid sisters too. When she dunked me beneath the foam and held me under, I floated in the water as though in the womb, hearing the beat of her heart pulsing in tandem with mine. Sealed in the warmth of the liquid around me, as if ensconced in the vessel of my incubation, I heard the melodies of the nereids' lullabies, sung to me before I had hands and feet with which to crawl. I smelled the sweet blood of my creator, the substance on which I fed before I had fangs to subdue. I could see the portal from where I came into being, the light that beckoned me forth and promised me an eternal existence. I floated in the abyss forever, as I shaped my own creation, watching the genes of my father envelop those of my mother, the nature of my being taking root in the darkness of the immortal's womb, shifting in form as though becoming were an undecided and fickle state of existence. I knew the love that embraced me, her love, the eternal mother who relinquished me to the gods for the promise of immortality. Consumed by the maternal, devoured by the creator greater than us all, I heeded to the profundity of life, the ephemeral and fleeting essence of the flesh, the everlasting nature of the soul. I was just about to see the One when a force yanked my infant body up and out of the water. Peleus had found me, having come upon the shifters in their perverted ceremony of induction.

"Thetis!" His voice shook the rocks that surrounded the bay. Nereus and his daughters fled beneath the waves, but my mother was pulled up and tossed onto the deck of my father's ship.

A shifter's demeanor is as malleable as her physical form and thus Thetis eventually pacified her husband, making him forgo his anger. King Peleus did not forget, however, and as soon as I was old enough to speak, he sent me away to be raised by another. I did not see my father again, for he died in the jaws of an Aegean fish. They say nothing was left of him but the macerated stump of his right arm and the hand that bore the great king's Myrmidon signet ring, the only circlet he ever wore. When I was stolen from my mother, she went into a toxic rage and pined away, but within hours of Peleus's death, she shifted and disappeared into the sea.

I saw Thetis again years later when the pinch of the deadly arrow sent poison into my veins, but she fled as quickly as the life of the Amazonian queen I killed at the battle of Ilium—ah, Penthesilea! I still recall the ichor of that raging beauty—it was dried and stuck to my sword when the arrow's toxin bit into me. I remember the touch of her frizzy strands against my cheek, as I sent my blade into the side of her neck. Her savage blood sprung from her throat like the arched water of a fountain in Chios and she dropped her spear to stifle the wound with her delicate fingers. The blood gushed from between them, and I longed for it when I woke with a vampire's thirst.

When the poison reached my heart, Hades rushed up to meet me. I do not remember the numbness, the acute sting of death, but recall the sublimity of resurrection. Three days after they mourned for me on the shores of Ilium, I rose from the ground and stood transfigured beneath the light of the moon. My rugged helmet, blazoned shield and bronze sword were gone, but I no longer needed them, for I knew what I was—I always had—though I could not embrace my true nature until I abandoned my citizenry among the living. From that first day of my rebirth, I saw the world in black and white until I only saw red.

3 November. — The taste of the girl's blood haunts me still, and I now know withdrawal's burdensome ache, that for which my beloved had warned me.

"If you consume her blood once," he had said, "you will never stop."

"I have tasted pregnant women before," I had said. "Besides, she does not appeal to me."

"This girl is different."

"You find her that potent?" I had hoped my voice would not betray my jealousy.

"Yes," he had said. "Even for the strongest of us."

It had not gone unnoticed that he meant me specifically.

"It is simply blood, my darling," I had said. "Have I not yet proved my resolve with our rations?"

"I am not questioning your ability to resist her, Vincent." Our conversation frustrated him.

"Then what are you questioning?"

"Her ability to deny you."

"I did not realize you found me so irresistible."

"I am not joking," he had said. "Your appeal to humans is unlike anything I have ever seen."

He referred to my superior state of immortality. For the past hundred years or so, I have experienced a heightened communion with my victims—my aura is now divine and draws them to me. No other vampire enjoys this kind of magnetism. It is reserved for me, the progenitor. My allure is irresistible, for its cardinal nature, but the attraction is never sexual. More enlightened individuals will sense my gnosis, and sometimes take me for the Deity. I had not explained this to my beloved, for he was too inexperienced to understand and I could just barely comprehend it myself. But also I had not wanted him to think it was the reason he desired me so. I wanted him to believe he loved me freely.

"She is ignorant of my station, and too young," I had said.

"She may only be a child, Vincent, but she is also alone and frightened and will cling to any olive branch you offer."

4 November. — The bloodless have made their way up to us. The howls draw closer every hour. Something has aroused them. We are quiet, living mostly in the dark, and Evelina sleeps despite the time of day. I told her the baby makes her tired, but her wounds have also taken their toll. I fear they may be infected since she is forced to cover them with incense to mask the bloody scent and the oil irritates her lesions.

I have considered our options, but the thought of leaving is unpleasant. My energy-infused high has long since faded and I cannot do battle without another feeding. Our situation is bleak and—

Later. — This evening in the pitch black of the villa, as Evelina slept in the bedroom at the back, I caught the whiff of another. The scent of fresh blood was unmistakable. I anticipated a man's arrival, as the pungent odor of ichor grew with each passing moment. When he reached our door, he used a key to unlock it. I waited in the shadows for his entrance.

I know you wonder if I hallucinated, if I imagined him into being with my bloodstarved mind, but if you had been there you would have been as surprised as I to see the young man fall through the entryway of the villa, wielding a machete and carrying a large rucksack. He kicked the door shut as fast as he had opened it, slamming it closed with his back. I watched him, undetected in the dark, ready to pounce. The door thumped behind him, as the bloodless clawed at him from the other side of it. Their howls rose to a fevered pitch like a cacophony of crickets in thick springtime air. The man's expression was more determined than frightened, as he pushed his whole body up against the door.

"Shit," he mumbled.

Sweat dripped from his brow and I could practically taste the salty stench of his skin on my tongue. He would not appeal to me if I was in a position to choose, but like this he would do. I waited a little longer to see what would happen since I did not think the door would give way, though I was prepared to intervene if it did. When the howls lulled, he smiled. "That's it bastards," he said. "Suck it in."

When the cries of the bloodless ceased, I did not think it was because they had dropped to the

109

ground one by one like stones falling on concrete. I assumed something drove them away, and the mystery aroused me.

When all was silent outside, the labored breathing of my guest drew my attention. The young man let his body slide down the door until his bottom hit the floor. He tossed his head back with a sigh, and rested it on his rucksack. He dropped his machete to his side, and reached over his body with his free hand to pull his other arm up and across him. When his head slumped to the side, I knew he was no longer conscious. I held off my attack, though he would have been easy to take—his machete is no match for my speed. His ability to skirt the bloodless intrigued me and thus granted him a stay of execution. He had obviously used something to make his way through the swarm and into the villa. There had been no gunshots or explosions, and he had not arrived in a vehicle. It was as if he came through the swarm with some kind of immunity.

After watching him in his stillness for several minutes, I was surprised when he moved again. Finally revived, he slipped his good arm from the strap of his rucksack and pulled the injured one out slowly. He winced and cursed, as he freed himself from the bag. With one hand, he placed the sack in front of him and threw his legs around it. He rifled through it, pulling out a round canteen. He brought the jug to his mouth and dug his teeth into the cap, turning it three times before yanking it off. He spat it from his mouth and raised the jug to drink, downing it in one long swig then placing it on the floor before reaching into the bag again. He rummaged through before finding the item he sought.

When he pulled out the flashlight, I slid behind the drapes. He threw his light on the room, spotlighting the ceiling, furniture, floor and windows, but missing me entirely. When he left his light on the bookcase in the corner of the room, I knew he searched for something specific. He struggled to stand, his lame arm dangling at his side. He looked unsteady but regained his balance when he took his first step to cross to the bookshelves. Once there, he stuck the flashlight's end in his mouth and sifted through the books. "Shit," he mumbled.

His wounds were pungent, filling the room with their odor. He winced, as he reached for a book way up on the top shelf. He was forced to use the stepstool near his feet and when he finally pulled the book down, I could see it was a large photo album. With his good arm, he carried it across the room to a table in the corner near the window. The flashlight was still in his mouth, but he pulled it out once he put the book down. He opened the album and shone his light on its pages, as he examined each one. When he found what he was looking for, he held the light on the page for a moment and then peeled out the silver photograph. He smiled, as he shone the light on it. He placed the photo in his vest pocket, and threw the flashlight around the room again.

He inspected the villa next, rifling through drawers and cupboards and sniffing empty cans. I was certain he could smell Evelina's incense oil and wanted to know who was living there in his absence. I followed him closely, knowing his machete was still at the front door but a small hatchet hung from his belt. He tiptoed from room to room, and I hoped Evelina still slept, though the slammed door would

111

have woken her. I was relieved she remained in her room until I had come for her.

As he made his way down the hallway toward her, he put his ear to each door. When he reached hers, I closed the gap between us and stood directly behind him. He listened at her door, and I concentrated on not killing him if he opened it. When he reached for the knob, I came out of the shadows.

"Who are you?" I said.

He did not try to grab his hatchet, for he fainted at the sound of my voice. I caught him in my arms and tapped softly on Evelina's door. She had been waiting on the other side and threw it open when she heard me. "A creeper?" Her look of fright was almost as expressive as his had been.

"No," I said. "Just a guest."

I carried the young man back to the front room and laid him on the sofa. Evelina stood behind me, afraid he was dead.

"Fetch me the oil," I said.

I wanted to mask his scent, more intent on keeping him odorless for the bloodless than indulging in his savor. I opened his vest and lifted his shirt. His bare chest aroused me, exposed as it was. The cut of his abdomen, rising and falling with his breath, made my subtle fangs itch and they dropped despite my effort to keep them up. While the girl was out of the room, I took a quick nip from the inside of his arm where the vein sits just beneath the flesh. I pierced the skin ever so softly with the point of my fang and sucked up the blood that pooled in the crevice. The ichor hit my core with a jolt, charging my heart. His cocktail was far more potent than Evelina's, though not as delectable. His

112

taste in fact proved how hers had ruined me for all others, even as I relished the high from his.

When Evelina returned, I spread the oil on his chest and arms, which was how I discovered his dislocated shoulder. I gave the girl the bottle to hold and placed my hands on his joint where bone meets socket. "I think I am about to wake him," I said.

When I snapped the shoulder into place, the young man let out a shriek, his eyes locking shut in pain. I slapped my hand over his mouth to smother the cry.

"Shush," I whispered. "I mean you no harm."

When he opened his eyes, they welled with tears. Evelina stood behind me, watching with apprehension. The young man breathed in heavily and then spoke with a strident voice. "How did you get in here?"

"The same way you did," I said "The front door."

"But it's surrounded?"

Elizabeth and I had scaled the trellis on the side wall to reach a window overlooking the valley below at the back of the villa. The front entrance had been impossible to breach with the bloodless pacing the villa's doorstep, but the isolation at the back of the building made it worth the effort.

"There were none when we arrived," I said.

"Shit," he muttered. "That's impossible."

"They couldn't smell me," Evelina said. "I mean, us."

"How did you travel past them?" I asked.

He evaded my question and changed his posture, sitting up to look at me. The room was still dark, but Evelina held up a candle that allowed him to see my frame. I was not sure if he knew I was

113

with another, but he tried to hide his surprise. His tune changed when he saw the girl and he treaded lightly. "How long … you been here?" His words were disconnected, as though he had a hard time stringing a sentence together. He drew in a deep breath and then his whole body fell backwards into the sofa.

"Is he dead?" Evelina asked.

"Just unconscious. He is probably starved."

I ordered her to bring me the grappa from the cupboard and when she returned, I dripped a bit of the liquor on the man's mouth. The aroma seemed to revive him and when he finally came to, I forced him to take a proper swig. He kept the bottle at his lips until he had downed enough of it.

"Are you hungry?" Evelina's small voice softened him. He shook his head, and let it fall back again, though he did not pass out. He fell into a deep slumber until the sun brought in the morning sky.

5 November. — I slipped out of the villa, leaving Evelina to watch our guest while he slept. The air was thick with the fog that rolled in over the mountains. The odors of a salt sea and rotted bloodless mingled, making one fetid aroma. The swarm I had heard die away from the doorstep was actually still there, but the bodies were fallen on the cobblestones and decomposing at the villa's entrance. Inanimate piles of flesh, unmoving as corpses are wont to do, stared up at me. I kicked the first body and stepped on its limbs, the brittle form breaking beneath my foot. I leaned over and looked into the face of the bloodless woman whose nose and eyes were eaten away as though buzzards had climbed in and feasted. Her flesh looked green,

114

drained as it was of all its juice, and dried marrow was visible beneath the skin.

I waded through the fallen swarm, inspecting each body as I went. They had not been punctured or visibly wounded, nor were they burned or macerated. Their debilitated state mystified me, and I knew only one person could explain. When I headed back to the villa to speak to the young man, the sun threatened to burn away the morning fog.

He was awake and sitting up on the settee when I came in through the front door. "Going out is risky," he said. "Don't you think?" The smell of his blood distracted me for a moment and I pictured myself tearing into his neck. "Shit," he said. "You okay?"

"Perfect," I said. "How is your shoulder?"

"Feels like hell," he said. "Evelina is getting me some aspirin." He pulled his arm closer to him and winced.

"I can tie a sling around it if you would like," I said.

He seemed reluctant to let me touch him, but gave in when Evelina returned. I was not the gentlest of paramedics, though he wore a brave face for the girl. She was at ease with him already. They had obviously struck up a conversation before my arrival, and I almost regretted leaving her alone with him. I had assumed he would sleep for hours. When she asked him about the photos that hung on the walls, I paid little attention.

"You're in every one," she said.

"It's my father's home," he said. "We were close."

"Do you live with him?" She asked.

"I used to," he said. He winced, as I pulled the scarf into a knot. When I finished with his sling, I took up a post near the window on the opposite side of the room. I decided to wait to ask him about the bloodless.

"Where is your father?" Evelina asked.

"Gone," he said.

"I'm sorry," she said.

She sat down beside him on the settee and touched his shoulder. The young man shifted his body, though he did not flinch. I could see he welcomed the girl's embrace.

I will be more cautious about leaving them alone from now on. She is vulnerable and too easily charmed by silly men. I do not care he is the first human she has spoken with since Marco. She has grown used to the company of vampires, and I will not have her safety threatened by a garish young man.

8 November. — His name is Helgado Tarlati. He has been with us for two days, sleeping and eating. He is exhausted, if not completely dehydrated, but seems revived by the bit of food Evelina has coaxed him to eat. I am not happy to share her meager rations with him, but she insists. At this point, I do not know what to make of him. He tells us the villa belongs to his father. He is young— nineteen he says.

"When it all began, my father refused to leave," he said. "It took months to convince him to evacuate."

"Did he die on the road?" Evelina asked.

"He'd have stayed if I'd let him. He would've died here … in peace."

116

I watched the two of them, as they exchanged brief histories. They spoke about their dead loved ones in the same stoic manner.

"I had to destroy the body," he said.

Evelina reached out and patted his hand where it rested on the table. The tightness in his mouth seemed to relax at her touch.

"It was torture," he said, "but I forced myself to watch. I wanted to see his flesh melt, I needed to see it bubble and boil on the bones."

The question faded from Evelina's lips, as she caught up her breath and stifled her desire to know why. She seemed to pull back a bit, moving her hand from his ever so slightly. I do not think he noticed, but I could see the tempo of her breathing change, as the rush of blood that flowed through the lovely vein in her neck sped up. Her cheeks flushed and I could barely contain my fangs.

"The torment of losing him led me on a wild chase into the desert," he said.

"The desert?" Her small voice indicated she had not yet recovered from his admission. She did not know what to make of Helgado Tarlati.

"I was enraged," he said. "I wanted to kill every one of those blasted things with my bare hands." He took a deep breath and held it for a moment. "Maybe I had a death wish—maybe I just wanted …"

"To be like one of them?" Evelina said.

"I just wanted to feel something even if it was that."

Death has no feeling—I resisted adding to the conversation.

"I was lucky," he said. "I don't know how I survived."

"What happened to your shoulder?" Evelina asked.

He grinned. "I have no idea."

"But it was pulled from the socket," she said. "You must know what happened."

"When I got to the main square at the bottom of the village," he said. "Something caught me."

Evelina's eyes opened wide. "A bloodless?"

"Bloodless," he said. "That's a weird thing to call them."

She blushed and my mouth tightened. My fangs ached for a bite.

"A group of them surrounded me," he said, "forcing me through a small opening between the picket fences that border the shops on the main street." He had gotten caught in the fence, as he crawled through. "My rucksack got stuck."

"Oh no," Evelina said. She was fixated again, holding her breath, as he told the story of his narrow escape. Her fear of him was waning, her pulse newly racing.

"But before I could panic," he said, "I felt a ... I don't know, like a rough tug on my arms. They were out in front of me like this." He raised his good arm straight up above his head. "I was belly-down on the ground and it was like this jolt of cold hit me, it grabbed me like a vise around my wrists. I couldn't see what it was but the next thing I know, I am being pulled with this intense force."

"What was it?"

"I have no idea," he said. "It was too dark and it just disappeared. But the pain ... whoa."

"Your shoulder?" He nodded, seeking her sympathy. "How did you make it to the villa?" She asked.

118

"Shit luck, I guess."

Evelina blushed again.

"I've always been lucky," he said. "After papa died, I went further south—into the desert. I ate whatever I could find—flowers, grubs, anything— sometimes I went days without food. I only stopped to help ... and kill. But eventually I didn't run into anyone, and it felt like I was the last man in the universe. I thought ... I felt like ... forget it." He faded away for a moment, seeming to remember something he wanted to forget, then continued, telling us that he found shelter at an abbey. "Mount Oliveros," he said. "It's a monastery on the top of a peak in Tuscany. When I saw the sand-colored brick, I touched it just to make sure I wasn't hallucinating."

He smiled then and looked at Evelina. They sat beside each other at the small dining table in the kitchen nook. They seemed to forget they were not alone in the room, and I shifted in the doorway where I stood to remind them.

"The monastery had a drawbridge ... like a castle," he said. "As soon as I approached the entrance gate, the bridge was lowered and the great iron door opened for me."

"Were you scared?" Evelina asked.

"Of what?"

"Anything—everything," she said with a giggle.

His grandstanding bored me, as he shook his head, once again faking bravado for the girl. "A monk came to greet me as soon as I crossed over into the darkness."

"They were safe?" Evelina asked.

"They are totally isolated, living separate from everything, they haven't experienced it yet."

"How is that possible?"

"They don't have communication with the outside world."

"But …" Evelina was confused. She could not detect his lie. I am in fact familiar with that particular area on the coast of the Ligurian Sea and know of no monasteries there.

"They fed me and gave me fresh clothes after allowing me to take a hot bath," he said. "They even gave me my own room and I slept for like fifteen hours straight or something."

"But did you tell them?" Evelina asked.

"I wanted to, but I couldn't. Every monk takes a vow of silence and I had to do the same if I stayed."

"But how could you not tell them?" The girl's voice cracked. "What if one of them dies?"

"I was sworn to silence."

"But you could have passed them a note."

"I tried," he said, "but Brother Clemente wouldn't accept it."

"But …"

"Their Order forbids them from receiving info from the outside world."

"Why did they take you in then?" Evelina asked.

Ah-ha! She was paying attention—perhaps he will be forced to admit his lies.

"Their only activities are prayer and meditation but if a stranger comes, they have to offer him a seat at their table in case it's an angel in disguise."

"Oh," Evelina said. "That's beautiful."

I could not believe he filled her head with such nonsense.

"They're men of God," he said. "They believe everything that happens to them is his will." He looked up when he said *his.*

Evelina pouted a little. "But if they die, they'll all become…"

Bloodless.

11 November. — I often write long into the night. The boy sleeps in his father's bedroom while the girl uses the room across the hall from him. On the second night he was here, he took his rucksack and slipped into the room quietly after Evelina had gone down. He turned the lock in the door after he closed it and dragged a chair over to lodge beneath the knob. He did not trust me, though I have yet to show him how treacherous I can be. He and Evelina have grown close. His shoulder seems to be healing, which I think is due to her attention. She fawns over him. They eat together and talk about childish, petty human burdens, though the other day I overheard him ask her about me.

"Vincent saved me," she said.

"Were you alone?"

"No," she said. "I had a stepfather—and a sister."

He was quiet, though I knew he wondered about her baby. Evelina showed now and her condition was obvious.

"Vincent's not the father," she said.

"I didn't want to pry."

"It's okay," she said. "The father was Marco."

"He's gone?"

"Yes."

"I'm sorry."

"Oh no," she said. "It's for the best—he's—he was my stepfather." Helgado sighed. "After my mother died," she said. "He took care of me and Lucia."

"Lucia?"

"My sister," she said.

"Did your mother die in the plague?"

"No," she said. "I guess she was lucky."

"So Marco—"

"He never touched me before," she said. "I was a lot older when we—"

"I'm sorry Evie," he said.

She sniffled, obviously upset by their conversation. "It's okay," she said. "My baby's the only reason I'm alive."

"How so?"

"If I wasn't carrying this baby," she said, "Vincent and the others would've … uh."

"Others?"

I stepped into the room to deflect any unwanted truths. Needless to say, the conversation died with my entrance.

Later. — This evening, when Evelina had gone to her room, I followed her. "You must be careful with our guest," I said.

"Why?" She asked. "Don't you trust him?"

"I cannot afford to take such chances."

She looked at me softly and reached for my hand. "I won't leave you," she said. "I promise."

She thinks I am jealous. I am not. I am merely being cautious. I know she will not leave me—I would never let her.

15 November. — Things have been cozy for several days and I itch for Evelina's blood. I will need to recharge again soon. I have not fed since the nip I took from him the night he arrived. He is a distraction, though, as my curiosity about him fills my thoughts. This afternoon I asked him about his plans.

"I wasn't really going to stay," he said. "But this injury is really holding me up."

"Were you heading somewhere in particular after coming here?"

"No definite plans," he said.

"Why did you return to the villa?" I switched my tone to something less interrogative.

He sat at the dining nook, polishing his machete. He could not know how ineffective his show of intimidation was. "I needed to get something," he said.

He was a bit evasive but I avoided conflict and let it drop until Evelina woke from her nap. She was our best referee. If I could have stolen a bite without his knowing, in the meantime, I would have. I would do anything to quell the desire I have for her blood.

When Evelina was back at his side, she was able to get the answers I could not.

"What is that?" She asked.

Helgado had pulled a small paper photograph from his pocket, a rarity even before the plague. Obsolete since 2029, they had been replaced by glass-plated holograms. The photograph was torn but he held it by its edges anyhow.

"I've never seen one," Evelina said.

He passed it to her carefully, showing her how to hold it lightly between the tips of her fingers. She exhaled softly before she smiled. "What a beautiful woman!"

"My mother," he said. "Papa took that one a few days after I was born."

"That's you," she said. "Look Vincent!"

Aloof as usual, I only looked over at the image when she insisted. The woman, his mother I suppose, stood in a trite pose on the front steps of the villa. She held one hand up to her brow to block the sun and the other around the bundle at her chest. I could see the family resemblance since she looked about Helgado's age when the photo was taken.

"She left us," he said.

"What do you mean?" Evelina's voice was small but strident. "Did she die?"

"No," he said. "She just disappeared one day from our garden."

"Without saying goodbye?"

"I don't know," he said. "I was still a baby. Papa didn't talk much about it."

"So you've never met her?"

"I was a baby. She had trouble, I guess."

"Was she sick?" Evelina asked. "Why do you need the picture now?" She gave it back to him, and he studied it again.

"I couldn't remember her face," he said.

"Do you think she's still around?" Evelina asked.

He contemplated the image for a moment. "Yes," he said. "And I need to see her."

"Why?" She asked.

"I just do," he said.

He gave her a sour look, but then seemed to regret it. He patted her on the back of the hand before withdrawing to his father's chamber for the night. The girl went to bed shortly after.

16 November. — I slipped out for food this evening once the sun went down.

"No," Evelina said when I told her I was going. She was upset at my decision to leave, and I will admit I was rather surprised by the effect it had on her. I was certain she would enjoy some time alone with the boy.

"You will be safe here," I said. "With Helgado." I had already lectured him on watching her in my absence and making sure she was safe.

"We'll be fine," he said. "But how'll you get past them on your own?"

The howls have intensified over the last few nights, and the neighborhood is still infested.

"Same as you," I said. "I would imagine."

Slightly depleted, I convinced myself I had enough strength for a quick run into the village. Evelina needed food and Helgado had told me about a neighbor's storage shed several streets over.

"Mr. Rabizzi's place is white with a black roof and green trellis on the front wall. It's hard to miss. The shed is in the back, probably still padlocked."

He offered me his rucksack, bolt cutters and flashlight. I was not going to need the tools but I took them anyway. Before I left, Evelina stopped me at the door. "Take this please," she said, shoving a little vial into my hand. Her pale complexion evinced the gift.

"You must not do this," I said, returning the vial. "I cannot."

I would have relished the taste of her blood again, but that was the problem. Like opiates to an

125

addict, there was no return. I believed I had finally recovered from my fits of desire for her taste—I could not fall for her again.

"Please!" She pleaded with me softly so the boy could not hear.

"Keep it for me," I said. "I will be back." She looked wretched when I left, but outside the fresh night air cleared me of my empathy. I love the feel of darkness on my skin.

The bodies that once lay on the front step of the villa had dissolved into a black, tarlike substance. Spread across the cobblestones, the tar acted as a barrier to keep all the others away. I did not stop to examine the substance, but propelled myself over the ooze to reach the other side of it. I noticed a few bloodless wandering across the way and one stuck in a fence further down the hill. I made use of Helgado's directions and hurried to the shed two streets away. As I turned the second corner, I slipped into the garden on the left and made my way through the hedges at the end.

Everything went smoothly until I saw the white house with the black roof and green trellis, where a large swarm of bloodless communed on the front lawn as if waiting for me to arrive. I dodged them, tucking into the side yard. I needed to find a way around to the back without crossing the front, so I decided to climb the neighbor's wall and get onto the roof where I could reach the shed from there.

A sense of familiarity, similar to the one I experienced the night Helgado arrived, gnawed at my gut. I was not alone, though the horizon offered me nothing but open space and the howls of bloodless. I rushed across the roof, barely touching the peak, as I hopped to the one next to it. When I got to the back of the house, the yard was empty but the swarm in the front was close. I dropped down onto the grass and pulled out the bolt cutters, as I rushed to the shed. I wanted to preserve as much energy as I could, and foregoing the use of my talons would help. The padlock hung on the door intact, if only a little rusted. I was quiet, as I pinched the metal and snapped the lock open.

The clang of a bell in the distance interrupted me, as the clock in the village square sounded. It was the first time I heard it since our arrival, but the mystery of its clanging did not distract me from my mission. I slipped into the shed, grateful the howls faded, as the swarm moved toward the center of town. I hustled to shove cans and jars of preserves, packages of dried meat and fruit, and bottles of water into the rucksack. When I had filled the bag, I loaded every one of my pockets, and then closed the shed behind me, placing the broken padlock back through the bolt.

I headed around the side of the house with the heavy rucksack, still able to maneuver my way through the streets efficiently, but when I reached the last leg of my journey up to the villa, I encountered a swarm greater than the one I had dodged on the front lawn. I assumed the bell diverted all of them, but obviously a larger group eschewed the distraction and were now making their way through my very path. The howls escalated when they sensed my presence. I ran despite them, barreling through the herd with all my force, which is when I realized the bloodless were drawn to my own clanging, as the bolt cutters dangled at my side. I ripped the tool from my belt and tossed it away, redoubling my effort to knock down the bloodless, even as they grabbed for me. As I rounded the last corner up the hill, I could see the front steps of the villa and pushed my body beyond its state of depletion, seeing stars before lunging forward and hitting the ground. As though in slow motion, I had tripped over the decayed corpse at my feet, landing prostrate on the concrete.

I raised my hands to cover my head before the swarm could close in on me. By some turn of fortune, I noticed the spot of tar on the body that had tripped me up, and rolled toward it, ripping the leg from its socket. I held the gooey poison up to the masses, and like sparrows fleeing the hay-man, the bloodless ran in all directions, falling over one another to get away. I picked myself up and raced the last few feet to the villa, flying in through the door and throwing the rucksack down before I could rejoice at my near escape.

"Thank God," Evelina said.

"Where is he?" I did not waste time, wanting to know his secret then and there.

"In his room," she said.

I went down the hall and banged on his door, opening it at the same time. "What did you use?" I asked.

"What?" He looked at me confused, a feigned expression no doubt. He knew exactly what.

"What did you use to disable them?"

"I don't know what you mean," he said.

I hate to admit it, but I lost my cool. I reached for his throat and pulled him toward me.

"Vincent," Evelina's voice, deeper than usual, pulled me from my rage. I dropped my hand and stepped back. "Please," she said. "Please don't." She had slipped between us when she saw Helgado puff up his chest. "Don't fight," she said to Helgado, knowing she would have a better chance getting him to back down than me. He looked at her and then turned away from the door.

"Come with me, Vincent," she said, leading me down the hall to the front room. I do not know why I followed but I suppose her hold on me is stronger than I thought. "You can't hurt him," she said. "We need him."

I do not need him, I wanted to say, and he is nothing to me and the moment I know his secret I will crush him. But I resisted.

"You're exhausted," she said. "Starving." She reached for my hand and placed the vial in it again. "Please," she said. "For me."

"I need to be alone," I said.

She retreated, locking herself in her room for the night, but only after thanking me for my effort. "Because of you, the baby and I will eat tomorrow."

I would give anything to down the tiny vial, or to suck the blood directly from those blushing cheeks. I want it—I need it—but I will not have it.

Later. — Her blood teases me more with each passing hour and I would love nothing more than to drink every last drop—baby and all. But he is a nuisance. I know he keeps a secret, a solution to deter the bloodless, to destroy them, and unless I can discover it and take it from him, his only use to me is as a donor—a poor replacement for the girl, though an acceptable feed nonetheless.

Her attachment to him grows and I suspect she is unwilling to part with him. If he decides to leave, she may even want to go with him.

129

My heart aches, Byron. I feel heavy and I miss you. I am so tired, fed up with this task. I long to be with you again—an impossibility, I know. You and I have been robbed of the life we were promised the moment I gave you that piece of myself. We are cheated—stripped of everything.

17 November. — My suspicion is confirmed; he wants to take her with him. I overheard him knock on her door when he thought I was asleep. They could not mask their whispers despite his slipping into her room.

"Come with me," he said.

"I can't leave Vincent."

"I can protect you," he said. "My strength is back. My shoulder is better."

"No," she said. "I won't leave without him."

"He's no good for you."

"He keeps me safe."

"I've seen the way he looks at you," he said. "He leers—like you're his possession or something."

"It's not like that."

"Something's not right with him," he said. "He looks sick, like he's always starving. Is he anemic or something? He's so ..."

"So what?"

"Tired looking," he said. "He doesn't sleep much does he?"

"You don't know him," she said. "Besides, he's just worried for us that's all."

"What about those scars? Did he give you those?"

"No," she said. "Just stop it. You don't know him."

"So what," he said. "I can feel it ... in here."

130

"No."

"Why is he helping you?" He sounded agitated now. "Does he love you?"

"It's not like that," she said.

They struggled to keep their voices in whispers.

"Do you love him?"

"He made a promise to keep me safe."

"To who?"

"It doesn't matter. He's loyal—he's like a father to me."

"Like Marco was?"

"That's not fair. You don't know what we've been through. What he's been through."

"We've all been through hell."

They were silent for a moment.

"He can't save you," he said.

"And you can?"

"Yes."

"We all have the same chances out there," she said. "What if you get attacked—what if you die or turn?"

"What if he gets bit and dies? Or turns?"

"That'll never happen."

"Oh ya, right," he said. "He's invincible— bullshit! He's just as vulnerable as the rest of us."

"You don't know him."

I could hear one of them cross the room and sit on the bed.

"Evie," he said. "I love you."

"You do?"

"Yes, Evie. Evie. Evie. I am madly in love with you! You're so ... beautiful and smart and funny and ... ohhhhh, you've turned my world upside down! I can't live without you."

"But—"

131

"Come with me. Please!"

His begging made me sick. He was a pathetic boy and I could not believe he thought she would find his pleading attractive.

"We can make a beautiful life together," he said. "I promise."

"How can we make a life in this … world?"

"I have a secret weapon."

"What?"

"I know how to defeat them."

"Who?"

"The bloodless."

"What do you mean?"

"It's …" He paused and then shuffled toward the door.

"What are you doing?" She asked.

"Just checking." He went and sat with her on the bed and whispered, "It's a seed from a plant." I heard every word of his secret.

"Why didn't you tell Vincent about it?"

"I just told you why. I don't trust him."

"That's what he wanted to know when he came in," she said in her full voice.

"Shush!"

"But you've got to tell—"

They were silent again and I assumed he had stopped her from speaking the best way he could. I could hear the smack of their kiss and then the springs of the bed creak when she broke the embrace.

"No," she said. "Tell me about this plant."

He sighed like a petulant child. "I've almost run out of it," he said. "When I was attacked at the fence, my bag was torn and I lost some. I am down

132

to only a few stalks and that's why I have to leave. I have to get more."

"Where?"

"Not far from here," he said. "I have a map."

"Then why can't we both come with you."

"No," he said. "We have to go alone."

"I don't understand." He sighed again. "But Vincent can offer us both protect—"

"I knew I was going to meet you," he said. "I knew I'd find you here."

"How could you?"

"The shaman told me."

"The what?"

"Shaman," he said. "The man of divination I met in the desert."

I could not believe he continued to spin his outlandish tales.

"He's a Métis tribesman," he said. "He told me all sorts of things about the future—that's how I knew I'd meet you. He told me the photograph would lead me to you."

"The one of your mother," she said. "That makes no sense."

"Don't you see," he said. "That's why I came here. I was destined to find you."

Neither of them whispered now.

"And so what did he tell you about Vincent? This fortune-teller?"

"Not a fortune—never mind," he said. "He didn't say anything about him. He just told me I had to come and get you and take you with me no matter what."

"This is crazy," she said.

I tried to read her voice, to learn if she believed the foolish liar or not.

"The shaman said all that?" She sniffled; he had upset her with his lies. "He's wrong," she said. "Vincent is the only thing—the only one who can keep me safe."

"Just listen to me," he said. "The shaman was right about everything else so far."

"Like what?"

"Like my injury, the seeds, you."

"But ..."

"You have to come with me," he said. "You have to trust me. He's no good for you. I can keep you safe. I'd never let anything happen to you."

I did not think Evelina would betray my trust, that she would tell him my secret. He would wear his fear on his sleeve if she did.

When he left her room a few moments later, I decided to make him pay for his treachery. Since he and Evelina had grown close, he had stopped locking his door at night, and when he fell back asleep, I entered his room. He was beneath the covers, but it was easy to slide them off of him. I grabbed hold of his newly healed arm and yanked it from its socket again. I was swift, already out the door and back in the front room when he jolted awake from the pain. His scream shook the house and Evelina ran to his side to quell his nightmare. When she saw his arm dangling from its socket, she called for help.

I snapped his arm back into place and told her to fetch the sling. "You must have pulled it in your sleep," I said.

I assumed he was in too much pain to speak when he did not answer. Evelina returned and I tied his shoulder in place and assigned her to play nurse.

When I left them, I was satisfied there would be no more talk of leaving without me.

18 November. — This morning I went in to check on him. Evelina was still by his side, but had dropped off to sleep with her head on his pillow. Helgado was awake.

"She needs to rest in her room," I said.

The sound of my voice woke her. "I want to stay," she whispered.

I left them alone again, but was not surprised when she came to fetch me an hour later.

"Helgado needs to talk to you," she said.

I did not bother to ask what about and headed into his room.

"I wasn't telling you the truth before about the monastery," he said. "I had written Brother Clemente a letter telling him about the plague after all." Evelina came into the room with me but he asked her to wait outside. He needed to keep his lies separate and straight. "I couldn't leave without warning them," he said. "But as I was leaving, the friar stopped me and broke his vow. He told me that God had spoken to him and given him a message for me."

He paused for a moment, either for dramatic effect or, most likely, to come up with something convincing.

"He said, 'Man has warded off the devil since the beginning of time. This plague, too, shall be conquered. The dead are not returning in the name of God, but come as warriors of Satan. Let the Almighty Son of God enact His revenge upon these days. Do not give in to temptation. The Lord has a great plan for you. Go into the desert, a message awaits you there. Go in peace, my brother.'" He looked at me as though he expected me to say something that would suggest his monk's words were riveting. I denied him the pleasure and said nothing.

"When I left them," he said. "I headed into the wilderness and that's where I found Farouch."

I restrained my laughter at the silliness of calling his made-up shaman Farouch.

"He's a Métis shaman," he said. "I smelled the smoke from his pipe first—it was blowing across the clearing from where he sat in front of a huge red teepee." He smiled and I wondered if a bit of delusion had not infected his fabrication. He may very well have imagined his vision; the desert sun has a way of draining a man of his senses.

"Whoa, did he make an impression—his stature was ferocious. And he was a giant, kind of like you. I thought I was hallucinating. He was bare-chested, wearing nothing but loin cloth and prayer beads, and had stripes of red and white paint on his cheeks and chest. His skin was brown and leathery, like he'd been in the sun for years. And he didn't really speak to me with words, but somehow I knew he was inviting me into his teepee."

Helgado was able to describe the inside of the tent more elaborately than I would have given him credit for. He has a vivid imagination.

"The interior was bronze with large stripes of gold and silver," he said. "And it shimmered in the firelight—and the smoke—the smoke from the fire pit went up through the opening at the top of the teepee and a little pot-belly kettle sat bubbling on a rack just above the fire. The steam climbed the walls of the tent and twisted itself around the smoke, as both escaped the hole at the top together." He paused again and then proceeded to detail the furniture and accents. "There was a small stool next to the fire and a mat of straw that was lying on the ground at the back of the tent," he said. "And several clay bowls with purple powder residue were turned on their sides, and a few pestles and glass containers scattered across the floor—everything was stained plum color." Finally, his shaman spoke. "Miitshow was the first thing he said aloud, and I don't know how, but I knew what it meant—he wanted me to sip from his cup. It was filled with a thick, sticky substance that numbed my tongue. It had a funny taste—familiar but not really. I can't describe it, but I can still feel it on the tip of my tongue."

He said its texture was like honey, but not sweet. He guessed it was a mix of blood and sap. When he drew his tongue across his top lip, I thought of blood—his blood.

"I downed it," he said. "And then he offered me a drag off his pipe. That's when he started chanting. I could've sworn the fire rose and fell with the sound of his voice."

Helgado closed his eyes and began to chant softly. "Toñ Periinaan, dañ li syel kayaayeen kiichitwaawan toñ noo. Kiiya kaaniikaanishtaman ..."Almost possessed, he did not stop until he opened his eyes again and said: "Answichil—Amen."

It was the *Our Father* in Michif, the language of the Métis. Since Helgado's expression was blank when he recited, I could not tell if he had actually slipped away in that moment of recall. "Sorry," he said. "The shaman taught me that and I haven't forgotten."

I was beginning to get bored with his extraneous details, but I did not want to distract him from the cause and so I let him continue.

"When the sun went down, the fire lit up shadows in the tent. Things in the desert were creeping all around us. The shaman chanted, outmatching the rise of wails coming from the dead outside. That's when I saw him produce a dark seed—it was the size of a macadamia nut." Helgado reached into his pocket with his free arm and produced the very same seed. "He rolled it between his thumb and forefinger like this," he said. "And then trapped it in both his hands and rubbed his palms together really fast. After a few seconds, the seed disappeared and there was this plum-colored powder in his palms. With his hands open, he moved to the fire and blew the powder into the flame. It went up in the smoke and out through the hole at the top of the teepee."

I could guess what happened next—the bloodless dropped all around them.

"One by one," he said, "the shadows outside the tent fell like dominoes. And when the last wail was silenced, the shaman stopped chanting. 'Waapow, waapow' he said pointing to the door of the tent." Helgado told me he looked out and saw the bloodless toppled over one another on the ground. "They didn't rise again but melted into a black—"

"Tar?"

"Yes," he said. "The powder from the seed causes them to melt or something. It's like magic— or acid. They just fold under the power of the seeds—and not just the seeds but the whole plant too. The shaman calls it the Dilo plant."

138

That the deterrent to this plague is found in the natural world should not surprise me. Nature's way of correcting herself, I suppose. She thrives despite the erring ways of man. "What does the plant look like?" I asked.

"I never saw it," he said. "But the shaman said it had a thick yellow stigma and five large droopy brown petals ridged on their outer edges. The seeds are in the bulb, and the bulb is at the bottom of the style. But the plant has to be flowering or they'll be no seeds."

It was a story for Byron. He believed the virus had a natural enemy, though he thought it would be found in man rather than the earth. Since I had little else to go on, I believed the boy's tale. "Does the seed have to be made into powder for it to work?"

"I don't know," he said. "I've always broken it down."

"And how many of these seeds do you have?" I already knew the answer.

"Not enough," he said.

"Can the plant be cultivated?"

"I don't know," he said. "I never tried."

He was holding back on the map, so I pushed a little harder.

"Where did the shaman find these plants?"

"At the base of a bluff off the coast," he said.

"Which coast?"

"The Ligurian Sea."

It was not far from where we were. "We need to get more," I said.

"I know," he said. "The bottom of that bluff— that's where I'm headed. They'll be flowering soon and I didn't expect to be here this long."

I caught the blush that rose up his neck when he reached behind him for the map. It reminded me I was hungry.

"He gave me this and told me to go back to my father's villa before going to the bluff," he said. "He told me I needed to pick up the photograph, but he didn't say why."

I am certain that was not the first lie he told me throughout our conversation.

"Will you come with me?" He had accepted the necessity of my being one of his traveling companions. The bluff would be impossible to scale without my help, as would protecting Evelina. "We have to leave," he said. "Tomorrow if possible."

"May I see the map?" I asked.

"It stays with me," he said, though he held it out to me. "I'm sure you understand."

But of course I understand.

Later. — Evelina woke in the middle of the night and came to see me. I had just finished preparing our provisions and was about to get out my pen and journal. She looked soft and lovely with sleep still in her eyes. She is a temptation for the strongest vampire, even as the incense pollutes her smell, that luscious scent that always lurks somewhere between my nostrils and the back of my throat. I cannot wait to taste her again.

"I'm frightened," she said.

"You are safe with me."

I could only allay her fears with the same mantra I had been conditioning her with since the start.

"I don't believe you," she said.

"Why not?"

"Because you haven't fed," she said. "You're starving and depleted and you can't possibly protect me in this condition."

Though she sounded slightly hysterical, she was right. I was struggling. "I will feed when I can," I said.

"Why have you avoided feeding from us?"

I thought her question was ridiculous until I realized I had denied my nature without thinking about it. Why had I not taken from the boy? I could have indulged here and there, especially if I knocked him out first. The stench of humanness had clung to me ever since I resigned myself to saving the girl. "I am still satisfied from ..." I do not know why I had difficulty voicing it. I had tasted her blood, fed off her sustenance—her child's life source—and was desperate for more, but in doing so I had broken my promise to my beloved. I did not want to be reminded of that.

"But Byron wouldn't want you to starve like this," she said.

Her mention of Byron darkened my mood and I scowled without realizing I was doing so. Evelina reached out her hand and placed it on my cheek.

"You are handsome," she said. "But not when you look angry."

My fangs dropped at the touch of her skin against my cheek. I threw my tongue up to quell their itch. "Go," I said. "You need to sleep."

She let her hand drop and my desire died.

"I won't survive this journey without you," she said. "I can't." She reached into the pocket of her robe and pulled out the vial. It was filled with fresh blood. The aroma nearly destroyed me. "If you won't do this for me," she said. "Do it for Byron."

141

If only she knew what she asked of me. If only she knew that drinking her blood was the last thing my beloved would want me to do. If only …

I took the vial from her hand and tucked it into my coat pocket. She left me alone then with these empty thoughts and the temptation to drink her blood a second time.

19 November. — We left this morning before sunrise. Helgado and Evelina waited for my signal on the steps of the villa. I set off ahead of them to the main square to ring the bell in the tower as a distraction for the bloodless. I confess I was more than capable of accomplishing my task. Sometime before dawn, I gave in to desire. Her blood coursed through me with vigor, as her baby spiced the mix and made her serum more potent. I was high when I left the villa, steeped in the ecstasy of those few drops from the vial. I slipped past the bloodless without effort, agile and strong.

When I scaled the side of the bell tower, I was elevated enough to see the entire village and the villa on the top of the hill where Evelina and Helgado waited for my signal. I struck the bell with the ridge of my newly hardened hand over and over again, drawing the bloodless to my call. The side streets emptied, as ailing bodies crawled and stumbled into the main square. When the street was clear, the boy led the girl over the mess of tar and down the path I had taken several days earlier.

Once I had corralled the bloodless in the main square with my bell, I flung myself from the tower to the peak of the chapel beside it. I flew from rooftop to rooftop until I reached a safe place to land and made my way up the streets to the shed. Evelina was relieved when she saw me, throwing her arms around me. Helgado reloaded his rucksack and a second bag.

"We have no time," I said, sweeping Evelina up in my arms and tossing the half empty bag over my shoulders. "Now," I said to the boy.

We headed out of the yard and down the street to the fence Helgado had crawled through on his way up to the villa. I put Evelina down and told him to go first. He had some difficulty sliding through the opening with his injured arm, but I gave him a hand and he braved the pain. Evelina went next, slipping through easily even with her large belly. I tossed the bags to Helgado, pulling his attention away from me, and leapt over the fence. Evelina saw me and smiled. She knew I had fed.

By the time the sun had risen, we were miles from the villa and it was lost to memory. My mind wandered, as we made our way through the overgrown vines of the vineyards.

"Can we rest?" Evelina's voice broke the silence. I did not think of stopping. Since I had enough energy for both of us, I reached over to pick her up but she pulled away. "I don't think that'll do it," she said. "I feel … I need to sit."

"Is it the baby?" I asked.

She nodded.

"What are you feeling?" Helgado asked.

"Just a little pain," she said. "A cramp—a stitch, that's all."

We stopped between a row of vines, making a little place for her to rest on the ground. I laid my coat down and helped her sit on it.

"Maybe she needs something to eat," Helgado said. He looked through the bag to see what he had. "Nuts, apricots or dried jerky?" He asked.

"None of those will do," I said. "She needs protein." Byron had told me the girl would require plenty of animal flesh to enrich the growth of the baby. He suggested I hunt small game for her, feeding her the livers and hearts if she would suffer them. I had neglected his command since we had enough canned food at the villa. "I will have to get her something fresh," I said. "I will be back."

I instructed Helgado to mark a perimeter around them with some of his powder.

"I only have a few seeds left—"

I stopped him with my scowl. His frugality made me livid. "If I am not here to defend her—"

"Okay, okay," he said.

I waited until he rolled the seed in his hands and spread the powder around them before taking off through the grapevines. When I disappeared from his line of sight, I sped up, flying through the rows of flowering vines, picking up animal scents as I went. I reached all the way across the vineyard to the neighboring fencerow. The scent was strong in the brush, where game hid in the thickets. The shaded foliage marked the hunter's hour, late in the afternoon when the gregarious plant-eaters escaped from their burrows to pick the sweetest berries on the briar. I scoured the overgrown patch for the dark eyes of the rabbit. The smell of the cottontail was getting stronger.

As I awaited him in stillness, my mind strayed to human times, to the ephebic prince I stalked much the same. Troilus became my game too, as I sought his bright eyes in the somber temple. When I found him crouched by the altar, I almost did not kill him. He seemed worthy of my sympathy. The boy could not even fake an aggressive countenance. Lithe and elegant, he was a vision of femininity. He was surely a male adolescent but everything about him was unmanly. When he spoke, falsetto notes relayed his message. It was the whine that caused me to do it, his aggravating whimper made up my mind. I decapitated him with my sword, placing his torso upon the altar and his head in a bowl at his feet. I rode away from the temple with his blood still dripping from my sword. Wrath owned me then— they were warring times.

It was not long before the rabbit came out to greet me. I caught him up in one hand, and cracked his neck with the other. As I flew through the rows back to Evelina with the kill on my belt, I sensed the other. The vampire's presence crashed into me and I could only hope he did not reach them before I did. When Evelina's scream roared through the vines, I redoubled my pace. When I reached her, she was alone.

"Helgado," she cried.

"Where?" The vampire was close—I could feel him. Though he had not gone far with the boy, I was torn. I did not want to leave the girl alone.

"That way—go," she said. "Please go!"

I swept her up in my arms and carried her with me, as I followed Helgado's scent. We had gone maybe half a mile when I found Rangu feeding on the boy. He was limp in the arms of the old vampire, bent over him and sucking the blood from his healthy limb. He was on his second puncture; the first was in Helgado's clavicle. The boy was still alive, if just barely. I put Evelina down and rushed

Rangu, knocking the vampire clear off his feet and several yards into a row of grapevines. Helgado flew from his arms and landed somewhere on the soft ground. Rangu resisted me, as I held him to the dirt—he was recharged with the blood-high settling in. He pushed back against me, hissing and giggling, and threw me off, sending me several feet into the air. "Not this-s-s-s time, Du Maurier!"

He stole through the vines back to his prize. I jumped up and over the rows, planning to cut him off at the pass. When I caught up with him, he had reached Evelina. She was trying to stop the boy's bleeding, protecting him with her body, her hands covered in blood. She screamed for me, as I leapt on Rangu before he lunged for the girl. His iron fangs clamped down on my wrist instead of her flesh, as I pulled his head back with my arm.

We wrestled through the row of grapevines, twirling and spinning, until I had my arms around his neck and lifted him up off the ground. When he finally loosed himself from my grip, it was he who got me down, slamming me on my back, showing me the sky above, as he crashed down on top of me. Buried beneath the weight of his body, I kept my chin down to hide my neck. He attempted to take off my head, as he burrowed his honed talons into my jawline. His formidable fingers clawed their way into my skin, as his murderous eyes grew yellow with rage. Whether fate or luck, I do not know, but a chorus of howls broke our concentration when a swarm swooped in and yanked Rangu off me. As if dropping from the sky, ten, maybe twenty bloodless surrounded Rangu and ripped into him with their wolframlike jaws. They must have smelled Helgado's blood on the vampire and wanted it for themselves. I had just enough time to roll out from under him and into the next row of vines. Rangu called out to Brahma and Shiva before his voice drowned in a cacophony of trills. I could not save my old friend and rushed back to Evelina.

Though the swarm was distracted, it would not be long before they headed in our direction. I could only hope no others closed in already. When I reached the girl, I saw that Helgado was in bad shape. Evelina had done what she could to stop the bleeding, but he needed to be stitched up if we were to save him. I had to get them to safety first and so I picked up Helgado, balancing him on my back, and then took Evelina in my arms and ran to the place between the powdered vines. Once we reached the coat, I laid Helgado down and directed Evelina to pass me the medical supplies.

"Can you save him?" She was hysterical and sobbed ceaselessly.

"You have to calm down," I said. "I need you to do this." Unable to get a grip on herself, I was forced to comfort her. I put my arms around her and pulled her to me. Between her smell and the boy's open wounds, I grew dizzy. "You will have to do this," I said in my most serene voice. "I do not have the strength to stitch him."

I had used up so much energy in the last hour I was almost depleted again. The bloody wound on Helgado's clavicle had coagulated, but the bleeding from his arm was another matter. I held pressure on the opening and instructed Evelina how to stitch the skin. I eventually covered my nose with my free hand until the wounds were sealed and the blood had stopped. By the time Evelina had finished, she was calm and I coaxed her to eat a little of the rabbit I

147

had caught for her. She ate the liver before falling asleep between me and the boy. He is still unconscious and if he pulls through the night, it will be a small miracle.

20 November. — We spent the night outside. The powder from the Dilo seed acted as our safe house, repelling the bloodless that wandered the vineyard. Helgado regained consciousness shortly before sunrise. He did not remember any of it and believed me when I told him he had been dragged off by a beast.

"A wolf?"

"They are known to roam these parts," I said. "So close to the mountain border."

"It came out of nowhere," he said. "I couldn't even protect—"

"How do you feel?" I hoped to evade any details about my saving him. I was relieved he had not seen Rangu.

"Tired I guess," he said. "Sore like hell too."

"You have lost some blood," I said. "Drink this." I handed him the mixture of grapes I had crushed into the canteen of water. I thought the sugar would help get him moving. He took a little swig and lay back down on the coat.

"I'm queasy," he said.

Evelina was awake and gently wrapped herself around him, caressing his forehead. "Just rest now," she said. He drifted off to sleep again, and I thought she had too until I heard her small voice. "He's not going to die, is he?"

"No," I said.

"Why did your friend do that?"

I could not answer her question in a satisfactory manner. There was no reason—and every reason. It is our nature to feed on them, nothing else. I recalled the horror of Rangu's face, as the swarm yanked him from me. He would suffer their bites just as Maxine and Jean had and would lose himself to a punishment no one deserves, if he had not already.

The low rumble of thunder pulled me from my thoughts. Sheltered from the wind in our little enclosure between the vines, I had not thought to look up at the sky. The storm clouds had already rolled in, making the sky dark as ink. Water would be the death of us. I quickly packed up our things, waking Helgado and easing Evelina's fright. "We have to find shelter," I said.

Helgado was groggy when he woke and could not stand, let alone walk.

"You have to carry him," Evelina said. I did not have the strength to carry them both and the bags—she knew this and offered to walk. "I can keep up," she said. "I promise."

Before we left, I tore some of the branches from the vines and gave them to her. "They still have powder on them," I said. "They will act as a deterrent."

I tossed the bags over one shoulder and carried Helgado on the other. Evelina walked in front of me, waving her vines back and forth. I was annoyed I had to carry the boy and the girl was left on foot. I clung to her, as she set the pace. The rain had not yet begun, but the sun was nowhere and flashes of lightning menaced the sky. Each time thunder broke, Evelina stopped.

"We have to keep moving," I said. "Quickly."

When I hunted the rabbit the day before, I spotted a winery. I had planned on bringing Evelina there last night before the attack on Helgado, but his injuries held us up. When we got close enough to the building, I could see the large open doors. I did not hear any frequencies, or smell any humans, and so we proceeded carefully, stopping on the threshold before entering. I listened for movement, for howls, and when I did not hear anything, I guided her in.

The dark warehouse smelled like rotted fruit—and death. Evelina held onto the cuff of my sleeve, as I steered her through the blackness. An enormous vat sat in the center of the room and we disturbed the bed of flies that had settled on the spoiled pith, as we moved past it. The gnats surrounded us in another sort of swarm. "Close your mouth and eyes," I said.

We rushed through the infestation to the only door at the other end. I suppose I should have thought before throwing it open, but I was eager to get us out of the pests and into fresh air. As soon as I slammed the door behind us, I realized we were not outside. The howls pitched with the smell of the humans. Evelina screamed and clutched me tighter. I dropped the bags, and pushed Helgado and her up against the door, covering them with my body. The small swarm at the other end of the storeroom kept their distance, and I had enough time to formulate a plan. I lunged forward, kicking the beam that held several large keg shelves in place. When the shelves came down, so did the wooden barrels. They rolled onto the swarm of bloodless, toppling them over like a ball hitting pins.

With the bloodless distracted, I made for the roof. Using what strength I had left, I grabbed Evelina and Helgado together and scaled the shelf anchors up to a hatch in the ceiling. When I got to the top, I threw it open and climbed outside where the wind was fierce and raindrops ran down like strings without a break. I looked for a shelter for the two of them but could only find a small ledge near an exhaust vent. I put them down under the mantle, telling Evelina I would be right back. "Don't leave us," she said.

I had no time to console her and tore back down the hatch to get the bags. I landed on the shelf I had knocked on a slant. I slid down to its end and peered over the ledge. The bloodless were scattered, clawing at the wall opposite the door. They climbed on top of one another to get away from the potent seeds, sitting in the pocket of the rucksack. I slipped down to the floor and retrieved the bags, scaling my way back up the wall anchors and out onto the roof again. It was only a matter of time before frenetic, able-bodied bloodless would be clambering up to the humans. I needed to get us back inside.

I rifled through the rucksack and felt for the last three seeds. I took one and headed down the hatch again. I rested on the slanted shelf and rolled the seed in my hands just as I had seen Helgado do. But I could not make it into powder. As much as I clapped it between my hands and tried to break it, the ball would not dissolve. Finally, I realized my nature prevented the seed from breaking down. My skin was not skin but a casing that resisted heat and the seed would never soften in my hands.

I rushed back up to the roof. The rain pelted harder now, as electricity fired up the sky. A quick glance out to the fields alerted me to the coming bloodless. The human scent, no longer masked by incense oil, drew them to the winery. I pulled Evelina from Helgado. "I need you," I said.

"What?"

"You have to break the seed."

"I won't leave him."

"You have no choice," I said.

"No!"

I picked her up with two hands and ripped her from Helgado's side. She cried out but I carried her to the hatch despite her protest. I set her down hard—I was enraged. She had triggered something in me with her refusal and I wanted to expose my fangs. It took an incredible amount of strength to keep them drawn up. My voice was not my own when I scolded her and threatened to throw Helgado in the pit of bloodless if she did not make the powder. I ignored her cries, as I pulled her down onto the shelving with me and forced the seed into her hand. Frightened, she obeyed her master and rubbed her hands together, rolling the seed between her palms. Like magic, the ball softened into powder.

"Hold your hands open," I said.

Having regained my composure at the sight of the powder, I took her hands gently in mine and blew the purple dust out over the bloodless. Even before it settled to the ground, the swarm scattered, all sixteen of them collapsing almost instantly, as death arrested them once again.

"Stay here," I said.

"No!" She clutched my arm. "Not again."

I was softer now, telling her I had to get Helgado out of the rain. She let go and I flew up the hatch, barely reaching him in time. Several bloodless had ascended the side of the building, using each

152

other as a ladder to get up. I swept him and the bags into my arms and rushed back to Evelina. I sealed the hatch with an anchor I ripped from the wall.

I am exhausted now, my only consolation the girl safely beside me. The two of them are asleep and will most likely sleep through the night. In the morning, we will try to make an escape.

21 November. — We spent another day inside, the rain not letting up until sometime this evening. The boy needed the extra hours to recover and Evelina slept most of the day too. This unexpected stay, however, has depleted our water supply and we will need more tomorrow. I plan on leaving here in the morning whether the boy is ready or not. We cannot stay here any longer, as the bloodless decay all around us, making the room reek of infection. I do not want to risk Evelina getting ill. She needs a safe place to rest.

I would be lying if I said it was easy to resist finishing off the boy. I could take his map, the girl, and get the seeds with a healthy fill of blood in me, but something keeps me from doing it. Someone. You—Byron—my beloved, you are making me soft. It is all for you—this is my gift to you. I promised you I would keep her safe and I vowed to save the living—human and vampire. I miss you so.

Later. — While Helgado slept, Evelina spoke to me as if in a dream. *We need to leave.* Her sad eyes haunted me. "In the morning," I said.

She held my gaze. *You must feed.* "No, Evelina." *You must.* I must. *Yes, you must.* I cannot protect you if I do not. *You must.* Her head fell to the side and I could smell her skin. *You must.* Helgado

153

stirred in his sleep. I am starved—weak. *You must.* They will die if I do not. *You must.* I am our only hope. *You must.* The blush of her skin overwhelmed me; the nape of her neck begged for my puncture. *You must.* I will be gentle. Blood from the vial is one thing, but taking it directly from her is quite another. *You must.* My spine tingled, the back of my throat clenched, eager for her blood. I caressed the base of her neck, bathed in the smell of her skin. *You must.* I sunk my teeth in deep, closing my eyes as I pictured another, as I penetrated her flesh with the daintiest of fangs—I would not dare let my iron rods out. *You must.* The blood crept down my throat, as I lured it from the punctures at the base of her neck. The high was immediate, almost crippling in its pleasure. I forced myself to control the thrill, as it shot through every corner of my marbleized frame, touched every inch of my insides and made my hair stand on end. *You must ... stop.* When her body went limp from my indulgence, I quit and held her in my arms, pulling her to me, as she recovered from my feeding.

"Thank you," I whispered.

I laid her on the ground beside the sleeping Helgado and climbed out onto the roof to writhe in my ecstasy beneath the full moon. I will savor the taste of both mother and child for eternity.

22 November. — We left the winery this morning. I walked the perimeter before we set out, my senses fired, acutely aware of every single living organism within a mile radius. I could hear the rats, as they scavenged in the weeds, the birds, as they nested between the vines, and the worms that hid in the earth from both of them. The rabbits would be awake, burrowing for their breakfast and I would

154

catch a few before we left. It was good to feel godly again, potent and almighty.

Neither vampire nor bloodless were in the vicinity and when I reached the back of the building, I discovered that the tarred bodies lying inside had acted as a repellent. I flew to the fencerow to retrieve my fresh game, catching three rabbits this time, each one bigger than the next. I slung them on my belt after skinning them with my talons. I pulled a couple of sticks from the hedges and brought them back with me to the winery, plucking some grapes before heading in to get Evelina.

"What are those for?" She asked.

"Breakfast," I said.

"No, the sticks?"

I handed her the grapes, noticing she had pulled her collar up on her neck. "Repellent," I said.

I wrapped the ends of the sticks in a cloth dipped in the tar from the bodies in the storeroom. I gave one to each of them. Helgado was faring better but his shoulder was still in a sling and his wounds were swollen. Evelina steadied him on her arm when we left. They walked ahead of me together. He had consulted the map before leaving the winery and was convinced he could lead us to a well of fresh water from an Apennine stream. When we arrived at the spring a few hours after we set out, they rested while I filled the canteens.

"We'll head out of the montane region," he said. "We have to head west toward the coast."

Evelina looked tired. "How far?" She asked.

"Do you need me to carry you?"

She shook her head.

"Here," he said. "Eat something." He handed her a strip of jerky but she refused.

155

"I'll take the heart," she said, pointing to the naked rabbits on my belt.

I ripped one off and tore it open, digging out the heart. It slipped from her grip when I handed it to her, but I was swift enough to catch it up before it hit the ground.

"Whoa!" Helgado said. "How'd you do that?"

I had not meant for him to see my swiftness.

"What?" Evelina said.

"He was so fast," he said. "Like lightning speed or something."

"What are you talking about?" She said, stuffing the entire heart in her mouth. "You're still a bit foggy. He just caught it, that's all."

Although we have not spoken about my feeding, I can see its effect on her. Her desire for the animal's organs, the blood—she is addicted to it now.

When we headed back on the road, Helgado walked alongside me, keeping Evelina between us. "Uh," he cleared his throat. "Thanks for saving my life."

"I will do anything to keep Evelina safe," I said.

"Ya," he said. "I know, so, um, thanks for that too."

He showed gratitude as though she were his charge to protect. He forgets she is mine—and always will be.

23 November. — It has been another full day of walking and Evelina is exhausted. We have stopped for the night not far from the sea cliff. We have not come across another soul on our trek. The repellent continues to work, and I am still satiated and strong. I have not needed to expend too much energy as of

156

yet. I carry the girl sometimes but the extra weight is barely noticeable. The temptation, however, is another thing.

Tonight I sensed the ominous presence, that energy the boy brought with him to the villa. Non-threatening, indistinct, it seems to come only after the sun goes down. I am waiting for it to reveal itself to me since it is so keen on following us.

We are on the ledge of a rock face bordering the sea cliff. Our camp faces the water and is tucked under the rock overhang that serves as our roof. A small opening lies in the rock behind us, but the cavern is surely empty. When we arrived, it took some coaxing to convince Evelina she was safe here. Helgado built her a fire and I offered to fetch her a fresh catch.

"Don't go," she said softly. "Don't leave me."

"I'll keep you safe, Evie," he said.

His effort is in vain, for she only feels safe with me. Her attachment grows by the hour. As I carried her, she clutched at me with both hands. She has a difficult time resisting my aura, and Byron would not be happy with me for making her suffer the mild rejection she experiences every time I leave her. "I promise to return before you wake," I said.

Helgado used another Dilo seed for the perimeter, though he protested. We are down to our last two. "If it makes her feel safe," I said. "You will do it."

He did not bother to argue. He would not risk looking stingy or careless. I watched him spray the purple powder on the ground, the ledge and the surrounding rocks before I dove over the cliff into the sea.

When I returned with a handful of grouper, both of them were asleep and the fire had gone out.

24 November. — Today was a more memorable day than most and I will do my best to record it. At sunrise this morning, the nomad's arrival hit me with a blow to the gut.

"Ce mai faci, Du Maurier?"

Evelina and Helgado were still asleep when Wallach greeted me on the cliff's edge. I was not in the most viable position, cornered as I was with two humans. I told him it had been a while or some banality like that. We had never been companions and were barely acquaintances. He was seeking Veronica, no doubt.

"Not her," he said.

He has a gift for reading facial expressions and gestures, even the slightest of ticks can tell him what someone is thinking. "Then who?" I asked.

He stayed on the perimeter, hovering just outside the powder. I moved toward him, trying to draw his eyes away from Evelina and Helgado. When he looked at the two of them sleeping, I wagged my finger, assuring him they were off limits. He breathed in deeply—I can only assume to take in their aroma.

"Do not even let it cross your mind," I said. "They are mine."

He grinned, but I could read expressions too and knew he was slightly tortured by the impossibility of having them.

"I will not hesitate to take off your head," I said.

"Mi-e sete," he said. My Romanian was rusty but he wanted blood, though he did not look too starved. "I've eat-en already," he said. "But … mi-e sete."

He was thirsty, despite the blood he had found in the mountains. Animal blood was sufficient for temporary survival, but not as filling as human ichor.

"Te rog," he said. *Pleeease!* It was not beneath him to beg. He leered at Evelina's swollen belly, I was sure he could smell the baby. Her scent is potent.

"Nu," I said, scowling and holding up a hand, talons and all. He could certainly read that.

"Pardon." His shoulders dropped and he stopped leering. "Rangu told me about her," he said.

"Have you seen him?" I asked.

"Da," he said, picking at his teeth.

"Recently?"

"Nu," he said. "Unde este Rangu?"

He did not know about the vineyards. He could not—he was not there, or I would have sensed him too. I debated telling him about his partner. "I have not seen him since the catacombs at LaDenza," I said. "He was hungry and I offered him a blood substitute."

"Sânge fals?" He marked his scorn with a high-pitched laugh. "He'd sooner drink animal blood."

"Like you?"

It was an insult to openly accuse a vampire of drinking animal blood, but I could smell the family of chamois he had fed on hours earlier.

"Îmi pare rău," he said. "We can't all travel with our own personal blood sack."

His volley from Romanian to English made me dizzy. Each time he spoke, it was as if he switched

159

personalities; the English one refined, the Romanian brutish.

"I have not seen Rangu." I settled on that, knowing he would not believe me either way.

"Mincinos." He repeated the accusation in a low voice, spitting out the word rather than speaking it. His posture shifted as though he made ready to pounce from his haunches. He was crazy to think I would not tear him apart if he attacked. I thought Evelina was awake now, for how could she not be? "Mincinos—mincinos—mincinos!" *Liar—liar—liar!*

I stepped forward and pressed my hand up against the seething Wallach. He was smaller than I but had far less to lose. "You killed Rangu!" He screamed.

I told him that was ridiculous, but my expression betrayed me. He swiped a taloned-hand across my face, nicking the edge of my chin and neck. I threw my head back and leapt up before his second blow scratched across my shins. I landed with a sweep that knocked him off his feet. He sprang back up, kicking me with his heels, and hopped onto a nearby rock after regaining his balance. He was agile, his diet of animal blood giving him strength. But I was faster and stormed the rock he stood on, catching him by the arm. With my talons gripping his wrist, I twirled him around, sending him into a tailspin across the rock face and into its ridge. He slammed into the ledge with the thrust of my force, his head dropping back and colliding with the edge of the rock. The entire wall shook behind him.

When I saw his face again, it was covered in blood. Vampires do not bleed—the thrust of my hit caused him to disgorge the drink of chamois he had scoffed down in the mountains. As the blood spouted from his mouth, he clenched his throat. "Nenoroc—" He choked on his word, as the crimson fountain spurted without end. When a rumble came from above, I looked up to see the boulders drop from the rock face. I dodged several, leaving the nomad to his fate, as I ran back to Evelina on the ledge of the cavern.

Imagine my horror when I saw my girl was gone. The rocks came down with a fury and my only escape was into the cavern. The bags had disappeared, and I could only hope the boy had dragged her inside for safety. I headed into the darkness, taking in the air, tasting her on my tongue despite the rankness of damp and death. As I made my way in deeper, the mouth of the cavern closed when a large boulder fell on the ledge and sealed the opening. The light vanished, as my lone voice echoed through the tunnels. "Evelina," I roared.

Easy to track, I followed her scent, as I inhaled it—consumed it. Even in moments of danger, my desire for her blood aroused me. She would not get far without light, and I looked for the gleam of the boy's flashlight. A colony of bats clung to the stalactites above me, their sonorous squeals diverting me for a moment—I hated bats. As I made my way deeper into the cavern, heading into the core of the rock, I could hear the sea in the distance. Water sloshed around my boots, as I cut through the puddles, moving too fast to actually get wet. I breathed in the air, gripping her scent between my teeth. I no longer needed it since I could feel her pulse in me. We were in communion now, her blood coursing through my body, making her a part of me.

161

When I found her, crouching against Helgado in one of the cavern's small cavities, she could not see me.

"Stay back," he said. "I can hear you." The boy flashed his light in my direction.

"Vincent." Her strident voice alerted me to her fright.

When she tried to come to me, Helgado held her back. "No," he said. "He's dangerous." He shined his light on me and I did not feign dodging its brightness. "Who was that?" His posture was hostile, but nothing like Wallach's. "Why did he attack you?"

"He wanted Evelina." I was calm, finding no threat in this poser of a man.

"Sick fuck," he said.

"A rockslide has sealed the entrance," I said. "You will not find a way out."

A rush of pain—or perhaps pleasure—danced in me when the girl whimpered.

"What?" The boy was panicked. "Is that guy in here too?"

"No," I said. "Are you all right, Evelina?" I moved toward them and he pulled her closer. She struggled to get out of his grip and into mine. He was a fool for thinking he could keep her from me.

"She's fine," he said.

"Evelina," I said. "Are you fine?" I used my voice to entrance her, as she silently awaited my rescue. "I will make us a way out," I said.

"How?" The boy flashed his light about the cavern, remarking the inescapable situation in which he found himself.

"Trust me," I said.

I waved them to me and Evelina coaxed Helgado to step forward. I led them back the way I

162

had come, following the smell of the sea this time. I found where the cavern's wall was wet and offered the tiniest cracks of light. Before putting my fist through the rock to make us an exit right there in the cavern, I placed Helgado and Evelina far enough away to be safe, and where he would not see my enormous strength. "Shut off the flashlight," I said.

He was obedient now, realizing he was at my mercy. With the two of them huddled out of sight, I blasted alternating fists into the rock wall. Piece by piece it crumbled, as I whaled into it and tore through the cavern within seconds. When I made enough of an opening, I stepped out to see that I was on the other side of the mountain. The salt air rushed to meet me and I knew we faced the sea. Before me stood an expanse of green, the wild grass caramelized in the morning sun; we had reached the bluff.

Helgado had started to lead Evelina toward the sunlight when I turned back to them. She pulled one of the bags beside her and I rushed to take it from her. "Thanks," she said.

"I'm not even going to ask how you broke the rock," he said. "Not even going to ask."

He walked a little ahead to the center of the greenscape and threw his rucksack on the ground, dropping down beside it and yanking it open. He pulled out a canteen and took a sip before offering some to Evelina. I helped her sit down beside him, but he only moved over a little and rifled through his bag.

"Can you reach the apricots?" She asked.

He tilted the bag toward her, making her reach for them herself. She pulled out several other things before finding the fruit.

"The sea is that way," I said.

Helgado got out his map and compared it to the landscape around us. "I think we're close," he said. "There's supposed to be markers in the cliff above it."

He got up again and walked toward the edge of the bluff. I stayed with Evelina and perused the surroundings. They were peaceful, empty. The chaos with Wallach was far now, somewhere on the opposite side of the rock.

When the boy returned, he told me there were three massive rocks jutting out from the center of the water, each one indicating the location of the plants. "We made it," he said. His hostility had turned to excitement.

"When Evelina is rested," I said. "You can show me."

"I'm going down," he said.

"How?" Evelina looked up at him. "You can't climb down a cliff."

"Oh, and he can?"

"Better than you," she said.

"You will stay and watch over Evelina when I go," I said.

The brave fool did not protest since the vertical drop was at least three hundred feet and he would not be able to scale it with or without injuries.

"The plants are supposed to be blooming at the base of the cliff," he said.

"Under the water?" I asked.

"No," he said. "In a grotto between two rocks. That's why you can't see them from up here. Farouch said it was a small opening marked by a spear that's been stuck in the rock forever."

"Help me up please," Evelina said. "I want to see this spear."

"You probably can't see it from way up here," he said.

I wondered if it was not another one of his tall tales. We left the bags on the grass and walked over to the edge of the bluff together. Evelina used me for support while he went ahead of us. When we reached the edge, I held Evelina, as she leaned over and looked first.

"In there," he said.

"I can't see anything," she said. Helgado pointed downward with his good arm, but she failed to see his marker. "I don't see it," she said again, stepping back.

"May I?" I asked.

She moved to the side and let me take a look. Like her, I saw nothing but sea and foam at the bottom of the bluff. The only indication of a hollow in the rock was the trail of water suctioned into a crack.

"I know they're there," he said. "We just have to figure out how to get you down the wall. I have my gear—"

"I will not need gear," I said.

"What are you like a cliff diver or something?"

"Something," I said.

"Well, are you a strong enough swimmer," he said, "because it looks lik—"

"Leave it to me."

Helgado looked at me with confusion, if not incredulity, but then resigned himself to the situation. It did not matter how I got down, as long as I came back up with the plants.

165

"You should go now," he said, "before you lose the light."

"Tomorrow," I said.

"But we—"

"Tomorrow."

I would not leave before setting up a safe place for Evelina to rest, and I wanted to wait the night to make sure no others arrived.

Later. — As I write this, I sit on the edge of the bluff, looking at the waves below. The sea is rough where it meets the terrain but tomorrow's climb will be easy. I am high—charged with the boost from her blood. She gave herself to me again hours ago when the boy was already asleep. I barely put up a fight. I wanted it. I needed it. I am no longer ashamed. My vow to Byron was broken the moment he asked me to deny my nature. I have accepted our trade-off, her safety for my survival. The thing that keeps my stone heart beating—for my heart does still beat—is the one thing I will never resist. It is the blood, but also the power—the divinity I am fated to engender. The numbness, the vibrating ecstasy, the fire in my belly, all tell me I am becoming the other.

When I was finished, she placed her small hand on my cheek then slid it down to the corner of my mouth. She put her slender fingers between my lips and ran them across my front teeth. When she touched the sharp points of my bloody fangs, she withdrew her hand. The spell was broken. She wiped the drops of her own blood on her robe and went back to lie beside the boy. She can never unfasten this yoke between us.

25 November. — At dusk, the benign presence finally revealed itself.

I headed down the bluff early this morning, as soon as the sun rose. The two were sleeping, but I did not want to waste time. I thought I would have to make several trips if the plants were in fact in bloom, but I had no idea that the first trip would eat up the entire day. I carried the empty rucksack on my back, as I scaled the side of the bluff. I stole swiftly down the rock and reached the surface of the raging sea, the water exploding with anger only Nereus could muster. It splashed up at me, as if inviting me to sink in and play.

I used my claws to get to the place where the water was sucked in through the rock. The edge around the opening was slick and I had to grip the stone with my talons to hold myself steady. The splintered tip of what was once a spear marked the spot. The opening was tight, but I was able to slip inside, keeping a grip on the rock. By this time I was soaked and my marble frame was made even heavier. As soon as I got through the crack, the hollow opened up inside and I found myself in a natural grotto with vaulted ceilings. The ground was well below the sea, but I found a small ledge on the inner rock to stand on.

Raised up from the pool, I inspected the rock walls. The opening was nothing like the cavern, this hollow filled with vegetation. The rocks were vibrant and alive, covered in green and yellow algae—moss grew in abundance, as crabs skidded sideways through the aquatic brush. The overgrowth was so thick I could barely see anything else. With it and the mist from the sea, I wondered if I would have trouble recognizing the plant, until I caught a familiar whiff that evoked a memory so strong I did not feel myself drop in and under the water. I succumbed to a Stygian darkness too impenetrable even for a vampire. Engulfed and floating as though in space, my mind was like a sieve, everything pouring out of it save one ancient memory.

When I was a boy, I was taken to Mount Pelion to see the sibyl who lived in a cave much like this one. I recalled her damp walls, the dreariness of her hovel decorated with shoots and sprouts. She had frightened me with her crooked looks. She had no teeth, and her cheeks were sunken, framed by matted strands of hair that hung down past her feet. When she petted my face with her ugly fingers, I gagged on their smell of sardines and cloves. "S-s-s-s-alt water—cherries-s-s-s-s kiss—and this-s-s-s," she said. She held out a clay pot filled with water. A flower with large petals and a thick yellow stigma sticking up out of its center floated inside. Its fragrance was both sweet and savory, like cinnamon and olives. Unforgettable and rare, I had never seen it before or since. "Thetis-s-s-s," she said, "sótéria." Her eyes rolled back into her head and her mouth clenched into a tight wire. Her voice was low and sonorous, as she chanted *sótéria—Thetis—sótéria—Thetis—sótéria*. I recognized my mother's name but not the other. The foolish sibyl's words meant nothing to me until now—now they mean everything.

When light finally reached my eyes, my head was propped up on the ledge of the grotto, my body still submerged beneath the water. I was struck by the serenity and clarity I felt at the memory. I could smell the cinnamon and olives of the flowers in the hollow. I had located the Dilo plants and they were

168

in bloom. *Thetis*—they were my mother's flower, the ones that would lead to my salvation—*sótéria*.

I pulled my body out of the water. It seemed as though I had lost hours, transfixed by the smell and memory of the sibyl. The sun barely reached the opening, as I made my way along the rock shelf to the flowers, guided by their scent. They were just out of reach and I had to drop into the water to get to them. My body was as heavy for me as a slab of granite is for a human, and I was forced to propel myself up and out of the water with little leaps to prevent from going under again.

I picked the largest plants, the ones with the most blooms. I used the rucksack as a vessel for the flowers, keeping them immersed in the saltwater like the sibyl warned. I used the second bag for the seeds at the base of the tubers. I spent some time pulling up the smaller plants and stripping them of their seeds. By the end of the pruning, my body was tired from the constant thrashing of the waves in the grotto. I tried to leave by scaling the inside wall again, but I could not balance the bags and use my talons at the same time, so I had to tread through the water, holding the bags above my head, hoping to avoid the undertow a second time.

When I finally reached the opening, I was able to carry the bags in one hand and use the other to grab hold of the outer edge of the hollow and pull myself out of the water. I was relieved to be in the air again—a much easier element for us to move through. With the bags on my back, I scaled the rock, noticing the onset of dusk. When I reached the top of the bluff, I tossed the bags onto the landing in front of me, and then climbed up. But as I was about to swing my legs over the top, I received a blow to

169

my chest and throat that sent me back down. I thought I saw the boy peer over the edge, as I fell through the air.

I slammed into the raging water and sank straight down in the sea. The blow at the top of the bluff had not been as bad as the thrash my body received breaking through the water's surface. It took me a moment to reverse the direction of my descent and torpedo out of the water. When I finally came crashing up from the sea, I flew higher than the most determined mullet, leaping onto the rock and scaling the bluff and over its edge in time to see the boy making off with the bags and the girl. He pulled her across the clearing and toward the opening in the rock on the other side of the greenscape. I approached them undetected, as I caught up in one leap. When I tore the girl from his hand, she screamed in horror, and he stopped, seeing me catch her up in my arms.

"Evelina," he said, dropping the bags to reach for the machete at his side.

"No," she screamed at him. "Don't!"

I put her on the ground and faced the boy. She clutched my boots, sobbing and begging me not to kill him. "The traitor must be punished," I said, my voice booming through the clearing, rebounding off the rock face. I stepped away from the girl, taking one long stride toward the boy. I wrapped my hand about his neck and squeezed until his face turned red and I released him again to the ground. The girl sobbed and moaned and her distress got the better of me, keeping me from taking his life for the moment.

He caught his breath and did not relent. "You're the devil," he said. "A demon!"

"Is that so?" I found his little tirade amusing since I was a bit of a devil, one who was going to steal his life.

"You're going to kill Evie's baby," he said.

The humor in his accusation was slightly greater than the rage I felt for him in that instant, and I released a belly laugh.

"I saw you ... you ... and Evie."

I leaned down and looked him in the eyes, smiling with an open mouth. He cowered and turned away. "Saw what?" I asked.

"I saw you b-b-b-b..."

"Bite?" He could not say it out loud, and kept his eyes on the ground. I turned back to Evelina, toppled over and clutching her stomach. I flew to her side and dropped down beside her. "The baby?" I asked softly.

"I didn't tell him," she said through her sobs. "I promise I didn't tell him—he—he—he saw them." She reached up and touched the two small points on her neck. I knew she had not betrayed me. She never would—she is as much me, as I am.

"No," she said, looking past me. As though in slow motion, her cry warned me the foolish boy had raised his machete and was dropping it on my head. The metal blade hit my stone skull and bounced off without making a chink. My turn was so swift it happened outside of time and I caught his blade up in my hand, ripping it from him before he could regain his grip on its rebound. I launched his machete clear across the greenscape and out to the sea. "This ends now," I said.

"No," she cried. "Please don't kill him."

"Stay out of this Evie," he said. "Do your worst, asshole."

I grabbed him by the hair and dragged him across the clearing all the way to the edge of the bluff. I ignored his wails until he suggested he knew my plan. "I know ... what ... you're going to ... do," he said.

"Is that so?" I made him look at me, wanting him to see the face of his death. I unleashed my iron fangs, and opened my mouth wide. I have been told this look is the most frightening my face can wear. For him, I did not hold back.

"Please," he said almost breathless. "Pleeeeease—don't kill—"

"It is too late to beg for your life, boy."

Wrath seized me and would not let go. I had not felt this kind of rage since that foolish Agamemnon stole my booty. I wanted to rip off his head too, and drain him dry.

"Ev—" I choked his words, yanking his head back to admire the gleam of his brown skin in the twilight. I closed my eyes, letting everything drop away, and the rush of anticipation for his blood, satiating my insides, drowned out the girl's cries. My throat tingled in its preemptive hesitation, as it awaited pure pleasure. But as I was about to sink my iron fangs into his flesh and tear into his skin with abandon, her hands covered my mouth—her stone cold hands. "Please," she said, "release my son."

When I opened my eyes, I saw the face of a vampire I did not know, though I recognized her. She was the new mother from Helgado's photograph, but her eyes were empty now and her skin and lips drained of color.

"Please," she said.

Though I did not release the boy, I drew my fangs back up, dissatisfied and dry. This was the benign presence I had felt since Helgado's arrival. His vampire mother had followed him, kept him safe, yanked him through the fence, and rung the bell in the tower to call the bloodless away from the shed. She had stalked us since leaving the villa and now begged me to spare his life.

She stepped back from me and held out her open palms. She would not fight, knowing I would relent with her surrender. I dropped the boy on the edge of the bluff and stepped away from his mother. She was different, like no other vampire I had seen. Her eyes were bloodshot, her irises purple, her skin white like chalk, not smooth and silky like most. The boy pulled himself up from the ground and stared at his changed mother. "No," he said. "No … you can't be …"

"I am," she said softly.

By now Evelina had made her way to us with her face red and swollen and streaked with tears. I looked down at the boy and smiled. He received a punishment worse than the death I had promised him. He would suffer the humiliation of knowing his mother was not only a vampire, but cloned with artificial venom.

26 November. — I am transcribing Alessandra Tarlati's abduction and transformation as it was told to me.

"I was twenty-three when Peder Karlsson took me from the garden of my home. My baby was sleeping in the shade of the lemon tree and I was pulling up the weeds from between the patio stones. The prick in my neck felt like a bee sting. Everything went dark—almost immediately.

When I woke, I couldn't move my arms and legs. I couldn't even tell if I was alive or dead. I was in complete darkness. Then I heard the girl's voice—she asked me my name. Hers was Berenice. We whispered in the dark, lying side by side as we were. When I finally felt the numbness leaving me, I reached over and touched her. We held hands, as we suffered the burns. Our throats were on fire. She was the first to say the word blood. She wanted blood. I didn't know it was what I wanted until she said it. I could smell everything around me—wet snow, bark, smoke, cedar, mulberries, cocoa, mint, basil. Everything, every scent, was right there in the darkness with me. But the desire for blood became impossible to ignore. I was tortured, desperate to feed. I tried to bite Berenice, but I could not move close enough to her in the dark. I tried to catch her hand up in my mouth, but I only ever got my own.

I lost all track of time in the darkness. I prayed for death, not realizing it was impossible. Then one day, I began to see through the darkness. I started to make out shapes and that's when I saw Berenice for the first time. She was more dead than I, a corpse in full rigor mortis. I snapped her hand off when I pried mine from it. We were locked in some sort of crate together, no longer human—but animals. My scream blew the lid off the crate and I flew out of my prison, destroying the shackles that held me down.

I was not alone. Fifteen other women had been taken with me—all of us made into this. Peder had wanted a harem of vampires, but ended up with a brood of vipers instead. He constantly pitted us against each another, forcing us to fight for blood. A fang match, he called it. Several of the girls hadn't reached their full potential and suffered the effects of

174

the artificial venom—some couldn't digest the blood and starved from the inside out. I was one of the luckier ones. I am full vampire.

We eventually freed ourselves after the outbreak. He got weaker—he couldn't find enough blood to feed himself and we took off his head. We escaped and I abandoned the others, heading to the last place I was human. The trek from the north was easy until I reached Poland—that's when I ran into more and more of them. Blood was hard to come by, but I don't need much to survive. That's one of the perks of being a cloned vampire. I can survive on very little blood. But now I'm hungry."

Later. — Alessandra was actually starving by the time she revealed herself to me on the bluff. She had planned on going back to a hill town several miles north of where we were, but was afraid to leave her son alone with me.

"The town is well protected," she said. "It's abandoned but populated with rabbits. They gave me a good boost when I needed it." Like Wallach, she feeds on animal blood to survive. "It's just as tasty as human blood—sort of," she said. "I can probably digest it better than you." I did not argue since animal blood is something to which I will never resort.

She has a nice smile. Her fangs are always down, and though she does not have a set of iron teeth and her claws are duller than mine, she has something about her that tells me she can fight if she has to. I like her, despite her petulant offspring. Evelina urged the boy to feed his mother, but he refused. He did not take his mother's change well, and if he had not become so attached to the girl, he

175

would have left. As it is, his mother convinced me to seek out the abandoned hill town since it was much closer than the villa.

"It's enclosed with walls," she said. "It'll be safe for the girl, and for all of us."

We left the bluff at sunrise and walked most of the day. We are spending the night en route to the hill town. I am willing to trust Alessandra. I do not care whether I am led to follow her by instinct or desperation, but she is harmless and will serve as an ally for now and certainly keep me from killing her son, a decision upon which I am still deliberating.

27 November. — We reached the hill town at dusk. It sits on a precipice overlooking the sea. Three sides of it are enclosed with a wall that is twenty-feet of stone. The front entrance to the town is marked with enormous wooden gates, one of which is almost off its hinges.

I carried Evelina over the threshold, but she had rewarded my efforts before we reached the town's outer limits. The high from her blood made me euphoric, as the sight of the medieval town made me nostalgic for better days.

"I am going to inspect the perimeter," I said.

I had the boy surround Evelina with powder in the town's inner courtyard, where I left them to wait for me and Alessandra, as we swept the outer walls, checking for a breach.

A large forest, whose trees hug the stone wall, some even hanging over it, sits on one side of the town while on the other, a vast slope heads down toward a grouping of trees several yards away. A drop-off leads down to the sea, protecting the town's rear, while the interior court and laneways are just as scenic. Cherry and lemon trees line the inside walls, reviving the eleven stone dwellings and utility hovels that have been abandoned for centuries. With the proximity clear, as neither vampire nor bloodless nor human are close, the hill town feels safe and peaceful, unlike any other hideout since the cathedral, and I have decided to call this home for now.

28 November. — This is as good a place as any to make a haven for the girl. She can have her baby here. It would be reckless and serve little purpose to return to the villa despite its comforts. We are in the wilderness, and this abandoned town has not seen people, let alone bloodless, for decades. Here we can build our future, little by little. Here we can sustain human life. The girl is resolved to making this her new home. I told her we would set her up in one of the hovels and give her some privacy and, if she is lucky, things will start to seem normal.

I know what I must do with the plants. When I saw the cherry trees, the sibyl's message was clear. I will make saltwater beds at the base of them and plant Thetis's salvation there. The plants will bloom and eventually form a natural barrier to keep out the bloodless. The solution seems too easy, but the hill town is more fitting for us because of it. And that is what I need to believe right now.

We used the powder to make a natural perimeter outside the walls. The boy and his mother did the work. We had seeds in abundance with the plants I had plucked. With almost as many pips as a pomegranate, the bulbs carry a myriad of seeds in each.

177

I have not forgotten that we are limited in amenities here—she will be without hot water for a time, but not much else. I plan on making various hunts to scavenge for necessities. With the forest on our border and the sea at our feet, I can amass the natural resources we need, and will raid the nearest town for the rest.

The buildings here will give Alessandra plenty of shade in the daytime. She is still unable to face natural light. Only eighteen years vampire, she is susceptible to the sun—a vulnerability I hope will not hinder us.

Later. — Alessandra and I went out after the sun set to hunt small game for her and the humans. The herd of rabbits were scared off when we arrived at the hill town, but the clone has an amazing gift for tracking and she caught the scent of a family of badgers before I had even gotten a whiff of them.

"How did you do that?" I asked.

"I could feel them on the tip of my tongue," she said. "It tingles when I smell living things." She closed her eyes and rubbed her tongue across the bottom edge of her teeth. "There," she said. "There's a cluster of grubs beneath a rock over there." She pointed fifty meters behind us to a boulder the size of a melon. We stole through the forest to the site, and sure enough when I reached down and picked it up, its underside was crawling with larvae.

"Can you smell other vampires?" She shook her head. "You can pick up frequencies though, right?" I asked. It did not occur to me she would be unable to do so. It is one of our best features. I found it curious she had not heard my frequency at the villa, especially since I am the oldest, the one from whom all others come—cloned or not.

"I only knew you by sight," she said. "When I saw you in the village, I knew you weren't human."

I should say not, I thought, I am a god.

"You were so agile and strong," she said. "And you have a quality—a presence like no other." She smiled, bearing her fangs like a thirsty creature. She was captivated by me, if only a little. "I can't smell the bloodless either," she said.

"How do you avoid them if you cannot detect them?"

That is when she showed me her second incredible talent. She crouched down and launched herself at least forty feet in the air from her standing position.

She is an anomaly, a vampire like none I have ever seen. Byron would have thought so too. He would have loved to have known a clone. We had heard rumors, but never any success stories. Alessandra proves both a threat to our way of life and a boon. I can only hope her venom's fate proves more lasting than that of the synthetic blood.

2 December. — We have been busy building the nest while the girl rests. She actually looks well, and more maternal than I have seen her yet. Alessandra is teaching her the things she recalls from her own pregnancy, detailing the process of birth and what she will need to do to take care of the child. The boy is working hard too, obeying my commands and doing my bidding. We have planted the bulbs and repaired the roof of the girl's hovel.

In just these few days, the plants have taken root and are beginning to sprout already. It would make Byron proud that I have not forgotten my days of living off the land several thousand years ago. My beloved was never much of a horticulturalist despite his heritage.

"Your people were farmers," I had said to him once. "How do you think your first century Druids made their cures? I am certain they plucked them from the very same highlands you ran through as a child."

We had been discussing his frustration at growing Centaury for his Scottish herbal kidney tonic.

"Yes, yes," he had said. "I would have made a wretched Druid."

Yes, Byron, but I would have loved you all the same.

I wonder if we would have met in that first century of the Common Era when I rode into the northeastern region of Scotland to lay siege to the Caledonians. If Byron had been one of the many on that battlefield, would I have slaughtered him too? Would I have recognized my beloved?

I recall what he said then that seems so pertinent now. "The Romans made sure to demolish that Scottish way of life. I am certain my bloodline is more theirs than anything."

He had meant his human bloodline, but his observation about the Romans seems fitting nevertheless. For an empire to become the Empire, it must demolish another, and so on and so forth. That is the nature of history and that is why it exists—to tell the stories of fallen empires, and the rise of new ones. If one is lucky, history will live on. And if I am lucky, my history will continue to be written.

To be satiated, nothing is more pleasurable. I grieve for the feasts that were once so plentiful, the blood that flowed like wine at a banquet. I mourn the passing of time. But I still hope. I hope for the pulse-pulse of humanity to thrive once again, so that I may indulge this nagging urge I have to suck them dry.

4 December. — I have built flower beds that run along the side and back walls. I feel more confident we shall be safe against the bloodless, as long as the winter stays warm.

Alessandra's nose led her to a poultry coop last night, and she returned with a crowded cage of hens and one lone rooster. The fowl will be a nice addition to the girl's diet. She will enjoy fresh eggs and the occasional braised chicken leg. My next project is a small vegetable garden for her. She will continue to feed well, even as I am forced to abstain for a time.

6 December. — The blood of the hen dripped from the machete's tip, her death a sacrifice for the pregnant girl. Evelina's cravings for fowl demanded satisfaction, so I decided to appease them with one of the smaller birds. As I stripped the carcass in preparation to cook it on the spit, my mind wandered. The smell of the fowl's blood did not whet my appetite, but the neck of the bird lying severed on the block brought back a memory that made my mouth water for war.

Several years before the Common Era, I had returned to my human occupation as a warrior. My wont for sustenance was best satisfied by the warm blood I seized on the battlefield. I was a fit soldier and quickly received the honor of escorting my own one hundred into battle. Under the command of the Roman Governor of Syria and on the direct order of Emperor Augustus, I led my men into Sepphoris to quell the Jewish uprising.

My soldiers showed no mercy, snatching women and children, binding their hands and feet like fatted calves and throwing them into carts to be sold into slavery. The Jewish men were slaughtered like cattle, but only after being tortured. Their fingers were cut off, their faces maimed with hot metal rods and their soles skinned before their bodies were strung up on crosses. Their crucified flesh was left to scorch in the desert sun.

While my men worked to slay and hang the treasonous captives, I followed my nose into their hovels, tossing them in search of those still hiding. I was led into one home by the tangiest blood I had smelled yet. She was frightened, I could practically taste the sweat beading on her skin. It was only when I slipped into the hut that I heard her sobs. She was just a child, maybe twelve or thirteen, and was flat on her back on the dirt floor. Her sackcloth was pushed up over her waist and her legs were dropped to one side. She had brought her hands up to her face to cover her eyes against the soldier who stood over her tying his belt and readjusting his sheath. His sword had been removed and lay on the stone sill of the window. Fresh blood dripped from the blade, though I soon realized it was not the girl's. A severed chicken head had been tossed on the dirty floor at the foot of the sill while the decapitated fowl frisked about headless at the other end of the room.

I tucked into a recess and waited for the soldier to finish and leave, hoping he would not see fit to kill her. He had been ordered to keep all women and children alive but I could see he was not one to obey commands. I had to control my urge to pounce on the girl, her scent slowly getting the better of me. Her eyes were still covered, and for that I was glad since what the soldier attempted to do next was offensive to both man and vampire.

He picked up the severed head of the fowl and kneeled down in front of the girl, where he used his free hand to pry open her legs, pinning one of her knees down with his own. The girl squirmed in the dirt, her sobs amplified by their suppression. The soldier brought forth a growl from deep in the back of his throat, and then spat on the neck of the bird. Gripping it by the beak, he held it in such a way as to betray his intention. He planned on forcing the limp appendage into a place it had no business being. I could not witness such deviance without intervening and felt it only common decency to prevent further abuse of the child. Besides, I did not want him to spoil my appetite.

When I stepped forward from the recess, I told him he was done. The young man froze at the sound of my voice and the severed head dropped to the floor. He slowly got up and retrieved his sword from the window ledge, gliding it into his sheath. He barely looked at me, as he made his way out of the hovel and into the bright sunlight. I, however, would not forget the future prefect of Judaea, and when Emperor Tiberius sent me to keep an eye on Pontius Pilate in Jerusalem, I recognized the vicious boy straightaway. He was no longer the svelte Roman soldier with abundant curling tendrils I had encountered decades ago. The prefect had been transformed into a portly man with a drastically receding hairline that time had treated cruelly.

"Have you heard the stories of the rebel?" Pilate asked at my first meeting with him. "The militant's outlandish prophecies?" He threw a handful of figs at the plump tabby resting on the floor by his feet. He picked up another from the silver dish at his side and threw that one into his mouth, as he spoke. "His threats were intolerable," he said.

"I have heard the stories," I said. "A madman claiming divinity, nothing more. The court was right to decide his fate as they did."

My approval flattered the prefect, though he did not need it. He spent little time deliberating over the judicial decisions he had to make. Killing was his nature. For a man, he did not have much of a conscience. He had endorsed the death sentence issued by the Sanhedrin because he could not stand the heretic and had wanted to take credit for his capture. Neither Pilate nor the Jewish council could have predicted the repercussions of spilling that particular man's blood.

"Mmmm," he said. "So Vitellius sent you?" I nodded in agreement. "We shall have some fun then."

The threat my presence insinuated did not intimidate him. Rome was far from Judaea, and he believed he would remain the sole ruler of Jerusalem.

"The Jews grow restless with my show of power," he said. "They want me deposed." He balked at what he called their petulance. He had shaken some feathers on several occasions, toting idols through the streets, displaying relics where they did not belong, and most recently having two enormous limestone busts of Emperor Tiberius

184

placed outside the Hall of Hewn Stones. "Rome has ordered me to remove them," he said. "I assume that's why you're here?" His nasal voice was too coquettish for a man, though it suited his effeminate and aged appearance.

When a waiting-woman arrived with a large jorum of water, Pilate shooed the tabby aside. She greeted me with a drop of her head, exposing the luscious nape of her neck. I heard the pulsing rush of her blood beneath her golden skin, and took a long whiff of the air as she passed.

"The oils are redolent of the pomegranate blossom," he said. "Lovely, isn't it?"

He thought I was taken with the scent of perfume in her hair, but he was mistaken. His waiting-woman would surely die that night under the painful pierce of my aching fangs. She curdled the venom beneath my skin—her exquisiteness was potent. "Lovely," I said.

I held my bite, as she proceeded to lay her jorum at his feet. She kneeled beside the prefect and gently placed one hand atop his foot. "Your hand is cold, woman," he said. With all coquettishness drained from his voice, he scolded the woman. She shuddered and apologized softly, rubbing her hands together in her lap. She held them there for a moment before attempting again, as Pilate bragged about his reign of terror.

"I have a wonderful plan if you'll indulge me, brother," he said. "I'm thinking of teaching those Jews a well deserved lesson."

I listened to him, though I was wholly concentrated on the delicious waiting-woman at his feet. Perhaps he could see my desire or maybe he just had a hankering for horror himself, but when he reached into the folds of his toga, he withdrew a dagger. Quite casually, as he explained his scheme, he reached down at his side and stroked the woman's hair as though caressing the pelt of his tabby. She kept her eyes on the basin, continuing to wash his feet, as his hand ran over the crown of her head. When he ceased speaking, I noticed the subtlest of changes in his expression and a slight grin rose on his lips. As though sensing the shift, the woman tensed, and he grabbed a fistful of her hair. She gasped, as he yanked her head back and leaned over to force his mouth atop hers. Then, pulling away only a little, he brought the dagger across his chest and to the under side of her chin. She did not have time to surrender to her god before he dug the dagger into her neck and slit her throat. As the blood spilled down the front of her robe into the jorum of fragrant water and onto the stone floor, I licked my lips. I would need to find someone else for supper.

"As I have said, brother," Pilate continued with the girl's wasted blood forming a pool about her. "We shall call them up to the mount to see some … agh, I don't know … some urn buried beneath the stone or some fabrication of the sort." He sipped from a cup he had at his side and then tossed another fig into his mouth. He licked his fingers one at a time and then clapped his hands together. His eyes widened as though a brilliant idea were just hatched. "We'll tell them the holy mountain calls them to see the sacred vessel of their god. Ah! That's a good one."

I could not keep my eyes off the waiting-woman's nectar. Its smell teased me, even as the ichor slowly congealed. I was irritated by the waste.

"Are you with me, brother?" His words had escaped me and so I nodded. "You'll ride with my soldiers into the village to slaughter the swine."

I pulled myself away from the wasted treasure congealing on the floor. "If I may," I said. "Your Excellence." He giggled and I knew the title pleased him. "Will it not anger the Jews further and perhaps ignite unwanted tension with the High Priests?" I asked.

"Praise Bellona! It will be war!"

And so it was, though Pilate did not reign for long after that. Caligula showed the prefect no mercy, sentencing him without a trial and placing him in prison where he could either take his own life or gamble on exoneration in the other world. I was sent to Pilate's cell to deliver the verdict, and when I slipped into the room armed with an opal box, he rushed to my side.

"Hear me out, brother, before you speak," he said. "If my life has come to its end, take my soul. I've seen your black heart—your pointed teeth— your lust for blood. I know what gifts you possess." He whispered in the somber cell, his coquettish voice lost to fear.

I was not surprised he had discovered my secret. I did not hide my passion for blood as carefully as I could have. His ruthless ways brought out the worst in me. "I wonder if you are deserving of such a gift," I said.

"I assure you I am," he said. "I'll rule the world with powers such as yours—to die and be resurrected. What could be more potent?"

"I have yet to die," I said.

He moved toward me, reaching out his hand. He placed his palm on my chest and let it rest there for a moment. The sinister smile I had so often seen cross his face was now gone. His countenance was stone, shocked by the thumping of my beating heart. "But how ... please, brother, share your gift with me," he said. "Spare my death and make me like you."

I uncovered the lid of the opal box, where a rather plump scorpion lay docile in its corner. Its tail was relaxed and its stinger limp. Pilate stepped back upon seeing the arachnid, and shooed the box away with his hand. "I can't die," he said. "Not like this."

I placed the lid back on the box and put it down. "Brother," I said, "death is not unique to you, nor are you to it. Every man who devours life to excess will be ushered into death's embrace with regret and despair."

I let my subtler fangs descend and their points drop over my bottom lip. He drew in a shallow breath and held it. I told him to close his eyes and let grace bear him to the other side. He mistook my meaning and turned his face away, dropping his head to expose his neck. I let him go to his death thinking he would be reborn. He did not excite my desire, but blood was blood. When I unleashed my iron fangs and opened my mouth wide, I recalled the tasty girl in Sepphoris. She would finally be avenged of his brutalities, and hers was the only face I saw when I ripped open his skin and stole the life from him.

7 December. — This morning the boy warned me the smell of the cooked meat has drawn the bloodless near. We have not seen any until now, and I fear the plants are not grown enough to have an effect. Eventually Thetis's flowers will multiply and

188

their toxic seed will spread through the soil to create a natural fortress inside our walls, but for now the powder on the outer walls will have to suffice. The gate is sealed and I do not believe they will attempt to climb the fortifications lined with powder, but the boy stays on the battlement most of the day to stand guard. The parapet along the four sides gives us a full view of our surroundings, and for now we can keep watch.

"There's a small swarm down near the tree line," he said. "But that's it."

When I am up there, I mostly watch the west, where the sea crashes up onto the base of our cliff. Though we are several hundred feet up, I am wary of a water attack. If the bloodless rise up out of the sea, they will certainly scale the rock, adrenalized by the water. Rain worries me too; if a storm comes, we will have to hope the powder holds.

The other matter is the girl's health. She looks peaked, despite the protein I feed her, and she may be anemic. "The baby is using her up," Alessandra told me. "Draining the mother of her nourishment."

I am jealous of the unborn, for I must starve in the meantime. It has been a week since I last fed. I feel the pain of withdrawal, but am busy enough not to notice it every waking moment. Shortly after we arrived, Alessandra and I discovered that the only source for drinking water is a mountain spring running through the forest several miles from our walls. I fetch water almost every day, and before I left for the spring today, I saw the girl.

Her new home is a small two room squat with open windows and stone walls decorated with grass roots and cracks. The floor is a mix of cobblestone and dirt, and the thatched roof has been newly piled.

189

The boy and I repaired its holes before Alessandra swept out the floors and dressed the interior with several pieces of furniture recovered from the villa. Evelina has two stools, a small table, a raised mattress and several tapestries. She has other trifles, such as dishes and a washbasin, but the decor is more than lacking.

When I entered, she lay on the mattress with her swollen feet propped up, frowning at me with her changed face, distended and pale. Her smell is the same, though I cannot tell whether that is a boon or bane. It still tortures me, if less than the cessation of our communion. The bond we formed overpowers me at times, and I find it difficult to be near her. I would not have gone in to see her if she had not asked for me.

"Sit with me," she said.

"Is everything all right?" She shook her head and I sat beside her, placing my hand on top of hers. I thought of Byron. Had I somehow turned into him? Had he become me? I missed my beloved still, and would perpetually.

"I'm worried about you," she said.

I patted her hand with mine. "Ridiculous," I said gently. "You are the one about to give birth."

"But you're not feeding," she said, knowing my reasons. "You look sickly."

"I am a vampire, darling. I am supposed to look like death." My attempt to make her smile failed.

"Alessandra feeds," she said. "But she's not strong enough to keep us safe."

I would not tell the girl I agreed with her, though I did. Abstaining from her blood made me weaker.

"I'm frightened," she said. "I'm having bad dreams."

"What dreams?"

"They're coming."

"Who?"

I knew very well who. Her fears of being taken by the bloodless will never go away, and she has every reason to be afraid. They are even more relentless in their desire for her than I am. She knows her baby's smell will lure all kinds of predators to our door—bloodless and vampire. I have my own doubts about the war that lies ahead.

"Tell me about the dreams," I said.

She took a deep breath and closed her eyes. "They come from the ground—up through the stones, flinging them away as they crawl out of the earth," she said. "And sometimes they swing from the trees, over the walls, squashing the flower beds beneath their bare feet—and they're huge ... these men ... these monsters. They have skeleton faces and their hands are twice the size of yours—and they use them like big scoops to rip up the ground around us. And they steal ... they snatch the baby from my arms before suffocating me with their horrid tongues, and—they—they—catch me up in their teeth and they bite me all over—my arms, my neck, my stomach. And their teeth ... their teeth are like ... are sharp like—like—yours."

She was agitated and I placed my hand on the crown of her head to calm her. I told her it was only a dream, impossible fears that would never become a reality. I promised to bring her a sack of Dilo seeds to keep by her bed just in case. "It will keep you safe if I am not here," I said. "Both you and her."

"Her?"

I had known for some time Evelina was carrying a girl. The flavor of the child's blood betrayed her sex; I tasted it in her mother's. "You are having a girl," I said.

"But how—oh!" She took my hand and asked me to help her sit up. She was lighter than one would expect looking at her girth.

"Her scent is … like yours," I said.

"But you'll resist her, right?"

"Of course." I could only hope.

Later. — I have just returned with the water, and something I had not expected to find.

Before I left the camp, I faced the forest and took a long whiff of the air. I let my nose dig into the trees beyond the side wall, holding the scent in my nostrils, hoping to detect the faintest trace of blood ripe enough for drinking. I gave Alessandra the message to bring the girl a sack of seeds and told her I was going for water. I headed into the woods with the cart, as dusk settled in.

I cut through the trees, trailing the scent of a buck. I was disinterested in the animal for myself but wanted it for my girl. It would mean several weeks worth of food for her. It had been a while since I had smelled such large game. The forest had seemed all but abandoned by its four-legged nesters. I picked up speed, as I felt myself coming closer to the roe deer. When I spotted the reddish summer coat, I stopped several feet away. I watched in silence as the buck picked at the leaves of the brush. It seemed undeterred by the apocalypse ravishing the earth, unaware of the new predator hunting its flesh. I practically floated on air as I made my way closer to the animal. It was deaf to my approach, as it pecked at the briar root. It chewed the branch greedily and the forest echoed with the sound. All things dropped away, as I moved in sync with the buck's jaw, its chewing dictating the rhythm of my pace.

When I was a few meters from it, I crouched low to the ground and then stretched long as I propelled myself up from the path. My energy faltered and I barely made it off my feet. The twigs beneath me snapped and the startled buck looked back in my direction. I realized then I had been mistaken. I had not stalked a roe deer at all, but an emaciated corpse, pecking at the rotting flesh draped over the brush. I tumbled backwards, as the bloodless lunged in my direction. It did not attempt to bite me, even as it swatted at me with its mangled arms, protecting its find. I pushed myself up, grabbed the cart and took off in the opposite direction.

My delusions were getting the better of me. It was not the first time I had imagined something that was not actually there. I needed to feed. I raced through the forest to the ravine at the other side of the woods. The wheels of the cart bounced off the ground, as I dragged it behind me. I could hear the water rushing and smell the fresh spring, as I approached. By the time I arrived, darkness had seeped in through the trees. I crept up to the water, careful not to arouse a swarm. I had a small amount of powder from one of the seeds hidden in my pocket and could only hope it would keep the bloodless away. I dropped to my knees and tasted the cold water, wishing it would somehow refresh me, reinvigorate my senses. But only blood—her blood—would suffice.

I sunk the canteens in the stream and when their skins were swollen, I corked them and slung them over my shoulder. I was feeling rather defeated, believing I was stronger than this. I failed at the sacrifice I was trying to make—anemic or not, I wanted to feed on my girl—and then I smelled it, the slightest trace of blood on the air.

Human blood.

I abandoned the cart and tracked the scent west through the forest. I slid past trees and tripled my pace, as the smell became stronger, sharper, its promise boosting my energy. I trampled pines, twigs, roots and stumps, jumped over shrubs and under branches, until I reached the end of the woods. As I stood on the cliff, facing the swollen expanse, I realized the scent came from a distance far greater than I could travel. I spotted the ship at the furthest reaches of the sea, carrying the human cargo along the waves. The smell wafted through the air like the beguiling charm of the Siren and I stood on the ledge, yearning to pull it to me. I watched it sail past the French Isle and into a port somewhere else, not realizing the swell of the waves put me in a trance— I stopped thinking and only dreamed.

I imagined hearing Evelina's cry from beyond the other side of the woods. My heart raced, as I dreamed of tearing across the forest path to scale the trees that hung over our walls. I would hop down from the branch, spilling the canteens of water across the grassy lane. I could even hear Alessandra, counting out the breaths, as the boy paced the girl's doorstep outside. He would greet me coldly before I grabbed him by the neck and dug my iron fangs deep into his jugular, ripping open the skin and draining him of his hot blood. I would toss his limp body across the yard, as the girl's screams tore through her hovel. I imagined her cry of pain would irritate me second only to her stench, the smell of her insides being ripped open. The taunts of her fresh blood would provoke me. The grace and discipline I spent millennia honing would be gone. I would not resist the child, the saccharine plasma of the newborn would be my dessert—its mother's blood filling my appetite. I imagined turning my iron fangs on Evelina, shooting my venom deep into her veins and making her mine—consecrating her my vampire!

Vincent come—I imagined the new mother disheveled, draped with bloodstained linens, her skin exposed in desirable places, the rush of fluid through the rivers of her arms, legs, neck, her perfect, ageless flesh—living flesh. *Vincent come*—I imagined caressing her lips with my tongue, wetting my fangs as they dropped and pierced the edge of her mouth, the swell of her juice, as the blood gushed to meet me, the sweet taste of Evelina, as it trickled down my throat, hot and sticky like boiled honey. *Vincent stop*—seconds away from tasting my imagined ecstasy, I succumbed to my frailty and dropped out of consciousness on the edge of the cliff.

When I woke, my vision was blurred and only a fragment of my fantasy remained. The urgency of tasting Evelina's blood had dissipated, the spell broken, but I was grateful to be far from her at that moment. I drew in fresh air, as I tried to revive myself, my thoughts. Human blood was all around me—the smell unmistakable. That heavenly fragrance of tin and cloves tickled my venom and piqued more than my curiosity. I leaned over the ledge and peered down the face of the cliff. I saw a

195

flicker of light tucked inside a hollow at the base of the promontory where the tide rolled up onto the sandy beach.

My talons did most of the work, as I scaled the rock to the shore. I struggled to keep myself from sliding a few times, my claws having weakened without her blood, but I kept my fingers engaged and dug my feet in. The stone crumbled beneath each kick of my boot, as I made clefts in the bluff for my climb back up. Sometimes just the promise of a taste is enough to give me energy.

When I finally reached the beach, I was several feet from the opening of the hollow and I sucked in the fresh blood. As I made my way to the opening, I heard voices, at least two men speaking a tongue I had mastered centuries ago.

"We need to leave," one of them said.

"We can't," said the other, "not until he can walk."

"We'll have to carry him."

"What?"

"We can't stay here."

"He's in too much pain."

"But we have to go."

"What if I catch us some fish tomorrow?"

"There's no fish."

"But what if—"

"We've got to go."

"Shush!" A third one spoke this time. "Do you hear that?"

"What? I don't hear—"

"Shush."

I pressed myself up against the rock just outside the hollow. One of the men poked his head out of the opening and looked around. He squinted, as he peered in my direction, but I had wedged myself into the rock and he could not see me. "It's nothing," he said, as he tucked himself back inside.

"What if she comes back? What if she finds us?"

"That isn't going to happen," the third man said. His voice was the most deadpan of the three. "She won't find us."

"Humph."

"What?"

"You think she—" The one who peeked his head out trembled more than the other two. "Never mind."

"No," the tired one said. "She wouldn't risk it."

"So what's the plan then?"

"I told you we've gotta leave first thing."

"How are we going to scale the rock?"

"We're going to follow the shoreline," the tired one said. "Till we find the best place to go up."

"What about your leg?"

"I'll be fine," he said. "Now let's get some rest."

The men fell silent and my fangs dropped, as I licked my lips in anticipation. But I hesitated and I am not sure why. With the grace I may have now considered a curse, I stopped to contemplate the use they may be to me over the long term. If I were to bring them back, they could serve me indefinitely with their blood. I would gain much more if I did not waste them all at once, and I was still intent on repopulating the earth. My mind spun, as I deliberated their fate, letting preservation win out— theirs and mine. I decided on a plan and somehow gathered enough strength to see it through.

I faced the rock wall again and dug in my talons. The clefts I made on the way down were invaluable on the way up, plus Alessandra had taught me how to spring vertically and I exploited my newly extended reach. When I got to the top, I headed into the forest toward the ravine. I tracked the bloodless to a little clearing of velvety grass littered with acorns. The oak trees made a natural pergola with their leaves.

The bloodless wrestled with a severed animal haunch and did not hear me approach. I had readied the strap from one of the canteens to use as a leash, planning to slip it over his wrists and drag him off by the arms, but when I reached for him, he scrambled forward, making a clumsy escape through the brush. He leapt on all fours like an animal into the bushes in front of him, leaving the haunch behind, but he did not get far when his flesh got caught in the branches. He howled when I tied the leather strap around his neck, so I stuck the haunch in his mouth to shut him up. I bound his wrists the best I could with his flesh worn away as it was. The horror of such decayed humanity made my venom freeze within my veins. I could not look the bloodless in the eyes—they were windows into a hallowed hell I would do everything to avoid.

Once bound and gagged, I dragged him back through the forest. When we reached the promontory, I dropped him close to the edge. I did not doubt he could smell the humans since he was agitated, and before I could free his arms, he rolled away from me and over the edge of the bluff. The bloodless plummeted to the sandy shore, hitting it with a thud that was drowned out by the crashing waves. I rushed down after him—he was useless to me tied up.

When I caught up to him, he was turning over in the sand. One of his legs barely hung from his hip, but he still clawed the ground with his bound wrists, trying to reach the humans. I snapped the binds off with my talons, and the bloodless used his hands to pull himself up, falling when he tried to walk. He was persistent though and crawled through the sand on all fours to reach his prey.

"What is it?" One of them said from the hollow.

"It's one of them," the tired one said.

"What should we d—"

"Shush!"

They thought if they kept quiet enough the darkness would protect them. The bloodless stuck out his tongue and lapped up the air, as he reached the opening of the hollow. The anticipation of tasting their blood teased the tips of my fangs and I felt a rush of heat through my cold body. My delicate points had already dropped again. The bloodless twisted his head and jut out his chin, raising his left hand, as he inched his way over the threshold. One of the men screamed and another yelled for Paul before I crossed into the darkness.

"Get it!"

"I can't see it," the other said.

The injured man shrieked, as the bloodless reached for him. He could not have seen the creature but must have sensed his proximity. The other two men cowered along the inside edge of the rock. The bloodless got hold of the injured one and was about to sink his jaw into his arm when I stuck my dagger deep in his neck. I reached into my pocket and pulled out some of the powder. The bloodless scrambled backwards, but not before I blew it in his face. He dragged himself away, deeper into the hollow.

I wasted no time reaching for the man's arm and sinking my fangs in before he knew who got a piece of him. He had passed out, but still fresh to taste. I siphoned the blood quickly with muted force, indulging in the thickness of his savor. I let the blood linger in my mouth before ingesting it and enjoyed my energy's rise with his ichor, relishing that familiar tingle. His blood was unlike the girl's, savory rather than sweet, but in some ways more potent. When I finished feeding, I let the man's arm drop. My head spun with delight and I barely noticed the other two cowering against the rock.

"He's gone," one of them said.

"Paul?" The other asked.

"You are safe now," I said, my voice rumbling along the walls of the cavern.

"Who—who—?"

The injured man stirred and muffled groans echoed in the hollow. I crouched beside him and placed a hand on his shoulder. The blood from his wound had clotted.

"Who are you?" The oldest of the three spoke first.

"I am from a village not far from here," I said. "We have a camp. It is safe."

"How did you—I mean, where did—"

"I was fishing along the shore when I heard the screams," I said.

The two men slowly came away from the wall. "We should make a fire," the older one said.

I pulled out the piece of flint I carry with me and struck it on the steel of my blade. The small

200

sparks eventually erupted into flame. Once the hollow was lit, the two men picked up their injured friend and laid him close to the fire. He groaned a little but had passed out again. They could see me now and the young one's eyes grew wide.

"Are you a viking or something?"

I smiled and offered them the canteens, which they drank greedily.

"Paul's injured," one of the men said. "His leg's hurt pretty bad."

"I have medical supplies back at the camp," I said. "I can bring you to it if you would like."

"You got food?"

"Enough," I said.

"Paul can't walk," the older man said.

"I can carry him up," I said. "I have a cart that we can use to pull him the rest of the way."

I planned on scaling the rock, using the clefts I had made to get us to the top. If we left in the dark, they would not fear the vertical rise as much and the light of the moon would be enough to guide them. I put out the fire and led them from the cavern. The young one, Tim, introduced himself when we exited the hollow. Beck looked the oldest of the three, and I carried Paul on my back while the other two followed behind.

The climb was difficult—for them, not me. I masked my strength by keeping their pace and followed them up, guiding them as we went. When we finally reached the top of the bluff, the men needed to catch their breath.

"How … how can you do it?" Tim asked me.

"I recently ate," I said. He could not appreciate the humor.

We headed into the forest back to the ravine. I kept their pace but I could not quell my desire to fly. Paul's blood had a strange effect on me. I could feel every single one of my nerve endings fire, as if a small electrical shock ran through my body. I was not inebriated, but also not sober. In the mid-seventies, Byron and I shared a girl so high on something we felt its effect. The barbiturate accelerated our senses and things looked unlike themselves. The field on our way back to the tombs at LaDenza was like a sea of toothpicks, standing upright and firm. Each blade scratched against our marble skin, as we moved through the grass. The sound was like nails on a chalkboard. Byron was soon sick and vomiting blood, as we made our way home. He recovered more quickly because of it. The blood plagued me until I washed it away with clean drink. Paul's blood was tainted the same way but I enjoyed its intensity. The vibrancy was a welcomed change to my starved state.

As the men slogged through the forest, I wanted to race. Time stood still and every single thing appeared to be made of stone—like me. The solid trees were like pillars standing at the gates of Zeus—the leaves were crystallized effigies strung up on titanium branches—the ground beneath my feet sounded with a great boom each step I took, the earth shaking as though its plates shifted every time I laid my foot down—and I smelled all the animals, dead and living.

We came across a trail of small game that looked like it had been drained of its blood, and the men tripped over the carcasses, as we passed. The darkness hid everything from them and they clung to me, as I led them through it. "We are almost at the ravine," I said.

When I saw two of the bloodless up ahead, I laid the injured man down and told the others to stay put. I checked the forest around us and when I did not see a swarm, I left the men where they were and moved toward the bloodless. I pulled out another little handful of powder—reaching into my pocket was like wading through syrup, my limbs were heavy and rigid, their weight almost more than I could bear—and moved slowly toward the fiends. When I was finally close enough, I brought my hand to my mouth and blew the powder at them. It seemed to float in midair, revealing each separate grain of dust. The bloodless could not flee the wrath of the plant and they howled when the powder stung them as acid ate skin. I returned to the men when the bodies dropped to the ground.

"Are they gone?" Tim asked.

"How did you do that?" Beck asked. "Your speed … it's impossible."

"You could see me?" I asked.

"One minute you were right here, and then the next—I could hear them—drop—it's like you never left."

Only I experienced the slow motion. "We have to keep moving," I said, picking up Paul and slinging him over my shoulder.

When we finally reached the ravine, I put the injured man down on its ridge and splashed water on his face. I handed the other two the canteens and told them to fill them. "I am going to head a little further down stream to catch some fish," I said.

Before I left, I pointed to the cart and suggested they place their friend on it to await my return. Their whispers reached me, as I disappeared into the shadows.

"How can he see in the dark?"

"He's not human," Tim said.

"What is he then? Cause he sure isn't one of them …"

I followed the edge of the ravine, noticing how the rushing water looked stagnate. I could see each droplet, as it clung to another and moved in a herd to the pool at its end. The water revealed its treasures to me, from the amebas sucking parasites off the rocks on the pool's floor to the trout wading just below the surface. I dunked my hands in the fresh stream and stabbed five fish, one with each talon, pulling them up and slinging them on the belt at my waist.

Before I could plunge my hand in a second time, I heard his cry. I rushed to the men, as the scream died on the air. The bloodless had caught Tim by surprise, grabbing him as he relieved himself behind a tree. Beck moved toward the bloodless with a broken branch but I beat him to it and stuck my dagger in its neck, severing head from spine. The fiend still had the chunk of human flesh between his teeth, as more bloodless gathered through the trees, enticed by the bloody wound of the injured man.

"We have to go," I said.

I put Tim on the cart with Paul, telling Beck to stay close. He kept pace with a jog, as I transported his friends, and his stamina surprised me. When we were near the village, the howls increased and a small swarm rose up behind us. "Keep moving," I said. "It is just through that cluster of trees." Another swarm gathered in front of us, blocking our path to the entrance, but the side wall lay straight ahead and

I knew if I could get us close enough, we would be under the aegis of the powder.

"Vincent!" Alessandra's voice rose as a beacon amidst a treacherous shoal.

The vampire bounded over the wall and rushed through the barricade of bloodless, forcing bodies to scatter, as she tossed a sack of powder at them. Two of them came at us, but I slashed them with my talons. Beck had dropped down under the cart to hide from the swarm and I told him to get up. "We have to move," I said.

Like a mother bear rescuing her cub, Alessandra grabbed the man and tucked him close to her body, bounding through the danger and up the wall to get him to safety. I followed with the cart and we were over the wall and in our haven almost instantly.

It is too early to know if bringing them here was the right thing to do, but I have already indulged in a second nip from the older one while he slept. I may have some explaining to do in the morning.

8 December. — The bloodless have arrived. The powder keeps them off the wall, but they linger nonetheless. Evelina has cotton in her ears to block out the sound of their feverish howls. I placed the men far away from the girl in the hovel I had been using as a retreat. A small mattress, a couple of stools, and a table—a remnant from the wood door that had once barred the entrance—make up its surroundings. I removed my personal effects, writing instruments and a small collection of books, and put them in the abandoned smithy. We fed the men, gave them candles and built them a fire pit. Helgado furnished them with a pile of wood and

Alessandra attended to their medical needs. "The man's arm is healing," Alessandra said shortly before dawn. "It doesn't look infected."

"Impossible," I said. "I saw the wound."

She smiled with those bright white fangs of hers. "I'm no doctor," she said, "but I wanted to try something on him." I raised an eyebrow. "I made a balm," she said, "with one of the seeds and a bit of salt water. I guess it's working."

"Just the powder and salt water?" I asked.

"No," she said. "I added the smallest trace of venom." She squinted as though fearing my disapproval.

"Your venom?" I was not surprised she used her venom this way—its natural byproduct is potentially curative. Since the clone is unable to reproduce, her venom is not harmful to humans.

When I went to see for myself, I confirmed her instincts had served her well. Tim's bite is healing rather miraculously. His flesh wound has closed up and is now covered with a scab.

"It's better," he said, as he pulled down his coat sleeve. "Whatever she put on it—it started to feel better right away."

"And you?" I turned to inspect Paul.

"Leg's a bit better," he said. "The sleep helped … but I was wondering if you had anything for this?"

He lifted his arm and showed me the puncture marks my fangs had made beneath his bicep. His small wounds were not healing and his skin was bruised. The barbiturates in his system, the lingering sores, the injured leg, all told me he was an ailing man. "I will see what I can do," I said.

Beck shrugged. "I'm fine," he said. "But hungry."

I left them, promising to return with more food. I would have to keep them fed if I was to continue eating too. Helgado met me, as I made my way toward the smithy.

"I need to speak to you," he said. He was abrupt, agitated. "Why did you bring them here?"

"Because they are human," I said.

"Blood," he said. "That's all you ever think about."

"Better theirs than yours, no?"

"So you'll stop feeding off Evelina then?"

I smiled—I could not help it. His ignorance got the better of me.

"Of course not," he said. "Why would you? But the baby—you better not touch that child."

My mood darkened with his idle threats. I raised a hand to his cheek and tapped it lightly. He tried to pull his head away but found he could not move. I had wrapped my mind around his and locked him place. My eyes penetrated his and I sneered, baring my subtle fangs. Using my deepest register, I told him I did not like to be threatened. I released him from my hold when his mother called to him from her hovel. She was inside for the day, but always kept an eye on her boy. He stumbled backwards and fell to the ground.

"Fuck you, Vincent."

I left him sitting on the pathway and went to seek out food for our guests.

Later. — These men have a secret. When I approached the hovel with their food, I caught the end of the following debate.

207

"He can't," Paul said.

"You must've lost it when that thing grabbed you," Beck said.

"But I have to go back for it," Tim said. "What if she finds it?"

"Shush!" One of them said.

"Don't mention her," Beck said. "They can hear each other."

"Do you think," Tim said, "he's like her?"

"Yes," Paul said. "He's one of them."

"We've got to leave then," Tim said, sounding slightly panicked.

"Where?" Beck said. "There's no where to hide."

"Why don't we just tell him?" Paul said. "He'll protect us."

"What makes you think that?" Beck said.

"He's been good to us so far," Paul said. "He saved us. And what about this? And yours too?"

"What about your meds?" Tim asked.

"I'm feeling good," Paul said. "Really."

"You're kidding, right?" Beck said. "You look like hell."

"Nice," Paul said. "Real nice."

The men fell silent and I entered with several cans of sardines and a bottle of wine.

"Perfect," Tim said. "Thanks a lot."

I bowed slightly and Beck leaned forward to mirror my show of respect, which is how I noticed the pendant around his neck. It was an emerald dragon set upon a flat gold backdrop. "May I?" I asked, reaching for it.

"Uh," he said. "Sure, it's nothing—just some cheap Chinese knockoff."

I examined the small dragon. It was Chinese, but I did not believe it was cheap. I recognized the Qing dynasty's emblem engraved on the back. The necklace was a relic belonging to Empress Cixi.

Beck cleared his throat, as I held the jewel in my hand. "Really," he said. "It's nothing—from an old girlfriend." He laughed nervously.

"A memento?" I asked.

"Yes," he said, "just a stupid memento."

I let the pendant go and it swung back and forth before Beck caught it up in his hand and tucked it back under his shirt. I could not begin to figure out how this man had acquired a necklace from the Qing dynasty, let alone a piece that belonged to its Empress.

9 December. — Although I had not been gone long, I felt a strong sense of peace when I looked at the girl's face again. When I went in to see her, she was standing, as Alessandra helped her walk off the mild contractions she had been having. Her hair was gently pulled up off her neck, exposing her nape, and I noticed the flush in her cheeks from the activity of her body. I could practically hear the pulse of her blood, as her heart beat in rhythm with mine. Despite the nip from our new arrivals, I could not wait to sink my fangs into her again.

"Stop staring," she said. She giggled before the pain made her pretty face contort. "Owww ..." She stretched out her expression through pursed lips.

"That's a girl," Alessandra said. "Deep breaths. In and out."

"Is the baby coming?" I asked.

"Not yet," Alessandra said.

"No," Evelina said. "You can stay."

209

When the bout of pain finally passed, Alessandra helped Evelina back onto the cot and then left us alone. Evelina tapped the mattress beside her and beckoned to me—a quick flash of my daydream made me hesitate before I sat next to her. The girl reached up and touched my cheek.

"You look better," she said. Her voice rang with the slightest bit of jealousy. She knew I had fed off the men. "I suppose you're no longer hungry?"

"No," I said. "Not at the moment." It was a lie. I could drink her blood until there was no more—famished or full.

She pouted, frowning a little. "Who are they?" She asked.

It was not a conversation I wanted to have with the girl.

"Just survivors," I said. "Like us."

"But where do they come from?"

They were not Italian—their English had no accent. They could be American, but I was not sure. "I have not asked," I said.

"Do they have bloodless where they're from?" Her naiveté astounded me.

"I am most certain they do," I said.

She tried to adjust her swollen belly, as she lay on her side, but needed me for leverage. I held her up and she shifted her body into a better position. She sighed heavily. "Alessandra says I'm due tomorrow."

"How does she know?" I asked.

"She says she can smell it."

I did not doubt the clone's prediction since her nose would certainly know. I smelled the baby too with the same intensity as she did, but not quite in the same way. I will have to occupy myself

210

tomorrow if it is true, if in fact the baby is coming. I cannot be around when that child is thrust bloodily into our world.

"Vincent?" Her small voice pulled me from my thoughts and I left her then, wondering no doubt what I was thinking, as I made my way out of her hovel. I could no longer take the smell.

Later. — The men are much more interesting to spy on than converse with. Their private debates prove entertaining.

"We have to get out of here," Tim said.

"And go where?" Beck said.

"Anywhere safe," Tim said.

"This is safe," Beck said.

"How can we be safe with him?"

"He hasn't done anything but help us and feed us," Paul said.

"And feed off us!"

"It's better than being on that ship," Beck said.

"Right," Tim said. "I know, but he'll keep us here too."

"So?" Paul said. "It's not so bad—we have food and shelter, and other humans too."

"The guy's a weirdo," Tim said. "He seems pissed off about us."

"But there's a girl," Paul said.

"The pale one?" Beck asked. "She's not a … woman."

"She's one of them too, you mean?"

"You can't tell? Didn't you see her jump over the wall!" Beck said. "And her eyes? Look at her eyes next time she comes in."

"This is crazy," Tim said. "We're going to die here."

211

"No," Paul said. "This is how we survive."

"How?"

"If he thinks we're useful," he said, "he'll keep us around."

"Right," Beck said. "We have to show him we can help."

"He knows we're good for blood."

10 December. — The clone was right, the baby is coming today. I am tucked in the smithy, as I write this, trying desperately to think of you, Byron, and not the girl. It is a challenge, my love. Her cries echo through the dusking streets. I am in pain too, trapped with the memory of your torture. An endless loop of suffering plays over and over in my mind, as I recall your writhing in the bowels of the dark cathedral. I can only ignore the image when I am fully engrossed in the occupation of our survival. But your end is always with me. I kept a vile of the blood substitute, a token of the poison that took you from me. The small trinket hangs about my neck, always next to my heart.

The baby is coming—but I will continue to write to you my beloved so that I may distract myself from rushing to the girl's side—another one of her screams rips into me, as she is torn apart by her labor. The temptation is great—I am longing to see it come into the world. The points of my fangs tickle my gums—they have a plan of their own. Perhaps I shall have just one peek at the blood dripping down the inside of her thigh …

Do not resist—come, she begs me.

Later. — The child is magnificent.

212

Before I went to Evelina, I locked up the men. I had found rusted manacles in the corner of the smithy shortly after I moved in here. I knew they would come in handy. The men were sleeping when I snuck in their hovel and tied the chains about their wrists. I plan on removing them in the morning.

I watched the girl from a distance, from the window unnoticed. It may seem odd I desired to witness such a human act, but the child's birth was of less importance to me than the blood her mother would spill—my blood.

"Push again," Alessandra whispered into her ear, as she stood beside her and held her up.

The girl bore down, using the vampire as leverage. The boy was there too, pacing uselessly in the corner.

"Bring me the water," Alessandra said.

He obeyed his mother and brought over the cup he had refilled.

"Evelina?" She asked. "How are you?"

She tapped the girl's cheeks and then lifted the cup of water to her lips. My girl did not speak. I could not see her face from the window frame, just her hair matted and clinging to the back of her robe. She was in a squatting position and I was reminded of the woman between the olive trees. I licked my lips. Her pain seemed to lessen with my presence, for she only moaned now.

"Push," the vampire said. "You're close." Alessandra bent down and looked at the girl's opening. "I can see the crown." The vampire called her son over and directed him to guide the baby out when he saw its head. "Just like I showed you," she said.

Helgado took his place between Evelina's legs.

"That's it, Evelina," Alessandra said. "Keep it up. You're almost there."

The girl's scream was foreign—it was low, guttural, demonic. Her head fell forward slightly and I heard the tearing of her flesh.

"Good girl," Alessandra said. "Push—that's it."

The girl moaned again and unleashed another cry unlike her own. The wail made her pain palpable and I bit into my lip. I was desperate in that moment to relieve her of it, to take her away from the horror she was forced to endure.

"One more!" Alessandra encouraged. "One more!"

All the force seemed to dissipate from her body with that one last push and she fell forward into the vampire, as the baby slipped into the waiting arms of the boy. The air was silent for a moment before mother and child both cried.

"She's here," Alessandra said. "You've done it, Evelina. Lucia's here."

Lucia?

Alessandra carried the girl over to her cot and laid her on it. The boy handed the newborn to his mother and she swaddled it before laying it on Evelina's chest.

"You can't rest yet, child," she said. "You need to feed the baby." The vampire coached the girl and the newborn.

I thought it would be difficult to resist the smell of the blood—I thought the new life would drive me insane with a vampire's lust, but it did not. The sentimentality of seeing the human life renew itself took hold of me, and I could not shake it. When I stepped away from the window, I came back to the smithy to record my cloying emotion—mawkish and shameful. I must climb the parapet and scan the darkness for the bloodless, for they should straighten out my—

Later. — Wallach has paid us a visit. When I heard the men call for me, their panic was tangible. A second cry for help rang through the streets, as I met Alessandra in the lane. "It's one of the men," she said.

"Stay with the girl."

I ignored the blood that stained her hands and made my way to the men. I had not sensed his presence—his frequency had gone unnoticed. I had been too taken with the birth, though I should have felt something.

Gone before I arrived, the nomad had left a devastating scene. Two of the men were still in chains, but the third was yanked from his manacles, drained and lifeless on the hovel floor. Tim's body lay in a pool of regurgitated blood.

"Unlock us," Paul said. "Before he returns."

"Tim ... he ... he," Beck said. "I—I—I ... can't ..."

"What did you see?" I asked, not knowing it was Wallach until they described him.

"A man—a strong man," Paul said. "Whistling some—some tune—like—I don't know—and he had these—pointed blades for fingers."

I unlocked the chains while Paul described the vampire.

"What ... what ..." Beck's words were few and disconnected.

"The screams woke me," Paul said.

I had not heard Tim scream.

"The girl's screams," Paul said. "I thought it was an animal." He told me that when he saw the chains, he woke the other two. "I thought it was you," he said. "The whistling—I thought it was you."

Beck leaned over the body of his fallen friend and sobbed. "Tim was closest to the door," he said. "Timmy ... was ... closest."

"I couldn't see his face," Paul said. "But I knew—I knew—it wasn't you."

"Did he speak?" I asked.

By now I had suspected it was the nomad, but when they described his voice, I knew.

"It was sinister, dark," Paul said. "And he was speaking Russian or something like that."

"Romanian," I said.

"You know him then?" I assumed there was no reason to deny it. "He just—just—jumped—pounced like an animal right on ..." Paul said, dropping his chin.

I was grateful I had been with the girl. If not, Wallach may have found her instead. Alessandra would not have had the wherewithal to take him. I did not need to guess why he stopped at Tim. He had vomited up the man's ichor shortly after consuming it. I assumed his affinity for animal blood had become so powerful he could no longer stomach human. "I need to take the body with me," I said.

I snatched up the remains before the men could protest and left the hovel. I will track the nomad and make him pay for his trespass.

11 December. — I spent the night looking for Wallach, but he is gone. Before I went out, I moved the men closer to the other two. I left Alessandra to

216

watch over all of them—in retrospect, probably not the most rash decision.

"Will we be safe here?" Paul asked.

It was a fair question, though one I did not answer. "You will not be put in restraints again," I said.

"Tim believed you—we all did," Paul said, "when you told us we'd be safe here." I could not change the past. "I still want to believe that," he said.

"I shall renew my efforts to keep you safe," I said.

When I left Wallach on the rock ledge near the bluff, I was certain he was finished. His appearance in my camp meant there would be others. Paul sat by the hearth, placing logs on the fire one at a time, while Beck lay on the stone floor with his back to us.

"I'm sure Tim didn't know what was happening," Paul said. "It was worse for us."

I was only slightly surprised by his narcissism.

"It was traumatic—the horror," Paul said. "He gripped Tim by the scalp and yanked his head back then stuck one of his long claws into his neck—right here."

Paul showed me the spot to which he referred. It was almost as if he needed to share the details with me.

"Right in the jugular," he said. "Blood went everywhere—and he stuck out his tongue and put his mouth on the wound—and then—"

"Shut up," Beck said.

Paul looked at me and I restrained myself from licking my lips.

"Just shut up," Beck said again. "Shut up."

I excused myself then, telling them Alessandra and I would be watching over them all night. I had already turned my back to go when Beck lunged at me. I had not seen him stand up. I almost laughed when I felt his tiny hand on my throat, but the steel of the pistol abated the urge.

"Kneel," he said.

"Beck," Paul said. "What are you doing?"

Paul moved toward his friend. Beck tried to close his hand around my throat but could not get a grip. He pressed the gun to my temple and though I did not feel the barrel on my skin, I knew a bullet at close range could do some damage.

"You're the reason he's gone," Beck shouted. "It's your fault—you killed him."

"Beck." Paul matched his intensity, enraging him even more. I was calm, as I strategized my escape—and his demise.

"No," Beck said. "If he didn't lock us up—we could've got away. Tim could've—I would've shot the bastard just like I'm going to shoot this one."

He pressed the gun into my temple, emphasizing each word with a tap on my skin. He was too excited to notice my flesh did not give under the pressure.

"Beck," Paul said, "you don't want to do this. Vincent's not to blame here."

"Bul-l-l-l-l-l-shit."

He was hostile, getting louder with each objection. I tried to seduce him with my words, using the melodic tone I had relied on so often in the good ole days. "I know your pain," I said, "I have lost loved ones too—"

"Shut the fuck up!" My charm was not effective with everyone.

218

He cursed and raged, as he squeezed my throat. He must have felt the texture of my skin, he must have noticed his grip failing; he could not damage my flesh and his hand probably hurt from the tension. I assumed he would tire before pulling the trigger. As I sat there with the raving man's barrel on my temple, I wondered how I had missed his having a gun. I suppose it never occurred to me they would be armed.

"You will pay for Tim's—" The man's grip faltered, as he swallowed his words. The gun went flying across the dirt floor and he fell to the ground beside me. I looked up at Helgado, standing over Beck with the butt end of his machete poised.

"The baby sleeps," he said in broken English. "I don't have … how you say … want this loud voices to wake her."

Paul nodded. "We're sorry," he said. "He's just …"

Helgado held up his hand to Paul, brushing off his excuses before leaving the hovel as discreetly as he had arrived.

I smiled—I would have never thought the boy would be saving me.

12 December. — I spoke with Alessandra when I returned at dawn.

"He is gone," I said.

"Will he be back?"

"I cannot be sure," I said. "But I doubt he only came for the men."

"The baby?"

"Her, Evelina," I said. "Me. Revenge is a strong motivator."

"He must be nothing to you," she said. "You can destroy him, no?"

Yes—but I thought I had. "I do not know how he made it past the bloodless in the field," I said. "He must have scaled the cliff from the sea."

"Didn't you feel him coming?"

I did not want to answer that—knowing I had not heard his frequency bothered me. I brushed off the question and asked about the newborn.

"She is healthy," Alessandra said. "Evelina is … well, she suffers a little I think."

"How so?" I had not felt her sorrow or pain since the nomad showed up. The death of the other has kept me occupied.

"She's asking for you," she said.

"Has she eaten?" I could not feed if she had not.

"No," she said. "She tells me she's nauseated."

I tried to subdue the pang of thirst that hit me when I thought of her suckling the child. "Is the baby feeding?"

Alessandra nodded as though nostalgic for better days, human days.

"And how did you handle all that blood?" I asked.

She sighed. "It was easy," she said. "I've fed on animal blood too long to desire anything else."

"You know human blood gives you more strength," I said. "It makes you—"

"I know," she said. "But I can't."

I respected her decision, though I could not understand it. I assumed her nature was inauthentic, as was her genesis. I felt sorry for her—it is no way for a vampire to live.

"Go see Evelina," she said. "She's looking for you."

Later. — I delayed seeing her for as long as I could. If she had not eaten, I could not taste the thing I wanted most. I did not think I could sit with her if I could not feed. When I finally gave in, I found her with the baby asleep in her arms. I could distinguish the two smells now—the mother's being the only one I desired.

She smiled at me. "You look hungry," she said. "Come, let me feed you."

It sounds macabre, I know. She held her newborn near her breast, but wanted to nurse me instead. I would not resist her for long.

"I'm ready again," she said. "The baby's here now and we can go back to like it was."

She dropped her head to the side and stretched her shoulder downwards. It was perfectly perverse to bite the nape of a new mother. My fangs dropped. I sat beside her and caressed her neck, as the boy came into the hovel.

"She has to eat first," he said.

I turned to him with a scowl. I could have ripped open his chest for the interruption.

"I'm fine," she said. "I'm not hungry."

I was not a complete devil. "You have to eat something," I said.

The boy took the baby from her and placed it in the bassinet, and then offered her a handful of cherries. She put them in her lap, plucking off the stem one at a time before popping them into her mouth. Her lips and teeth were soon stained red and I ran my tongue over mine in anticipation. I had never desired to kiss the girl until that moment. A blood obsession will do that—it can fool one into

221

thinking they are in love. I have seen many vampires fall into that trap. It never leads to anything good.

When the boy left, I sat down beside her again.

"What?" She asked. "Why are you looking at me like that?"

She sighed, as she bit into another cherry, sucking on it before chewing it up. I waited for her to offer herself to me again but her thoughts moved on to other things. She reached for the sack of Dilo seeds tucked beside her cot and clutched it in her hands. Clearly emotional, she started to cry. "I know they're coming," she said.

She could not have known about Wallach. We had agreed not to tell her.

"Who?" I asked. "The bloodless?"

"The ones in my dreams."

"The bloodless cannot breach the walls," I said. "Not with the plants there."

"These bloodless can," she said.

She was being foolish and temperamental but I was tolerant for the moment. I wanted to settle her down so I could enjoy my long delayed nip. The baby stirred in the bassinet and I asked if I should bring her to the girl. "She'll be fine," she said coldly.

"Have you chosen a name yet?" I knew she had named the baby after her sister but I was not sure if she had made it official.

"There's no point in naming her," she said.

"Why?"

"She won't live long," she said.

I admit I was taken aback by her austerity. "My darling girl," I said. "Do not let your feelings overpower you. They will pass."

"Feelings," she said. "They're not just feelings. I know—I know we're doomed."

I had never seen an outburst quite like it. She was willful and petulant, not like herself at all.

"Have I not kept you safe?" I asked. I did not match her melodrama but remained stoic, if not compassionate. "What more can I do?" When her despair shifted to adoration, I realized the boy had come back into the room.

"Alessandra wants to see the baby," he said.

He picked up the bassinet and carried it out of the hovel. Evelina looked away and sighed. I wondered if she was not suffering some sort of trauma from the birth, some sort of psychological side-effect. Byron had told me she would be hormonal, and perhaps even depressed after the delivery. I wondered if this was what he meant. I attempted to get up from her side to pour her a glass of grappa, but she held onto my sleeve.

"No," she said. "Don't leave." She took my hands in hers. "Do you still desire me?"

I never desired you—just your blood. "Of course," I said. "We are bonded now." I am obsessed, I freely admit it, but I can control my addiction if I choose. I can overcome anything—even desire.

"Now that the baby's here," she said, "what good am I to you?"

I ran the back of my hand along the curve of her clavicle. "Let me show you," I said.

My subtle fangs dropped anew and I opened my mouth slightly, exposing the points of my teeth to subdue the wildness in her eyes. "Show me," she whispered.

It sounds erotic, I know, but it is not really equatable with human sex. Perhaps sharing the pleasure of a hallucinatory drug is a more fitting analogy. Though my hunger for the girl is not libidinal, my lust for her blood is undeniable. I will suffer almost anything to ingest a drop of it. And some days, I feel like I have.

As I pulled her blood up into my mouth, letting it slide down my throat, I relished the shot of adrenaline it gave my heart, kicking it into beat. My muscles tensed with the power she gave me. When I felt our exchange come to a close, when her body collapsed in my arms, I withdrew my bite, but like a soft breeze upon a stone I felt Evelina's hand resist my egress. She held me in place, trying to prevent me from pulling out.

"Change me," she whispered. "Make me like you."

It was dangerously irresistible—a Siren luring me to the shoal. I hesitated before resisting her offer and she passed out in my arms. I had not done the irreparable, but making her faint was not the gentlest way to feed off her. She would be hungover for several days.

I basked in the rush of her blood, licking the ichor from my lips. I held her in my arms despite my wanting to fly through the streets, over the wall and into the forest, just to feel my renewed vigor. I was grateful to wash away the blood of the other two— hers was unrivaled. When she stirred, I caressed her cheek with the back of my hand. *Vincent.* Her small dreamlike voice was in my head. *Vincent.* I waited for her to open her eyes. *Vincent.* I returned the smile she gave me. "Evelina," I whispered. "How do you feel?"

She blinked her eyes and sat up, looking around the room. "Everything is the same," she said.

"You were not out for that long," I said.

"But why is it the same?"

It occurred to me then that she thought I had turned her vampire. I could not contain my laughter—the thought was ridiculous. When she pulled away from me, I released her.

"I told you to change me." Her petulant tone had returned. "I told you," she said.

I did not bother telling her I do not take orders from anyone, especially humans. "I will never make you vampire," I said. "I would regret your blood too much." My confession stung her, but I was honest nevertheless.

"I can't go on like this," she said. "I can't be human."

She ripped the neck of her gown as though it constricted her and slapped the inside of her arms, bruising the skin overtop her veins. When she began to wail, I got up and left her there. The boy rushed in with the newborn, as I was leaving. He did not have the courage to ask me what I had done.

13 December. — The perimeter is holding, though several new swarms have formed at the end of the field near the border of the woods on the other side. We have reloaded the powder on the outside of the wall and the plants are growing rapidly. They will be flowering soon.

No sign of Wallach, though I expect a return visit. If he got in as easily as he seems to have done, he will be back for more. I can only hope he will be alone again.

The men will stay put—even the traitor. I decided not to kill him, to give him a reprieve. We have taken away his weapons of course, and I have told them that I will not hesitate to chain them up if need be. In the meantime, I use them as watchdogs, keeping them on the parapet in shifts.

15 December. — It has been two days since I visited the girl. I regret hurting her, if in fact I have, but she forgets her place, and mine. Alessandra tells me she is doing better, though she still refuses to eat. I have ordered the vampire to cover both Evelina and her child with the remaining incense oil. We need to manage the growing number of bloodless outside our walls even if that means masking the scent of the most desirable humans in our camp. The men will have to do without—we barely have enough left for the girl and her newborn.

I did not want to leave, but we needed fresh water. I checked the perimeter before I left. I had cleared my mind, silenced my inner dialogue, so I could listen for his frequency. I heard the waves splash up on the rock, but no vampire. I heard the buzzing of vultures in the fields pecking at the howling bloodless, but no vampire. I heard the low voices of the humans, but no vampire.

With a sackful of powder, I made my way over the wall and back to the ravine. I could not ignore my heart's pounding, working to consume the girl's blood. My heavy feet crushed the soil beneath my boots, as I made my way past the bloodless. The powder kept them away, but I moved so fast they could not catch me if they tried.

When I reached the stream, I sensed something strange. I was not picking up a frequency, but a familiar feeling overcame me, as I pictured the faces of my missing clan—Maxine, Elizabeth, Jean, Stephen, Veronica … you, Byron, all came to me. I felt the pull of our union, our commitment to each other, our sacrifice. Sadness nagged at me, as I filled the canteens and lugged them back to the camp. I would not see those faces again—immortal beings I thought I would know forever. I will—

... — The date escapes me—I am guessing days have passed since my last entry. So much has happened—I do not know if I can record it all from memory but I am determined to try. My future is changed—our history too.

When I came back from the ravine, I was oblivious to any danger. I did not check on the girl, I went to the smithy and began my journal entry. You cannot imagine how I regret not seeing her, not tasting her again. But the past is irrelevant ...

I remember thinking about all the things I would have to do to prevent others from finding us. I recall his image, as I wrote the words that were my last—*will* was the final word my pen scribed before her scream tore up the lane. I smelled the smoke at once, and then I heard his frequency, his low grumble echoed through the camp. I rushed out of the smithy and flew the five paces to her hovel—but it was too late.

She was gone, the baby too, and Alessandra was ... was no more.

The clone's body was slumped over in the chair. He had slit her throat, almost severed her head from her neck. It had fallen to the side and rested on her shoulder. The cut was clean, made by the edge of a talon. She had not sensed his approach, the danger. The baby held her attention when he yanked her head back and dug his claws into her throat. She still had a smile on her face. She did not have time to say my name.

I had mere moments to put the pieces together. The fire was spreading, the smoke was thick. From the window, I saw the source of it. The plants were on fire, the inside of the walls in flames. I launched myself up and over the rising smoke onto the parapet, where I could see more. The flames wrapped around the walls, sparked by his accelerant. His frequency was dim but he was still here.

"They went that way," the boy said, as he pointed in the direction of the field to the north.

I could not smell her, see her, feel her—she had vanished.

The flames agitated the bloodless, drew them to the smell of flesh inside. It was not long before they got past the walls, past the flames, and into the camp. I had lost too much time and needed to catch him before he disappeared. I followed the frequency along the wall to the back where it was strongest—I knew he was there waiting for me. I faced the sea and looked out, relieved no bloodless rose from the water below.

"Răzbunare." The hushed word came up to meet me. "R-r-r-evenge s-s-s-sweet," he said. I looked down at the face of the famed impaler, the raging pyromaniac, as he clung to the rock beneath the ledge of the parapet. Vlad smiled at me with his metal grill, his iron fangs a permanent fixture of his vampiric face. "For-r-r-r Jean," he said. "If-f-f mine burn—yours-s-s too."

He scowled, as he released his claws and fell back toward the sea. His body pierced the water like a torpedo, speeding beneath the waves and away from the cliff. Lost to the deep, he left me with his damage. He had helped Wallach invade the camp, causing the distraction that allowed the nomad to get

228

the girl and the baby, and kill the clone. For revenge—all for petty revenge. He left with nothing but an empty satisfaction. But he would pay— revenge *is* sweet and primal and mine.

"No!" The boy's voice reached me up on the wall. "Vincent." His screams peaked—he was frightened. The bloodless came over the wall, burning in the flames but coming nevertheless. It was as if something greater than the smell of the men drove them to us.

I rushed down to get the boy. Several bloodless were closing in on him, backed into a corner as he was. He had a garden hoe and tried to hold them off. I sliced through the three of them, dropping them with my talons, and then threw the boy over my shoulder, carrying him to the smithy where I stored the seeds. We would use the powder to get the men out. "Have you seen the other two?" I asked.

"In the old bakery," he said. "Last I saw."

The two men had run into a hovel that had a second level, trying for higher ground. I grabbed the bag of seeds, my journal, and the boy. We crossed the street through the smoke. The air was thick and he could barely breathe let alone walk. I flung him over my shoulder again. The bloodless stayed clear of us with the seeds in my hand.

"Vincent." Paul's voice came at me through the smoke. The men were in the bakery but burning bloodless had trapped them. Beck was bit and Paul could barely stand. I will admit for a brief moment I questioned my intention. I should have fled, left them there amidst the flames and bloodless. I needed to track the girl—I needed to get out. "Vincent," Paul's second cry appealed to my heroic side.

The boy grabbed a pitchfork off the wall and ran toward the trapped men. He dug the prongs into the first bloodless and it dropped easily, aflame as it was. I destroyed the others swiftly and freed the men, pulling out the seeds and ordering them to make the powder. "We have to get out," I said.

"How?"

"Over the wall."

"But the flames," Helgado said. "We can't."

"Through the gate then," I said.

I believed the powder would make the bloodless disperse and we could walk right out the front door. The camp was a cacophony of howls and fiery roars. I could not see the bloodless, as I made my way through the lane with the men, tossing the powder around them. The market square was a scene of chaos—blind chaos. The smoke was thick but I could hear the frightened fowl cluck in their coop. I think it was at that moment everything slowed to a halt and the scene turned black and white. The smoke cleared and revealed the bloodless toppling over the walls as if aimlessly throwing themselves inside. They were like ants fleeing a poisoned hill, running away from something rather than to it.

Suddenly everything went mute and I was oblivious to the men screaming at my side. The sound of the camp's large doors flying open deafened me, as the barrier exploded, the wood splintering beneath a heavy blow. Only when the smoke escaped from the entrance, as if sucked through the opening, did I see the cause.

"Du Maurier." Rangu's voice boomed with wickedness, as I barely trusted the vision that came to my eyes. An insult to our kind, he was a demonic aberration worse than Scylla or Demogorgon—

hideous, gargantuan, transformed into something so unnatural I have yet to recover my senses. I cannot record the atrocity on these pages—but his guttural chuckle will haunt me always. "Vin-n-n-n-ncent-t-t-t-t-t!"

His appearance was not even the worst of it, for greater misery flanked him—my kin—Stephen and Veronica. Once lithe, beautiful, they were now transformed like Maxine into beaked, twisted, bulging-eyed creatures. Veronica stepped forward first, extending her hand. She made a trill sound that stung my ears and sounded like *join us-s-s-s-s*.

"I-I-I …" I stuttered, trying to reason with her but was barely able to speak. Stephen stepped forward, his blood-red eyes looking through me. His hair was disheveled with missing clumps and what looked like brain matter caught in its strands. He had obviously been bludgeoned in the head.

When Veronica came forward, I could not move, the horror of them both was too much. Stephen struck at me first, knocking me back thirty feet. The men had already fled and the bulk of the powder was gone, but it did not matter since it did not affect the bloodless vampires. Stephen came at me again, throwing his whole body on top of me. The force was violent, the momentum powerful. He pressed his face up against mine and I tried to see him as he once was, but could not. He was no longer one of mine. Rage filled me, sadness inspired me, and I reached for the nearest thing. When he had knocked me over, we toppled the water cart and one of its wheels was next to me. I grabbed it, ripping it from the axel, and slung it over his head. I threaded him between two spokes, crushing his malleable skull with the steel. When I got the wheel around his

231

neck, I used my talons to sever his head from his body.

Veronica came forward next, her shrill scream deafening me again. She reached for her beloved's body and yanked it off me, and then lunged for his severed head and attempted to place it back on his neck. I thought I was in a dream. She slammed the head down onto its body until it finally held itself and was newly fused together—Stephen was reborn. I did not have time to rise, for Rangu's bellow came from somewhere above me, and when I looked up, he hovered over me, black tar seething from his grin. "Rmmmph!"

I had few options, if any, to escape with the three surrounding me. I do not know why the clone popped into my head in that instant, but like a vision she did, and I stiffened my muscles, imagining myself up and out from the fray. My body heeded the image and sprang up like a stone from a slingshot. My momentum was great but then I quickly sank and landed somewhere behind them, though not out of reach. Veronica was quick and threw herself at me, knocking me down again. Her fangs latched onto my throat but she could not grip my granite flesh. I grabbed her by the hair and pulled her mouth from my neck. Her scalp came off in my hand and her bite regained its vigor. I put my other hand under her chin and forced her away from me. She was strong but I was stronger. I could have severed her head, but did not waste the time. I sprang from the ground and ran up the laneway.

"Vincent," the boy said. "Up here."

The men were on the second floor of the bakery, and I scaled the wall to reach them.

"We're trapped," Helgado said. They were trapped, but I could still get away. Beck lay on the ground, his leg bloodied and wounded, and the smell hit me with force. "Vincent!" Helgado said. "What do we do?"

His panic irritated me. "We have to get out," I said.

"How?"

"Into the forest," I said. "From there, we will see." My plan was shoddy at best, but I never intended to see it through.

"That's suicide," Helgado said.

"Beck can't walk," Paul said.

"I can, I can," Beck said through clenched teeth.

"Let's go then" Helgado said. "What're we waiting for?"

I was waiting for the bloodless vampires to find the humans—a fresh diversion. I suppose I could say I tried to save the three men, that I helped get them out, through the camp, over the wall and into the forest with me. I could lie and write history as I imagine it to be, but I am no liar—I am a vampire. This is where you will think me a villain perhaps, which is fine, just do not mistake me for a victim. I would save myself and find the girl. The horror of becoming a hybrid is enough to drive anyone to do what I did. I may seem cold-blooded now, but was far worse when I was human—war makes men brutal, makes them sacrifice morality, anything, to survive.

I tossed the injured man down to the abomination below. I ignored his screams, as I sank my fangs into the boy I had always considered my enemy. I drank Helgado's blood for vengeance,

233

without remorse. He passed out before I threw him down next. The other man did not stop me, but jumped from the second-story window to free himself. He broke his legs when he landed and the bloodless swarmed. He was the best distraction for me, as I made my way out the window and past the busied fiends tearing him apart. When I reached the parapet, I did not look back. I ran around to the rear of our hill town and launched myself into the raging sea below.

Save the girl—do it!

Byron's words haunted me and I thought of nothing else. I did not doubt my girl was still alive. I suppose I could feel her blood, despite my indulgence with the boy. With fresh sustenance driving me, I launched my body up and out of the water, clinging to the slippery surface of the rock. I made my way sideways across the stone using my talons, moving north along the coast in the direction Wallach had taken my girl. When I reached the middle point of the field north of the hill town, I scaled the rock to the woods above, where an abandoned hamlet lay on the other side of an arboretum. I could only hope he had headed there. The nomad had an hour on me, maybe less, so I moved quickly through the trees, knowing I did not have much time before Rangu and his henchmen would be on my trail. There were few if any bloodless left in the woods. They had moved into the hill town, used up by the inferno.

I knew which way to go—maybe it was instinct, or perhaps I smelled her, but when I came across the body of a fallen bloodless in the middle of the small woods, I was on to her. It was motionless, lying on the ground next to my first clue. I picked up

234

the Dilo seed and brought it to my lips. My fangs itched, it was covered in Evelina's touch, her sweat, her scent. She had grabbed the sack of seeds before the nomad abducted her. He had no idea she was the reason he was safe from the bloodless. I found the second seed twenty feet from the first, and the third was on the outer edge of the hamlet on the other side of the woods. I crossed the meadow and found two more. Closer now, I found another a few yards from the last. The trail ended near a small water mill with a dried out wheel and a lawn overgrown with poppies.

I recognized the blood in the air. The scent came from inside the water mill, something lodged in a compartment between two spokes and the hub. I reached in and pulled out the baby's swaddling blanket. It was stained with blood—not hers, her mother's. I clung to the blanket, holding it to my nose. My gums tingled and I could not resist placing the soaked linen on my tongue.

"Ce mai faci, Du Maurier?" He greeted me with a bloody mouth, stained with the spoils of rabbits and badgers. The smell of animal blood gave me the slightest relief.

"Where is my girl?"

"Not yours anymore," he said. "Îmi pare rău." His apology was dripping with sarcasm.

I wanted to throttle him, tear him in two pieces, maybe four, but I needed him. I needed to know where she was. I tucked the bloody swaddling cloth in my belt and approached him slowly. "You can keep the baby," I said. "I just want the girl."

"Da," he said. "Pardon." He smiled. "Mâine." *Tomorrow.*

"No," I said. "Now."

235

He toyed with the carcass hanging from his belt before ripping it off. He brought the rabbit up to his nose, savoring it. I suffered the nomad, as he bit through the pelt and slurped the animal noisily. When he was finished, he tossed it aside and then picked the fur from his teeth. "Veronica," he said. "I want her, and the girl is yours." He had to have known—he must have seen his progeny. "Unde este Veroní-í-í-íca?"

"Nu știu," I said. "She has not been with me for—"

"Rahat, mincinos!" He did not believe me.

"Îmi pare rău," I said. "I will tell you where she is if—and only if—you tell me where Evelina is."

He read me—he knew I was telling the truth now. "Spune-mi," he said.

I told him what I had seen in my camp, that they were just on the other side of the woods and they would be coming for me. I told him they were no longer like us.

"Răzbunare," he said.

"Revenge," I said. "For what?"

"Rangu."

He knew I had not helped my fellow vampire in the vineyard. I had left him for dead, saving the girl instead. He came at me then with hate in his eyes but he faltered and I grabbed him by the throat, crushing it, as I tried to squeeze his head off. "Where is she?" I said. "Tell me and I will spare you."

My talons pierced his weaker skin—the wild look in his eyes told me it was unpleasant. "Plecat," he said barely audible. *Gone.*

I squeezed tightly. "Tell me," I said. More tightly still. "Tell me."

His eyes dulled and he strained to open his mouth when all at once the blood from the rabbit revisited him. He vomited down the front of his coat and I tossed him on the ground. He started to cackle but I could not tell if he laughed or cried. "Bine, Du Maurier, veți câştiga," he said.

After conceding defeat, he said I had already lost her. He told me Rangu communes with the bloodless and leads them somehow. He brought them to my camp, made them climb the wall, and ordered them to rush into the fire. "I didn't know about Veronica," he said. "I didn't know … vampir meu." *My vampire*—she was no longer his, vampire no more. He said he did not know Vlad would be there, that the fire was a convenient distraction, a coincidence. But I do not know if I believe that.

"Does he have her?" I asked.

He shook his head. "She does," he said.

"Who?"

"Împărăteasă," he said. "She has the girl."

Resurrected by the great Xing Fu of the Zhou dynasty at the turn of the twentieth century, the vampire Empress had become a powerhouse in recent decades.

"Where?"

He gave me a bloody smile and winked. "El vine," he said. *He is coming.* "La revedere, Du Maurier."

I did not hear Rangu come, but left Wallach not wanting to get caught up. Between the men I found on my shore, the ship I had seen passing, and the reputed Empress, I knew where to go. The Genoese docks were not far and as I got closer, the smell of human blood confirmed my suspicion. When I saw the harbor, it evinced the abandoned world. Boats and yachts had been neglected, tossed on their sides, some even sunk altogether. The port's control tower had collapsed and was stuck, half in half out of the water. A massive cruise ship had capsized close to shore and was still eerily lit up by its emergency signals. Great cranes and container lifts were desolate, looking like visitors from outer space come to wreak havoc on the port and failed to return home. They stood guard along the water's edge like mechanical giraffes. When I looked out at the bay, I saw the cargo ship about a mile off the coast. I had found what I was looking for. It was the same ship that had passed by all those days ago when she was with me.

I made my way down to the shipyard, looking for a vessel to take me out to sea. I heard them, as I approached—their frequencies buzzing all around me. A flock of harmless, hungry vampires loitered on one of the docks, standing in a line, facing the ship as though willing it to them. The bloody smell was unmistakable and even I could not keep my fangs from dropping. Only one of the vampires acknowledged me when I approached. He was a starved looking fellow with a more peaked complexion than most. He saluted me with his free hand, the other cradling the fine sculpture he held at his side.

"You're an old one, aren't you?" His regional accent was impeccable.

"Ancient," I said.

He kept playing with his fangs, letting them drop over his bottom lip and then pulling them up again. "I haven't seen you here before," he said. "First time?"

"What is this?" I asked.

"Ho," he said. "You don't know? This is the jackpot, man. But where's your offering?" He looked me up and down. "Your payment?" He asked. "Gotta give her something to get on, man." He held out his sculpture for me. "It's a Pisano," he said.

The bust of a woman and child, probably the Madonna and Christ, was delicate, almost modern looking in its details. Its base was gone and it looked as if it had been ripped from a stone pedestal. I did not ask him where he got it—I did not care.

"You'll need something like this to get in," he said. "She doesn't accept junk."

"To get in?" I asked.

"The blood den, man," he said. "No golden bough, no ferry ride to the pleasure dome." He thought he was clever, smiling at his own wit, but I found him tedious. "You look well fed, man" he said. His eyes lingered on the redness of my lips. They betrayed my satiation. "Where do you keep your stash?" He sniffed the air around me.

I nudged him a little when he got too close.

"I gave up drinking the fiends," he said. "Couldn't take the stench anymore. Her den saved me, man. When the ship leaves, I jones until it pulls into port again. She gets the goods—I don't know where she finds them but man she serves the freshest blood."

He itched to tell me his secret, from where he had snatched his Pisano. I could see it in his bloodshot eyes. "Was it difficult to lift?" I asked.

He looked from left to right and then shook his head with a self-sufficient air. He leaned in and revealed his secret. "I tricked him," he said.

"Who?"

239

"The curator." His eyes narrowed and he looked past me. "You don't know him, man," he said. "Keep it that way—he's the devil."

The frequencies pitched, synching harshly when the ferryman launched his skiff from the cargo ship and headed toward the dock. The promise of blood agitated the vampires.

"If you do get in," he said. "Let me suggest trying the newest they've tapped—Zhi told me she just gave birth."

I do not think I heard another thing, though he kept babbling. My throat tightened and I saw red, as they say. I unleashed my iron fangs and dug them into his jugular, tearing it out with one bite. He dropped the sculpture when he reached for his wound but I caught it up before it hit the deck. His head fell back and I cut it clear off with a swipe of my talons. His body crumbled and I kicked it into the water, tossing his head in after it. The vampire who stood with his back to us turned and looked at the sinking body. "Thanks," he said. "He never stopped talking."

I waited impatiently for the ferryman to reach us, that transporter to paradise, though Zhi is nothing like Charon in his knotted rags and wiry white beard. The Empress's boatman is a rather elegant vampire, dressed in a traditional changshan with its Mandarin collar and low hanging sleeves, wearing his sleek black hair in braids tucked beneath a hat that matches the red silk brocade of his jacket. He is never without his slender opium pipe dangling from his mouth like a blade of hay.

"Hup, hup," he yelled, as he approached. He tossed his rope to the vampire at the front of the line. When it was wrapped around the dock tie, Zhi

240

motioned for him to step forward. "Liwù!" The ferryman called.

The first in line was a wretched looking creature turned late in his life. He stumbled, as he bent down to offer his gift and landed on his knees barely saving himself from falling into the ferryman. He regained his composure and reached into his pocket, pulling out a heart-shaped locket. "It is from the Stuart reign," he said in a thick English accent. "See the portrait?" He pointed to the small gold façade on its front. "That is King Charles the first," he said.

"Hmm." Zhi expressed his approval with sounds more often than words.

The vampire handed his prize to the ferryman. "The image was inspired by his execution in 1649," he said. "Inside there's a small piece of material that's soaked in the blood of the executed king."

The other vampires perked up when they heard the piece was drenched in royal blood. The ferryman opened the locket and brought it to his lips. His fangs dropped, as he touched his tongue to the ancient trace of blood.

"He was a martyr," the English vampire said. "His blood is sacred."

Zhi smiled at that and slipped the locket into a purse that lay at his feet. He motioned for the vampire to come aboard and called the next one forward. One by one, the vampires auctioned off their relics and pieces of art for a seat aboard the skiff to the blood den. I realized early on that the ferryman expected us to sell our piece with a bit of flair, detailing the history of the token. He would not be fooled, shrewd as he was.

241

"It's a Da Vinci," one of the more desperate vampires said. "A rare, lost diary." The ferryman refused the leather-bound journal. "It's one of his notebooks," the vampire said. "Look!" He opened the book and frantically turned its pages, showing the crude pencil drawings of circulatory systems and aircrafts.

"Jiǎ," the ferryman said. "A fake—fake—a fake."

He waved the vampire away with his opium pipe, and the swindler slumped, defeated by his failure. He tossed the book into the water, not afraid to admit his fraud.

"Piàn," the ferryman said under his breath. He knew a cheat when he saw one.

When it was my turn, I handed him the stone sculpture. "It is called *Madonna and Child*," I said.

The ferryman examined the piece and then pointed to its broken base. "Pò."

"Giovanni Pisano," I said. "The great Italian sculpture whose—"

"Pò. Pò." He waved me away with his opium pipe, and then pointed to the dock tie. "Shìfàng," he said, wanting me to untie the line.

When he refused to let me board the skiff, I considered jumping on it and tossing all the vampires overboard, though the ferryman would prove a sturdy contender. He was not one of the starved ones, his red lips giving him away. But nothing was to say that if I got to the cargo ship, I would be allowed into the den after killing the Empress's boatman.

"Please, brother," I said in my best Mandarin. "I have traveled far to taste the blood in the den of the Great Empress Cixi." My accent was rough and

242

my dialect even worse—the ferryman could not understand me.

"Zhi," the English vampire said. "Our friend was kind enough to relieve us of the fool." He pointed to the head of the other, floating now at the end of the dock.

Zhi looked over at the wandering head and took several quick tokes on his pipe, blowing the smoke out in figure eights. He narrowed his eyes and sized me up, inspecting my boots, coat, hands, and face. I was well-kept and anything but starving.

"Hup, hup," he said, motioning for me to board his skiff.

I untied the line and pushed us off before jumping in the boat. I left the broken sculpture of the Madonna and child on the dock, watching for my return. The English vampire introduced himself as Quinn, speaking in perfect Italian. "Smell that," he said. "That's lovely, isn't it?"

I assumed he referred to the human scent that got stronger as we got closer. Zhi piloted the skiff over the waves, holding it steady, as we bounded across the inlet.

"I've been a vampire since the fourth year of the Common Era," he said. Quinn could read minds without reading facial expressions, a rarity among us. "You are the ancient one," he said.

I nodded.

"How fortunate," he said. "I am honored to meet you." I was certain he could see my reasons for going to the den. "I am a friend," he said. "Not a foe."

"You suffer," I said.

"Who among us doesn't?" He snorted the air and stuck out his tongue. "It's really a burden, you know, more than a gift." Quinn had a charming smile. "But sometimes it helps," he said, tilting his head back to indicate the ferryman. "The weasel annoyed him," he said. "And I knew he hadn't made up his mind about you yet. You scare him a little."

As I should, I thought.

"Yes," he said. "As you should." I was in no mood to make friends but I had questions I wanted answered and he knew it. "She is a collector," he said. "Of fine art. Her ship is filled with the greatest works of art ever made." I assumed she amassed most of them after the plague. "Yes," he said, reading my mind. "She's been raiding museums since before it started." She trades blood for art. "I don't know how she keeps finding the humans," he said. "She just does."

We were getting close—the scent of human was all around us.

"Her ship will be in port until one of us conquers the curator." The weasel had also mentioned a curator. "He's staked a claim on the Museum of Oriental Art," he said. "He loathes the Empress."

"Natural rivals," I said.

"Aren't we all," he said.

I wondered what had become of my line—my descendants, as it were. Graceless and cruel immortals roamed the earth now, natural enemies, power-hungry despots. Too many young ones, too few great ones. But I am still and always will be the forebear—our origin.

"Being in your presence is quite something," he whispered. "I am somewhat awed."

I was untouched by his sentimentality, and thought of my girl.

244

"She must be extraordinary," he said.

I cringed at the thought of others feeding off her. I would destroy them all.

"Your rage will not serve you here, Achilles," he said. "The Empress has an army of vampires and each one more ruthless than the next."

The skiff pulled alongside the cargo ship, and the vampires stood in anticipation. Zhi tsk-tsked. "Zuòxià," he said.

They sat down again but like addicts they could not subdue their desire. They licked their lips and played with their fangs, contemplating the upcoming ecstasy.

The cargo ship looked tightly sealed, almost impossible to breach. I did not see an opening, except for the one entrance up on the quarterdeck. The structure stood at least twelve meters above the waterline and the only way onto it was the ladderlike gangway in its middle. There were small portholes lining the trim of the ship near the railing of its weather deck but the smooth and slick hull would be difficult to scale.

When the ferryman stopped his skiff beside the gangway, the guards on deck unlocked the metal hatch. A female vampire, wearing a traditional costume similar to Zhi's, awaited us at the top. One by one we climbed up to her and she ushered us inside. The outward appearance of the rusty cargo ship could not prepare one for its opulent interior. The Empress's vessel abounded with luxury. The bulkheads were lined with elegant tapestries and rich patterns made of the finest silk. The décor was lit by sconces hung every few feet along the passageway and one could see the works of art in detail. Sophisticated pieces of furniture marked the passageways, slim end tables and benches reminiscent of Louis XIII.

We followed the female vampire through several of these corridors and more hatches before finding ourselves in the Empress's famed blood den. The compartment was quaint but lush, containing a series of mahogany boxes with small gridlike vents that hung on the bulkheads. Long wooden pipes ran through the bottom of each box and down to the deck where they disappeared beneath it. A slim divan on which the vampire could recline, as he fed, sat at the foot of each box.

"Choose wisely," the female vampire said.

She gestured to the boxes, offering us her selection. The vampires rushed to them, sniffing each vent like a hound searching for truffles through piles of mud. Quinn was more discerning and chose to sniff only one. Before he placed his nose to it, he touched it with the tip of his fingers.

"May I taste, Youlan?" He asked.

Youlan was the Empress's attendant and the keeper of the blood den. She moved to the box like a nail to a magnet and pulled a pass key from beneath the hem of her cheongsam gown. She slipped it into the side of the box and opened a flap, reaching in for the tube. She motioned for Quinn to approach and hold up his index finger, and then she squeezed the tiniest drop of blood onto its tip. The other vampires flocked to Quinn's box, their hungry eyes watching him dip his tongue into the miniature pool of blood. Youlan was distracted when Zhi came into the compartment and stood at the den's entrance. He gave her a look and she locked up the box again, shooing away the hungry vampires.

"Choose," she said firmly.

246

I was disturbed by the monopoly of sustenance—it is barbaric, even for the cruelest of us. It is like a human bottling the air and selling it for no reason other than sheer power. We are sophisticated beings, far more evolved than human, but this scene made me wonder. We do not consume blood because we are addicted to it, we drink it to survive.

I had smelled the human blood when we boarded the ship—I had tasted every single slave on the tip of my tongue, as I climbed the gangway. None belonged to Evelina. "The one I seek is not here," I said.

Youlan ignored me and shrieked at Zhi. "Zhànshì!"

Zhi leaned into the passageway and whistled, calling six able-bodied soldiers to the compartment. The blood-depraved cowered near their chosen boxes, as the Empress's vampires rushed in, wielding deer horn knives. I suppose I was not surprised when they surrounded me. Youlan and Zhi had both assessed the threat, guessing I had come aboard for reasons other than the den. Their fear confirmed my girl was here, even if I could not smell her.

I was put in irons I might have freed myself from had I not also been suited with a flying guillotine. The vampires had placed a collar about my neck attached to a chain rigged to my wrist clamps. If I broke the irons, the chain would release the Damascus steel blade and decapitate me. I was led down into the bowels of the ship where the décor was even more opulent than it had been above. I passed the *Mona Lisa*, most certainly not a fake, several of Van Gogh's starry nightscapes and

Cézanne's card players. I recognized the blue-and-white porcelain of the David Vases—the cameo-glass vessel of the Portland with its mysterious ketos and love scenes, and the infamous Savoy inspired by the dress of a Sami woman. The Empress's collection was staggering and extensive.

They put me in a small compartment, a cabin with nothing but a berth and washstand with the most beautiful Roman jorum. "Empress Cixi has requested to see you," Youlan said. My clamps and headgear were no punishment, just precaution. The soldiers retreated but Youlan hesitated. "Why have you come?" She asked. Her Mandarin accent was thick, though she addressed me in Italian.

"For blood," I said.

Youlan emitted a unique frequency, it fluctuated rapidly like a stilted heartbeat.

"No proper offering?"

"Your ferryman rejected mine," I said.

She snapped her tongue against her teeth while sucking air in through her mouth, as she paced the small compartment, back and forth, gliding over the metal deck with her arms crossed and hands tucked into her sleeves. "He brought you here anyhow," she said. "Lucky you."

Lucky me.

"Sit tight," she said. "I'll be back for you soon. Try not to behead yourself in the meantime."

She slammed the hatch shut when she left, but I thought I heard a baby's cry, though it was ridiculous to trust my senses. I did not know Evelina was only two compartments away from me, as I sat there waiting for the Empress. I could not—she evaded me even then. Believe me when I say I tried

248

to smell her, tried to feel her, hear her, see her, but the girl had vanished from my insides.

When Youlan returned, she was with only two soldiers. They flanked me, as we walked through another maze of passageways. We climbed several sets of steps and eventually landed topside at the stern of the ship. I faced the open sea and embraced the air. "Come," Youlan said.

She guided me along the deck to a hatch with a hand-painted dragon across it. The slender green dragon in a field of cadmium yellow bayed at a scarlet sun. The lizardlike tongue and fangs of the monster were stark white but dripping with blood. It marked the Qing dynasty—I had reached the Empress.

"Jìnrù. Jìnrù," Zhi said, as he opened the hatch to greet us. He was more hospitable than Youlan. "Shénme." He wanted my guillotine removed. Youlan bowed to him slightly and took off my collar before unlocking the shackles. "Bèn, bèn," he said, punctuating with a tsk-tsk.

Once inside the deckhouse, I was left alone again. The Empress would be in shortly they told me. I was struck by the clutter of the compartment. Statues and porcelain figurines sit on every possible surface, a plethora of oil paintings and watercolors occupy every inch of the bulkheads, and the most imposing piece in the cabin is the life-sized canvas set in an oversized wooden frame in the center of all the others, a portrait of the Empress Dowager Cixi. The image is flat, lifeless without shadow or perspective. Her face is drained of all color and one cannot tell if it was painted before or after she became a vampire. She sits in front of a hand-painted dragon that looks at her as if he too reveres

249

her power. She faces straight out to meet her viewer head-on, unshaken by the dragon's leering eyes. A fan lies in her lap, its blooming chrysanthemum blurred by the shadow of her hands. Covered by decorative claws, her fingernails forebode the talons she now wields as a vampire.

I felt her imperial presence when she came in. Her frequency is garish, unmistakable. When I turned to greet her, I was not surprised to be looking at the very same visage I had studied in the portrait—flat and pale. She gestured for me to join her on the wooden daybed. I bowed slightly and extended my hand but she kept both of hers hidden beneath the loose sleeves of her ruqun. "I know you," she said.

She speaks Italian with only the slightest accent. She is fluent in many Western languages.

"Then you know why I am here," I said.

"You have boarded under a false pretense," she said. "And come into my den with thieving intentions." She kept her eyes on the mirror across from the daybed, admiring her reflection.

"I am simply here to reclaim what is mine," I said.

"Your face tells a different story." She studied me, almost disturbingly. "I have nothing of yours."

"The girl is mine," I said.

"Maybe she was once. However, I paid a fair price for her and never renounce a work of art once I have acquired it."

I thought it odd she considered my girl a work of art. "Is she not one of your blood slaves?" I asked.

"Slave? None of my humans are enslaved. They are donors giving freely."

"In exchange for what?"

250

"Their survival," she said.

I could not argue with that. Her humans were safe on the ship, as long as they were not drained past the point of living.

"My humans are valuable." She mimicked a frown. "I am sorry to disappoint but we are not the horror show you expected."

"Where is the girl?" I said.

"Which girl?" She said. "I have several, as you can imagine."

Force would get me nowhere, and a ship full of loyal vampires could be difficult to take if any harm came to her. I still had no idea how to get to Evelina. "My girl," I said calmly.

"I told you," she said. "I never relinquish a work of art once it's in my possession."

"You consider her a piece for your collection?" My tolerance waned, as it tortured me to know I was so close to the girl but unable to claim her.

"You don't?" She asked with a grin.

I considered Evelina one thing, and one thing only—mine.

She pulled a silver cigarette case from her sleeve, revealing her hands. She wore the same decorative finger claws I had seen in the portrait. Her pinky and ring fingers were covered on both— their tips as sharp as talons. She opened the cigarette case, keeping her ornamented fingers extended. "Cigarette?" She said.

When I declined, she took one out for herself and placed it in the whalebone holder she pulled from her other sleeve. She tucked the case back into the folds of her ruqun and stuck the cigarette holder between her slim lips. She sucked on it until the tip of the cigarette combusted, erupting into a small flame. "I may be willing to make a trade," she said.

I smiled. "Anything."

"How about Edoardo Chiossone's collection in the Museum of Oriental Art?" The Empress got up from the daybed and paced the compartment as she took long drags from her cigarette, sucking in the stale weed. "And the curator," she said. "Bring me his head."

"Of course." I did not stutter.

"Get me the collection and his head," she said, "and I will give up the girl."

Her cigarette had burned down to its ash and she had already placed a fresh one in its stead.

"Let me see her," I said. "In good faith."

She hesitated and took an extended drag on her second cigarette. "You may look," she said, "but you will not speak with her."

"But how will she know I have come—"

"Tut," she said. "Not negotiable."

The Empress left me then and Youlan returned to take me to the girl. My venom heated with the thought of seeing her skin, her neck, her face, her soul. The vampire brought me back to where I had waited for my meeting with the Empress. She led me further down the passageway and into another compartment, nothing like the one before. This one was empty, except for a small bamboo stool placed in front of a glass window. Youlan told me to sit on the stool and then slipped out of the compartment, closing the hatch behind her. The window was covered with a velvet brocade curtain decorated with Asian elephants. I sat and faced the window, waiting for the elephants to move.

I suppose I should have expected the vision I was given. She was a work of art, a living portrait of my girl. Posed like the painting in the deckhouse, Evelina was a mimic of the sitting Empress. The girl sat on a throne with her head poised and her hands placed in her lap, tucked into her loose sleeves. She wore the imperial costume of the Qing dynasty, a red and gold diyi embroidered with long-tail pheasants and round flowers. A crown graced her head, the exquisite headgear adorned with gold dragons and phoenixes made with kingfisher feathers, beaded pheasants, pearls and gemstones. My girl's dark brown hair was pulled back off her shoulders and away from her face. I could not tell if it was the harsh light that made it so, but her visage was paler than I remembered.

Evelina looked through me, unable to see me on the other side of the one-way mirror. The image of sorrow could not be more perfect when a single tear rolled down her cheek, the only sign she was not merely an effigy. I faltered, as I stood to approach the glass. I could feel her now, her blood flowing through my veins. The longing I felt for her taste was crushing. And then the curtain was drawn and she was gone. I still recall that image now—it is one I will never forget.

Youlan returned. "The Empress would like you to have this," she said.

It was a steel forged in an Iranian crucible and honed to a sharpness only rivaled by our talons. "My claws will suffice," I said.

"At least feed before you go," she said.

She led me back to the blood den where the other vampires had made their selections. They had been taken back to shore promptly after feeding. She

253

did not go to one of the boxes, but poured my blood from a decanter on a side table. The smell was unmistakable. When she handed me the silver chalice filled with Evelina's blood, I brought it to my nose before letting it kiss my lips. I drained the cup, as my subtle fangs dropped. I relished the ecstasy despite its ephemerality.

On my way back to the pier I was left alone to indulge in the perfection of my last blood high. I faced the dark city, as the ferry cut through the white caps of the waves. The sky was graying with night coming again. Gulls screeched above our heads, circling the sea for their supper. They hovered in the air as though dangling from a tether before spiraling into the sea below, their bodies striking the water like bullets from a gun.

"Tíhú," Zhi said.

He laughed and pointed to a family of pelicans fishing by the retaining wall of the harbor. The gregarious birds dunked their beaks into the sea then out again as though rocked off balance. He navigated the skiff as close to the waterbirds as he could without frightening them away, and with the swiftness of light and the quiet of silence, he dove into the sea and rose up among the fishing flock. He snatched one of their beaks, slicing the snout off the pelican's visage before jumping back into the skiff. The carcass of the waterbird sank, as the others took off bellowing. He opened the bird's bill and reached into its pouch for the fish it had caught. He consumed the sardines without offering me a single one. The Empress and her crew were well fed, for only a vampire consuming enough blood would desire human food.

When the skiff pulled up to the pier, I hopped out and onto the dock. Zhi did not toss me the line to tie up the boat but instead offered me the Damascus steel I had refused to take from Youlan. The silver sword was tucked into an embossed sheath with the insignia of the slender dragon. "Jiè cǐ," Zhi said.

He ignored my refusals and held the sword out until I took it. I obliged him only because it seemed as if he would chase me down the dock if I did not, and I had wanted to be on my way. As I stole up the abandoned streets, the sword hung from my belt, its hilt sticking out from under my coat like a pirate.

The vampires were all gone, and the bloodless too. The city was apocalyptic, its destruction greater than I had seen in the countryside. The whole of Genoa had been lit up and was still smoldering beneath its ash. I did not need to hear his frequency to know he was there, that he was the one I came for. Vlad had taken over the city—he was the curator they all feared.

I approached the museum from the street of palaces where tapering mansions narrowed my perspective and the groves of orange trees and blushing oleander would only bloom again in memories. The landscape of the Villeta Di Negro was still green and the water cascading from the gazebo still gushed out, Vlad having preserved his plot of paradise among the rubble. The entrance gates were closed but easy to scale, though they gave fair warning to all who braved passing them. The vampire had impaled heads on the spikes of the fence, the bloodless still howling despite their missing bodies. I barely noticed the head of the vampire added to the mix, an extended warning to his kind.

Vlad was alone—his sole frequency guided me, as I climbed the park to the museum. The building was barricaded, its front doors boarded up, but he came and went somehow, and when I recalled the vampire head on the spike, I knew its dampness was my clue.

I ran toward the gazebo and launched myself down onto the rock that touched the edge of the waterfall. I found his entrance above the pool on the first level of the cascade. I stepped through the curtain of water and discovered the tunnel he had bulldozed through the rock. I smiled when I heard the howls from deep within the chamber—of course he had set a trap for his visitors.

I went into the darkness, greeting the swarm of bloodless with nothing but my steel and a handful of seeds. Three came at me first and I tossed one of the seeds at them, but the bloodless were wet from the cascade's spray and the water agitated them, making their retreat a temporary one. Five of them pushed forward, howling and gnashing their teeth. They clawed at me with their bony fingers and I reached for the Damascus steel, using it to tear into them with its edge. I sliced my way through the tunnel, severing heads from bodies, amputating hands and arms, as they clawed at me. I realized by the end the impaler had shackled them to each other like a chain gang, keeping them from making an escape.

When I reached the metal portal to the museum, I smashed it open with my boot. The girl's blood pumped me up, tripling my force. The promise of another taste drove me to finish my task, though I lingered at the doorway to bask in the pleasure of my rage. The darkness was peaceful and I could see the hulking figures and bodiless heads of the sculptures

256

standing in the large gallery. Above me were several balconies that overlooked the main foyer and behind their black metal railings were glass cases that held the costumes of ancient Japanese warriors and samurai, suits of armor from Shang to Han. The bodiless panoply stood at attention for its vampiric overlord. The museum was still, his frequency steady.

I headed up the stairs to the first mezzanine, keeping my back to the wall. I held the steel out in front of me, though I did not think I would need it. When I reached the top step, I looked back down at the gallery below and only then did I notice the heads on the pedestals were not made of bronze but marble. Vlad had mounted the defeated intruders, vampire heads for no one to admire but him.

His voice boomed across the gallery from a public address system. "Bună seara, Ahile." Elongated consonants crackled through the speakers. "Pierdut-t-t-t-t?" *Lost?* The static interrupted his fuzzy cackle.

"Reveal yourself," I said.

"Nu sunt speriat, vechi grec." *You don't scare me, ancient Greek.*

His bellow blew out the speakers and the gallery fell silent. It occurred to me then that the only way the impaler could defeat me was by blowing up the very spot on which I stood. With him out of the room, that could have been my reality. The speakers crackled again. "Revenge," he said, "is that what you've come for?"

"I am here to make you an offer," I said. "A truce." Though his frequency was constant, his silence was unnerving. "We have a common enemy," I said.

"Împărăteasă," he said with aspirated esses.

"She has taken the girl," I said.

"Wallach's girl?"

"Mine—"

"What about mine!" He was volatile and unforgiving and completely perplexing.

"Yours?"

"Maxin-n-n-ne," he said. Maxine was Jean's progeny, not Vlad's. "My venomline," he said.

"Crocodile tears," I said.

"Du-te dracului!" *Go to hell!* His voice cracked and the speaker cut.

I saw the flame from the corner of my eye. The fabric of one of the costumes in the glass case beside me caught fire and soon the whole thing was burning. It exploded within seconds and I barely avoided the flying shards. His cackle erupted in the gallery but not from the speakers this time. His frequency was so strong it blew out my ears, as he swooped down from a balcony above me and landed in the center of the pillared heads. He glared up at me with steely eyes. His upper lip curled, drawn up by some imaginary wisp—the sneer his default mien. "She sent you," he said.

He could not have known.

"The steel," he said. "It bears her insignia." The blade was still readied in my hand, though the hilt was covered. "I have several in my collection," he said. "Damascus steel—the strongest metal-l-l-l." He smiled at me with his iron grill; he was the ugliest vampire I have seen.

"She will give me the girl back if I give her the collection," I said.

"And how do you plan on seizing it," he said. "By force?"

258

"I would rather not," I said. "I am looking for an ally."

Vlad grumbled something and placed his hand on the crown of one of the severed heads. "Ceea ce e în ea pentru mine?" *What's in it for me?*

"I will get you her blood."

"Sânge împărătesei," he said. "A costly price even for you."

"You know we can take the ship together," I said. "And all I want is the girl."

"One sip." He smacked his lips and ran his tongue across his metal grill. "One bite directly from your sweet source. Sângele ei."

His demand made my venom sour but I agreed.

"Veni," he said.

I still do not know how I convinced him to join me so easily. I had no idea he was such a fickle vampire. He catapulted his body upward from mezzanine to mezzanine using nothing but his talons. When he reached the top, he called to me again.

I took the stairs and met him on the upper level where he ushered me into a vaulted chamber off the gallery. The room was concealed behind a floor to ceiling tapestry of the Far East and a large metal door that looked like part of the wall. He lit several candelabra and the room came to life. One of its walls was covered in weapons—throwing stars, knives, swords, crossbows, spearheads, chains and daggers littered the concrete divider. An elaborate glass armoire, containing antique libation goblets from the great dynasties of China, sat across from the weapons display. The sealed chamber was full of secret treasures. I smelled the greatest one as soon as

259

I entered—a human girl hidden somewhere in the room.

"To each our own, Ahile."

I did not know if his statement referred to his girl or mine. I made on I was studying his wares, the goblets first and then the jade and bronze cups. When I turned my attention to the weapons, he busied himself with the floorboards. I will admit I was not surprised his girl was kept in the crawlspace beneath them.

"The ship is heavily guarded," I said. "We will have to take a boat to it before sunrise."

"We'll need a diversion," he said. "An explosion makes a fine surprise attack."

"Yes, a surprise attack."

"I have just the thing," he said.

I did not doubt it, as he perused the accelerants he had piled up in one corner of the room and picked up a porcelain jug. "Frumos," he said. "It was perfect for your plants."

My insides hardened but I stifled my rage. "At dusk," I said, "we will take a skiff from the piers of Il Crocifisso."

"Tedious," he said. "Let's make plans after we drink."

Vlad's tongue danced in his mouth like a serpent's. He reached down into the open floorboards and pulled up the girl. She was wretched, wasted and barely alive. "I'll take first bite," he said. The girl was limp in his arms.

"Why not bleed her and drink from the goblets?" I asked.

He looked at me with suspicion and then smiled with his iron grill. "Pact de sânge," he said. *A blood pact.*

260

He seemed flattered by my offer of ceremony and told me to choose the goblets. I twisted the lock on the door of the armoire with one of my talons. The cups were pristine, sealed up in the display case for years. I pulled a pair of pale jade cups with a porcelain base from the top shelf. The girl barely moved when Vlad pierced her frail skin with his talon. I handed him the first cup when the artery began to gush. The dark ichor oozed down the rim of the pale jade goblet. He filled it to the quarter mark and then handed it back to me. I passed him the second cup. When the girl's blood clotted, he pierced the inside of her thigh. He squeezed her leg but was unable to fill the second cup as much as the first. I insisted he take the more plentiful one. "She is yours," I said. "I only need a sip to seal the pact."

It was easy to appeal to his vanity. He switched cups with me and held his goblet up to the candlelight. "La nemurire," he said.

"To immortality," I repeated.

When the rims of our antique jade goblets clinked, his fate was sealed. I watched Vlad, as he licked his lips and placed the cup to his metal mouth, scarfing down the blood that would be his last. The girl's tainted ichor slid down his throat, dripping at the sides of his mouth and staining his lips. He licked the blood greedily, dragging his tongue along the inner rim of the goblet, and then sighed and tossed his empty cup across the chamber, knocking one of the spears off the wall. "Amar," he said.

"It is bitter," I said.

I had downed mine quickly, enjoying it far less than he did his.

"Nothing like my Evelina," I said. "But you will never know."

His pleasure faded and his mouth went taut. "What?"

"Yes," I said, "răzbunare este a mea." *Revenge is mine.*

He looked confused and then his face contorted with the pain. He reached for his throat and cradled his stomach, bending forward and dropping to his knees. He landed next to the wasted girl. "Ce-ai făcut-t-t-t-t ..." The convulsions began as his insides turned to stone. I cringed, as I recalled the agony of the blood substitute, the burning, the hardening, the sheer blow of it. It was easy to slip the contents of my cherished vial into his cup. Though I had wanted to save the last of the blood substitute as a souvenir, I did not think Byron would mind my using it to destroy the impaler.

I took the head of the Romanian boar and placed it in a glass case, a fitting end for a legend, living forever as a work of art. I left the museum with the head under one arm. The sun was already up when I arrived at the pier and the bloodthirsty vampires were waiting for the ferryman to come. A few of them admired my artifact but none named the vampire they all feared.

High with the promise of seeing her, tasting her again, I thought about where I would take her, how we would begin anew, and whether I was consolation for the family I had promised her. As Zhi launched his skiff and sailed toward the pier, I felt something like a sting within my veins at the anticipation of her blood. When the little vessel finally pulled up, the ferryman did not toss the line to be tied to the dock but motioned for me to come to the front. Some of the starved vampires groaned until they saw the treasure I held in my hands. I caught their whispers: *The curator was no more.*

Zhi examined the head and invited me alone onto the skiff, assuring the others he would return shortly. He did not tell me why I was given the private escort but I could guess. We skidded along the sea and I was up the gangway and on the weather deck with Vlad's head in no time. Zhi told me she was in the deckhouse awaiting my return. When I threw open the hatch to the cabin, Youlan stood in the corner and the Empress sat on the same wooden daybed she had been sitting on for our first meeting. Her visage was as stoic as ever and a cigarette dangled between the blood red lips of her slim mouth. She did not greet me when I entered, though Youlan gave me a slight bow by dropping her chin. She looked at her mistress and awaited her order. When the Empress finally waved her hand at the vampire, she exited the deckhouse through the hatch that led to Evelina. I anticipated her smell, but it did not come.

"The museum is yours," I said.

I placed Vlad's head on the bench beside her. She put her hand on the case and tilted it upward. "Jīngrén," she said, as she stared at the petrified visage.

"Not really," I said. "His pride got the better of him."

She peered into the glass, taking several drags on her cigarette. She blew the smoke at the figure and pulled the case closer with both hands. The semblance of a smile showed on her face, as she gazed at the stony head. I told her the museum was secure but her vampires would have to disarm the incendiary devices before they could gain access to the art.

"Yùcè," she said.

"He was predictable." I assumed Youlan had gone to fetch Evelina and I felt anxious for her to return with the girl. When she did not, I pushed the Empress to fulfill her part of the bargain. "Are you taking me to her?" I asked.

A gust of smoke escaped the vampire's tight mouth and rolled up into her nostrils, as she exhaled. She tapped the glass case with the palm of her hand and stood up. "Come," she said.

I followed her out of the deckhouse, as one of the guards waiting on the other side opened the hatch, anticipating our exit. She gave me a curt bow and ushered me into his company. He led me through the passageway I had taken to see Evelina once before. I sniffed the air trying to catch a whiff of my sweet morsel, but it was in vain. When we passed the compartment where I had viewed her from behind the glass, I knew I was close. I thought I felt her heart beat in tandem with mine. I could almost sense her warm touch on my callous skin. I would kiss her neck first, I thought, and then raise her in my arms. My mouth watered in preparation for her soft neck against my lips. She was close. I was close … so close.

The guard pointed to a compartment and I almost missed the smirk he tried to contain. Though his lips did not move, I could see the smile in his eyes. It was beneath me to reciprocate and I simply grunted, as I pushed him out of the way. I opened the hatch and went in. The smell of blood greeted me, though it was not Evelina's. I hesitated until I saw the shaded figure on the berth.

The light in the compartment was dim, as a lone candle cast shadows on the mantle. My girl lay on the berth with her hands gently across her stomach. She looked peaceful, as if asleep. She was still wearing the elegant imperial dress of the Qing dynasty but the gold and red embroidered diyi was stained with her blood. The mass of dried serum was clotted on one shoulder, and stuck in the hair that now hung over her left breast. The Phoenix crown with its gold dragons and kingfisher feathers was gone.

As I approached the sleeping beauty, I was certain I could see her chest rise and fall with her breath. She is only sleeping—I repeated the mantra until I felt her for myself and knew she was beyond sleep. I suppose I should have realized the truth sooner. I should have known the beauty for which I had embraced all hell was merely a transient fancy. I should have noticed the human features gone from her face, that she was merely an outline of what she had once been. I should have sensed the loss, the congealed and coagulated blood now fetid and dry on her ashen skin, no longer pulsing beneath it.

The black cloud of grief shrouded me, as madness and sorrow hit me in equal waves. I lamented her lifeless body like a father mourning his dead child, as I had grieved for my cousin long ago. Evelina's figure offered no solace, despite its tranquil perfection. She had taken her own life with the only weapon she could find. Her captor's decorative claw was still caught up in her nest of blood-clotted hair, and the gash in her neck revealed her fate, just as the wound in Penthesilea's nape had wasted her blood on the sticky Trojan air. I knelt

265

down beside the corse, just as I had done on the battlefield then.

Had I been human, I would have been breathless. Evelina was magnificent, her face an angelic effigy, her features drawn out and crystallized forever with budding youth. She was not dead but made divine, and the low murmur of her frequency told me exactly to whom she belonged. She was a child of the Empress now, a progeny of the Qing dynasty. I waited in anticipation to greet her, as her maker wandered somewhere else aboard her ship of masterpieces, Evelina nothing more than another opus for her collection—one that would live forever.

When the eyes of the novitiate fluttered beneath her closed lids, I knew she was on the advent of her transfiguration. Remorse and ecstasy consumed me all at once, and when her nostrils flared and her lips swelled and her jaw cracked with the pressure of their hardening, I was ready. I pulled her from the berth and into my arms, holding her to me. I readied the goblet of blood that had been placed at her side. She would wake with the unquenchable thirst and need we all experience, that commanding lust for blood.

Perhaps you read this now and question my joy at seeing her turned vampire since I had fought so hard to keep her human, but my sorrow fled with her metamorphosis, all my fear and wrath dissipating at the sight of her perfection. There was no need for her to be human any more.

A baby's cry rushed to meet me from somewhere deep beneath the metal deck of the cargo ship, echoing through the passageways. When the Empress saved Evelina from the clutches of the nomad, she had acquired the child too, a human newborn, the greatest treasure she could obtain. The child is safe here with the other prized works of art, as the most precious one among the whales of Cixi's collection. Evelina and I will protect her together. When the new vampire finally opened her eyes, the sound of her crying child seemed to aggravate her, as she recalled motherhood despite her change. Her first word upon waking was not blood—but *Lucia!*

THE END

CPSIA information can be obtained at www.ICGtesting.com
Printed in the USA
LVOW11s1333030715

444885LV00005B/150/P